M
Ren

ROBERT KIDD

M'Godini Publishing

Published in 2017 by M'Godini Publishing

ISBN: 978-1-5272-1022-6

A CIP catalogue copy of this book can be found in the British Library.

Published with the help of Indie Authors World

IndieAuthors
World

In memory of our beloved daughter Melodie 1960 – 1991 and to the mothers and widows of those who died at Wankie in 1972.

APOLOGIES AND ACKNOWLEDGMENTS

I must apologise to all my African friends for using the anglicized, but more widely understood name, 'Matabele' for the N'Debele people. However, I know that they will be pleased to hear that in researching their history, I came across an early map of present day Zimbabwe dated 1863 and the whole country is labelled MATABELELAND; in large capital letters. King Lobengula would have enjoyed seeing that.

The Zulu and Matabele spoken languages are not only graphically descriptive, the sounds and intonations are musical and lovely to listen to. The people are natural story tellers and I, like many other Rhodesian children, have very happy memories of sitting by their cooking fires sharing their sudza and relish and being absolutely entranced by their stories. Thank you all for these very special times.

In the account which follows I have used a few African names and words. Their phonetic pronunciations are given in brackets but sadly there is no way of reproducing their intonations.

It is not possible to name all of the wonderful friends who have assisted in the writing of this novel. But particular thanks must go to the Lee family, not only for providing us with a modern computer but also for their skill in recovering the whole of the original draft, which eight different viruses almost destroyed! I would also like to thank Kim Macleod and the team at Indie Authors World who supported me through the stages of publishing this novel, and especially Helen Baggott who assisted with the editing.

My ever supportive wife and grandchildren also deserve my deepest thanks for their encouragement, technical skills, patience and tolerance during this book's production.

Robert Kidd
Scotland 2017

INTRODUCTION

After four months on the voyage from Holland, Jan van Riebeeck landed, on the 7th of April 1651, at the Cape of Good Hope; the southernmost point of Africa. He was accompanied by his wife and son, plus eighty-two Dutch men and eight women. He had been contracted by the Dutch East India Company to establish the facilities for providing vegetables, fresh fruit, meats and water for their merchant ships on their way to and from India and the Far East. There was no intention of colonising but Jan van Riebeeck soon realised that the indigenous people were unreliable traders and it was therefore essential that the Dutch should grow the required foods themselves. He allocated plots of land for farming and inevitably, over a period of a few years a number Dutch and Huguenot farmers came and settled there; happy to be away from the religious strife in Europe and government interference. They became known as 'Boers'; the Dutch name for farmers. Collectively they called themselves Zuid Afrikaners (South Africans).

The major change came when Great Britain finally won the war against the Dutch in Europe and forced them to accept the terms of their peace treaty; a condition of which was the handing over of the Dutch East India Company's Cape colony. The Boers settlers were suddenly expected to pay taxes and to comply with numerous petty regulations, including military service against the local Xhosa people. The Boers were self-sufficient and fiercely independent people and strongly resented the interference in their lives. Many of them abandoned their farms and trekked north in search of vacant land to farm.

In 1836 there was a mass migration by the Boers, which became known as the 'Great Trek'. They travelled north by ox wagons, as far as 800 miles from Cape Town, and established two new colonies which they named 'The Orange Free State' and 'The Transvaal'. Unfortunately for them there were vast mineral resources buried deep beneath the rich agricultural soil which they truly revered and valued beyond any other riches. In 1867 diamonds were discovered in the Orange Free State near the town of Kimberly. Britain immediately annexed the Free State and laid claim to the mining rights. The Volks Raad, (the Peoples' Council), which governed the Boer Republic, objected vigorously with little effect. Shortly afterwards, alluvial gold was discovered near Pilgrim's Rest, a small town near the eastern border of the Boers' Transvaal Republic. A major 'gold rush' ensued and in 1886 gold prospectors found the richest gold field in the world. It was twenty-five miles from Pretoria, the capital of the republic. President Paul Kruger claimed the mining rights for the republic and they named the area 'The Witwatersrand'. The British government in Cape Town challenged this and ultimately annexed the Transvaal as well. Mining, with all the associated problems, had come to stay in southern Africa! Inevitably the next prize was to be north into mineral rich country which was occupied by the Matabele people. Cecil John Rhodes negotiated a deal with King Lobengula which became known as the Rudd Concession (See appendix i) This formal agreement pernmited miners and prospectors to settle in Matabeleland. This was the birth of Rhodesia. (called Zimbabwe since 1980).

It is against this background that the grandparents and parents of the characters in this novel played their parts, from 1890 up to 1980.

CHAPTER 1

✂ 1946 ✂

The woman was clearly angry. With her arms folded across her chest, as if holding in her emotions, she paced up and down the covered front veranda of her house. She stopped as soon as she saw her son jogging along the dry and dusty road in the distance. Her tense expression softened briefly as she proudly admired the sixteen-year-old boy. From his first day at school he had always run home, regardless of the fact that the midday temperatures in Wankie were seldom below 30 degrees centigrade.

As he approached, she refolded her arms and waited. He closed the small pedestrian gate and came up the steps onto the veranda.

"Greetings, Mother," he said in Zulu, as he put his school satchel down on the table.

Uncharacteristically she did not return his polite greeting but answered sharply, "Sit down. I have to speak to you." Like him, she was tall and slim and she towered over him as he slumped onto an old wooden Morris chair. Although he had some suspicion what it might be about, he certainly had not expected the ice cold anger in her voice.

"I had a visit from Mr O'Connor just an hour ago. As you know he is a very busy man and he does not normally trouble himself over the behaviour of school children, of which I would

13

remind you, you are still one. Mr O'Connor has been a very good friend to our family over the past eighteen years and I am ashamed that he should have found it necessary to come and discuss your behaviour with me."

"But, Mother," he interrupted.

"Don't you but Mother me," she said. "Just be quiet, boy, and listen to me. Mr O'Connor told me that you not only contradicted the new history teacher during his lesson, but you also amused your classmates by attempting to humiliate him with your superior knowledge. This not only shows bad manners, it also undermines the teacher's authority. You may think that you are something special but you need to learn a lesson. You would have received a good beating from your father if he had still been with us. Also, know that I would be perfectly capable of it too, if I chose to do so, but I have a better way. A beating would leave you with a painful backside for a week and then you would forget the lesson. What I have in mind is a lesson you will never forget. It involves humility; something which you are clearly lacking.

"I am told that you had the cheek to contradict Mr Ball, your history teacher, making out that he was in effect telling the class lies about the 1896 Matabele rebellion. Not content with undermining his authority, you had also passed a note round the class suggesting that a good nickname for your teacher would be 'umsende' – one testicle, as his name is Ball not Balls. This too was totally unacceptable behaviour. You could quite justifiably be regarded as 'a disturbing influence in the school' and you could be expelled. Think about the implications; especially just now when you are due to start sitting your Cambridge School Certificate exams in five weeks' time."

"But, Mother, I know the teacher was telling us something which was wrong."

Angrily she replied, "Have you not heard a single word I have spoken, or are you stupid as well as arrogant? This teacher has only just arrived from England and he is teaching what is written in the history books provided by the education department. Those books were written by English historians who never even lived in our country. There are certainly going to be mistakes but it is wrong for you to suggest that Mr Ball was making up lies. I am sure he is a good teacher; otherwise Boss Pat would not have chosen him for our school! Further, suggesting such a nickname might amuse your equally bad mannered classmates, but it was in very bad taste and you should be ashamed of yourself.

"Now listen well; you will have to act quickly if you hope to avoid expulsion. I have made an appointment for you to go to Mr Ball's house this afternoon, to apologise. You will put aside your stupid pride and overcome your arrogance. You will offer him your most humble apologies and promise that such things will never happen again. If he accepts your apologies, then your next step must be to tell your classmates precisely what you have done and how ashamed you felt about the note you passed round the class.

"For your information, Boss Pat mentioned to me that Mr Ball was the captain of his university's football team in England and perhaps he might consider coaching your school's team. Tell the boys in your class that it would be a wise move to change Mr Ball's nickname. 'Captain' or something like that might be a good alternative. Now it is up to you to sort out the trouble you have caused. It has to be your decision, not mine, but understand that it is vitally important to all of us."

"Mother, I am very sorry for what I have done. I will do all I can to put it right."

Finally she softened and said, "When we get over all of this I will take the time to tell you what actually happened to our ancestors in the 1893 and 1896 rebellions. Come and eat your lunch; it's probably stone-cold by now but you must not be late for your three o'clock meeting with Mr Ball."

She left him to his meal, went out onto the veranda and thought back to 1924 when she, Lisa Khumalo, had first met Patrick O'Connor. Nearly twenty years had already passed since then but during that time she had learnt a great deal about him and although they were employer and employee, they had become close friends. Patrick would have been surprised by the extent of her knowledge and the way she had built up a remarkably detailed picture of his life and the O'Connor family's from their conversations over those years. This was helped by their common languages and Patrick's communication skills, coupled with her female intuition and her natural curiosity about the sometimes strange behaviour of the white people.

CHAPTER 2

ᥫᯡ 1898 ᥫᯡ

Patrick O'Connor was born in 1898, in the small coal mining town of Newcastle in the South African province of Natal. He was the first child of a mother of Scottish descent and a father who had left his home in southern Ireland, planning to make his fortune in Africa. Patrick enjoyed a happy childhood, spending much of his spare time rock climbing and exploring in the nearby Drakensberg Mountains, usually accompanied by the Zulu children of his parents' household workers. Apart from becoming totally fluent in their language he learnt a great deal about the flora and fauna from them. In exchange he taught them English; which put them well ahead of their compatriots when applying for employment later in their lives. Without the barrier of languages they all became good companions and true friends.

After completing his schooling Patrick found employment as a junior clerk in the Newcastle Colliery Company's buying department. However, the work was repetitious, boring and totally unchallenging. Fortunately for him, after three months in the job, he was offered a junior position in the mine's newly formed African Personnel Department. He was a good communicator and his calm approach inspired the trust and confidence of others. It came as a surprise to him that the management had noted his potential and he was naturally delighted to become one of the staff members of the new department. His salary was increased slightly and he was allocated accommodation in a single quarters cottage in the mine's European housing estate. This enabled him to move out of his parents' home and gain relative independence for the first time in his life.

Patrick was enjoying his new work tremendously, but by 1916 Britain was suffering major losses in the world war against Germany and had embarked on a massive recruitment drive in the colonies, particularly Canada, Australia and South Africa. Like so many of the young men at that time, Patrick felt it was his duty to enlist. He volunteered to join the Royal Engineers in a non-combative role, thus serving for what he saw as a just cause. Having lived through the aftermath of the Anglo-Boer War with its slaughter of soldiers on both sides and the deaths of thousands of Boer women and children in the British concentration camps, he was unable to overcome his fundamental objection to fighting and killing. He was accepted by the army but the colliery blocked his release on the grounds that he was employed in an essential service. By mid-1917 however, the desperate situation in Europe resulted in changes to the South African call-up regulations and he was conscripted, released by the mine and shipped off, with about 500 other young men, to England. After four weeks' training he was sent to the Western Front in France. Like so many others, Patrick was horrified by the senseless slaughter and found it hard to tolerate the gross incompetence of those in charge; but he survived the war, serving with the Engineers until the armistice in 1918.

There is nothing like war for transforming a young man from happy carefree youth to physical and mental maturity; but inevitably it leaves its own wounds and scars. Patrick was no exception and he refused to speak about the war afterwards. A single sepia coloured photograph, sent from France to his mother, showed him with sergeant's stripes and that was the only record of his part in the war. In appearance Patrick had filled out into a sturdily built man, a little short of six feet tall. He had inherited his mother's blue/grey eyes and her calm composure. His voice was a deep bass and the slow measured way in which he spoke gave the impression of maturity and integrity. He invariably chose simple but apt words, almost as if he was conversing with a young child. Many unwary people fell into the trap of thinking he was mentally sluggish; whereas it actually hid a sharp and quick brain. He used this misconception to his advantage when he felt it was necessary.

On his return to South Africa, the Newcastle Colliery was happy to re-employ him, and he felt fortunate in being given back his old job. There had been major changes during his absence both at work and at his home. The colliery had expanded considerably and the O'Connor family had moved to the fast growing city of Johannesburg; the centre of the Witwatersrand gold fields. His father now held the position of chief buyer for the Brakpan Gold Mine and on the strength of this promotion had bought a house in Claim Street, Hillbrow, a moderately fashionable area of the city. Patrick's young brother, Shaun, had already completed the first two years of his five year electrician's apprenticeship at the East Rand Proprietary Mine. It was one of the richest gold mines on the Witwatersrand. It was known by the acronym ERPM.

Patrick's new job made him responsible for the welfare of about 1200 underground workers, a challenge that he was eager to meet. These men were of various nationalities, ranging from Natal Zulus, who formed the majority, to smaller groups of Swazi, Basuto, Xhosa, with few from Mozambique, plus some Matabele from Rhodesia.

Inevitably there had been tensions between the various factions so his immediate task was to get them to live peaceably with each other. This was not going to be easy. After very careful consideration he decided to change their housing arrangements. Instead of enclaves of houses for each nationality, he deliberately mixed them together, reasoning that as neighbours they would show more respect to each other. It was a radical step, based on his knowledge of the African traditions and he was prepared to gamble on it working. This was a major housing change from the multistorey accommodation blocks which the gold mines on the Witwatersrand had built for their male employees. There was absolutely no provision for wives and families. Patrick convinced his management to provide funding for a pilot scheme after quoting full details of the riots in the Transvaal gold mines. These had involved serious fighting between different nationalities. Even inter-tribal conflicts within the Zulu tribes were not unknown so the solution needed serious thought and forward planning. However, with the mention of the problems of prostitution at the gold mines, he clinched his case and he was given approval for all of the changes he had recommended. Building work started immediately.

The next step was to introduce the teaching of a common language for the mines' underground and surface workers. It was essential that various tools could be identified and that clear instructions be given underground in one common language. The same requirement applied to the skilled white miners and artisans who were a mixed bag of former coal miners from Yorkshire, tin miners from Cornwall, plus Afrikaans and English speaking South African artisans. Most of the latter spoke Zulu so it was decided to base this new language on Zulu, together with appropriate English and Afrikaans words. Patrick spent the following months training eight selected members of his staff as teachers. He had dictionaries printed and arranged for every classroom to be supplied with one of each of the tools commonly used underground. The new language was named 'Fanika Lo', meaning 'like this'.

The classes were deliberately made up of randomly chosen workers so that there was always a mixture of nationalities and, very wisely, he instructed the teachers not speak to the classes at all in their own mother tongues. The teaching method was simply to hold up and show a tool or item of equipment and say its name in Fanika Lo three times. Then everyone in the class had to repeat the name out aloud until the teacher was satisfied that they all knew that name and its correct pronunciation. The same technique was employed for useful verbs, such as; fetch, turn off, open valve, move, stop, find, hurry, etc.

Since most of the languages in the south and the east of the continent came from the same source, the majority of the African workers quickly picked up the new terms. The men from overseas naturally took a good deal longer to learn Fanika Lo and many of them resented being required to attend the classes and to be mixed with the Africans. It needed all of Patrick's tactful pressure to persuade them that it would make their own lives easier and safer if they could make themselves understood.

When one of the men stood out from the others as a quick learner and a good organiser, Patrick appointed him to the position of Assistant Head Teacher. He was a slightly older man and had worked for the company since leaving the Jesuit mission school in the nearby town of Ladysmith. His command of the English language was good, but he was never able to get rid of the rather comical Teutonic accent which he had picked up from the German missionaries who taught him English. He was known to the language students as Umfundisi (teacher) but Patrick preferred to use his family names, as given by his mother, which were Kumbula Zulu. It was an uncommon name and when they were better acquainted Patrick asked him about its origins. Kumbula explained that his name was given to commemorate the family's first born son who had drowned at the age of four, when trying to cross a flooded river. The name Kumbula, which means 'remember' or 'thinking back to happier times', was given to him because his parents believed that he, Kumbula, carried the spirit of their first son. This relieved much of their pain and grief.

The boost in industry following the end of the war had increased coal sales and Patrick was able to secure substantial additional funding for the construction of a sports arena and for a number of three bedroomed houses for senior married African staff. Unlike the gold mines, the colliery did not favour the building of multistorey blocks of rooms for the unmarried men, and concentrated on individual terraced apartments for their lower grade workers.

At the end of four years of intensive hard work Patrick and

Kumbula were well rewarded by the company following a very favourable report published in The South African Mining Journal. Because of this report the colliery's manager was asked to lay on a tour of the African township for a number of visitors from other mining groups. Patrick and Kumbula were given the task of conducting them around and answering their queries. At the end of a very successful day Patrick was approached by one of the visitors who introduced himself as Angus Mackay, the manager of the Wankie Coal Mining Company in Rhodesia. He told Patrick how impressed he was with what had been achieved and then asked Patrick if he would like to pay a visit to Wankie.

"I'm sure you deserve a break so what about coming up for a few days, all expenses paid?"

Patrick felt he could well do with a holiday and he readily accepted the kind offer, but sensed that he was probably being asked so that he could give them free advice on their own township planning. A date was agreed and Patrick immediately put in an application for two weeks' leave; his first break in a long time. He had heard excellent reports about Rhodesia and this would be a good opportunity to see if the country was actually as wonderful as the Rhodesians often claimed.

CHAPTER 3

ᛋᛉ 1921 ᛋᛉ

Patrick caught the Durban-Johannesburg overnight train which arrived at Johannesburg's Park Street station at six in the morning. It was a lovely crisp April day, so instead of hiring a taxi, he decided to walk, taking a shortcut through Joubert Park to admire the autumn flowers, the beautiful trees, and to enjoy the early morning sunshine. He then made his way up Twist Street, alongside the trams that served the entire area, and finally on to his parents' home at 102 Claim Street in Hillbrow. The size of Johannesburg interested him, having grown from a small gold mining camp in 1886, into a large thriving city.

Although he wrote regularly to his mother, it had been some time since he had last seen her and was shocked to see how strained she was looking. However, she gave him a tremendous welcome and once again he experienced the great love that had always flowed from her. He also received an enthusiastic reception from Buster, the family's boisterous pet Airedale, as well as from his young brother Shaun. His father joined them for breakfast but to Patrick's surprise he appeared distant as if suffering from a mild hangover. Shaun chattered enthusiastically throughout breakfast; mainly about his latest girlfriend and his very special new motorbike. It was an Aerial Four Square, which he was paying off weekly from his apprentice's wages. Patrick couldn't help feeling a small twinge of envy at the life that Shaun was leading; so very different from his own, in which there had been little time for any social life. In fact, having gone straight from boarding school to work and then into the army and back to a very demanding job, he had not had the chance to build up any social life.

After Shaun and his father had left for work, Patrick and his mother moved on to the sunny veranda where the house-maid brought them steaming cups of coffee. For a while they spoke of ordinary matters but Pat, ever sensitive to his mother's feelings, asked what was troubling her. After much hesitation and apology she finally told him that his father had recently been promoted to a managerial position and this, he claimed, required him to join the exclusive Rand Club, 'to meet and entertain all of the business people who mattered'. In the normal course of events this would not have been a problem, but because of what he regarded as his own rather humble Irish beginnings, he felt that he should spend a good deal of his time and money at the club buying drinks for his new colleagues. This meant that he was seldom home before midnight and not only was his health suffering but his increase in salary was of little benefit to the family. Another of her worries concerned young Shaun who with his great natural charm was attracting a number of rather unsuitable girlfriends; some of whom were a good deal older than him. All of this was causing his mother considerable anxiety, and she was naturally deeply concerned about their future. Patrick comforted her as best he could and resolved to speak to Shaun when he came back from his trip to Rhodesia. About his father, however, he felt there was really nothing he could do without creating a major disruption in the family.

That afternoon, Patrick and his mother walked slowly back through Joubert Park gardens, which she told him she often visited when distressed. They lingered there, enjoying each other's company and their mutual understanding. She was immensely proud of him and caused him some embarrassment by telling him that she looked upon him as the most mature member of their family. Still chatting, they walked down Plein Street and on to the station where the Rhodesia Railways train was already waiting. When departure time arrived his mother had difficulty in holding back her tears as he hugged her and kissed her on both cheeks before boarding the train. She stood on the platform; a solitary and lonely looking little figure, waving goodbye until the last carriage and the guard's van disappeared from sight.

Patrick's travelling companion introduced himself as Theo Odendaal; a young man who had been employed to teach the Afrikaans language at a senior school for boys in the small town of Plumtree in Rhodesia. Pat couldn't help but smile at the strange name, but he learnt from Theo that Plumtree was in fact a well-known school where boys from all over the country, as well as from further north, felt privileged to attend. Patrick and Theo found that they had a lot in common, and when they parted twenty-four hours later they shook hands, each expressing hope that their paths would cross again.

The rest of the journey to Wankie would have been rather tedious had Patrick not found and brought two excellent books from the Newcastle library, just before his departure; A Hunter's Wanderings by Frederick Courtney Selous; a big game hunter and explorer, and Mining Geology in Central Africa by Albert Griese.

The first book provided an excellent description of the topography and climate of Southern Rhodesia. The detailed descriptions engendered in Patrick a deep curiosity and unexpected affection for the country and its wildlife. From Selous's descriptions he learnt that the country was bounded on the east by the Inyanga and Chimanimani mountain ranges which separated it from the Portuguese territory of Mozambique, while in the west was Bechuanaland and the Kalahari Desert. Rivers form the northern and southern borders, the mighty Zambesi in the north and the sluggish Limpopo (which Rudyard Kipling describes so graphically as 'The great grey green greasy Limpopo'). In the context of African countries Rhodesia was classed as a 'small country', being just over one and a half times the combined areas of England, Scotland, Ireland and Wales. A large central plateau about 4000 to 5000 feet above sea level extends diagonally across from the east to the west and from this the land drops away and is known as the low veldt, being on average only 2000 to 2500 feet above sea level at the river boundaries.

Patrick learnt that the Kalahari Desert just beyond the western border influences the local climate in the Wankie area, making it hot during the day and relatively cold at night time. In the east the Inyanga and Chimanimani mountain ranges give rise to good rainfall for much of the rest of the country which has vast areas of grasslands and beautiful indigenous trees. It is ideal for grazing cattle and growing crops. It supports innumerable animal species, comparable in numbers to the best in South Africa. Apart from being a well-known hunter and explorer Selous's descriptions were superb, which Patrick thoroughly relished.

From Albert Griese's book Patrick learnt much about the early history of the Wankie coal mine. The author was a geologist and prospector from Germany and had a passionate interest in the precious and base metals, plus the geology of central Africa. He had travelled widely, mainly on foot, through the areas which were later to become known as the Belgian Congo, northern and southern Rhodesia. In addition to studying the geology of the countries he had listened well to the local people and noted which metals they used for making their tools and ornaments. He found that copper was widely employed in the south of the Belgian Congo and in Northern Rhodesia. Those people told him stories of the old days when copper had been mined on a grand scale and that the Arab traders had used black slave labour for carrying heavy ingots of copper to the east African coast for shipment to the Middle East.

Following a trip up the Zambezi River, to see the Victoria Falls, Albert Griese crossed the river above the falls in a dugout canoe, a highly dangerous thing to do as canoes were very unstable and frequently attacked by hippos. Added to the danger was the fact that the crossing point was less than a mile upstream from the Victoria Falls. Continuing on his way south he was told by the locals of certain 'black stones' which burnt like hard wood, and when taken to the bank of a deep gulley he instantly recognised the exposed edge of a coal seam. Investigating further he soon realised that what he was looking at was part of a vast deposit of high grade anthracite coal.

Without delay Albert Griese hurried south to Bulawayo, travelling on to the British South Africa Company's offices in the newly proclaimed capital town of Salisbury. The BSA Company held the sole mineral rights in Rhodesia, having tricked Lobengula, the King of the Matabele people, into signing a document known as the 'Rudd Concession' of 1888. Having obtained a prospector's licence, which was necessary before he could peg his claim on the coalfield, Albert Griese surprisingly changed course, spending the next three years prospecting for gold in central and eastern parts of the country. It wasn't until 1897 that he returned to Wankie to secure his claim for the sole coal mining rights. Luckily for him, no one else had done so during his absence. He actually claimed a single block of land covering an area of approximately four hundred square miles. Albert Giese did not personally undertake any mining operations, but sold the rights to the Mashonaland Agency Limited. They undertook further exploratory work but in turn they sold the rights on to the Wankie (Rhodesia) Coal and Railway Company in 1901. This company started shaft sinking and by early 1902 their first inclined shaft reached the coal and this is what later became known as Number 1 Colliery. Albert Griese's book went on to relate his mixed fortunes in the Australian gold rush, which was of no further interest to Patrick.

Patrick disembarked in Bulawayo from the Johannesburg train, which then continued on to Salisbury. He had a two hour wait in Bulawayo, the country's second largest town, before having to board the North train on the last leg of his journey up to Wankie. Needing exercise, he would have liked to have walked into the town of Bulawayo, but as the railway station appeared to be a fair distance from the town centre he decided to stretch his legs by walking up and down the long station platform instead. He was immediately reminded that he was in an English speaking country, for not only was the Union Jack flying above the station building, but all the railway notices were in English, and not 'twee taalig' as in South Africa.

It was early evening when the train pulled into Wankie station. Patrick had no difficulty recognising the tall figure of Mr Mackay and felt flattered that the mine manager himself had come to meet him. After exchanging the conventional greetings and pleasantries, Mr Mackay, in a broad Glaswegian accent, said, "I'm from Scotland and I don't go along with formality out of business hours. My name is Angus and I'll call you Pat, if that's alright with you?" Patrick readily agreed and immediately felt that this was a man he could trust and respect. They climbed into the manager's car and drove the short distance to the mine.

"My wife is away in Bulawayo on a two-day shopping trip so I would suggest that we have a couple of Johnnie Walkers first and then some dinner at the Mine Club. After that I'll take you to the mine guest house where you will be well looked after. Leave your suitcase in the car; it will be quite safe here. This is not Johannesburg"

"That sounds great to me. Thanks very much, Angus."

Over drinks and dinner they discussed a wide range of topics, also enjoying some friendly Irish/Scottish jokes and banter. The club dinner was very good and at around 10.30 Patrick was dropped off at the guest house. He unpacked the few things he needed, showered, and then gratefully went to bed.

*

Angus had warned him that work started at 7.30 on the mine, but still it came as a surprise to be woken by a 'tea boy' knocking on the bedroom door at six o'clock. It was another beautiful day with a slight chill in the air; a foretaste of the approaching winter. Being relatively close to the Kalahari Desert, the nights in Wankie could be very cold in the short winters, yet the summers were sometimes unbearably hot with temperatures frequently exceeding 38 degrees centigrade (100F). Later he heard from the locals that during those times the air was so still that not a single leaf moved on the trees

During the following days Patrick was shown around most of the mine, including the new hospital and clinic which were under construction, as well as the European and African housing. He was impressed by the underground workings of the mine, and last but not least, by the administration offices. Although the whole operation was smaller than the Newcastle Colliery, what pleased him most was that there appeared to be an excellent working relationship and pride amongst all categories of the staff members.

Angus Mackay met him at the club for a whisky after work on the first two evenings but on his last day Angus invited him home for dinner, to meet his wife. Patrick knew that an invitation like this would definitely not have happened in Newcastle. Although he was told that dinner was informal, Patrick went back to the guest house, smartened up, and enjoying the cool of the evening, walked to the manager's house at number 1 Victoria Road.

As Patrick had expected, the house was vast; a typical sprawling Rhodesian bungalow with wide verandas on three sides, all protected by green mosquito gauze. He made his way up the front steps and pressed the front doorbell. Within a few moments he was greeted by a lovely little woman, who introduced herself as Jeannie. Patrick couldn't have been more surprised as she was just over five feet tall but appeared to compensate for her lack in height by her lively manner and warm heartedness. With a welcoming smile she led him onto the side veranda saying that Angus had phoned to say that he would be a little late, so she was to look after him until he arrived.

Patrick was instantly fascinated by this charming little lady, and within minutes they were chatting and laughing together like old friends. She was interested in knowing all about him and made no apology for asking him all manner of questions about his background, his family and their origins. She was delighted when he told her that his father's ancestors had emigrated from Scotland and settled in the south of Ireland in the mid-17th century, and that his mother's parents had come out from Scotland fifty years ago to settle in South Africa.

"That makes us near cousins. I knew there was something special about you. Angus always jokes that the intelligent Scots realised that getting out of Scotland was most sensible thing to do." Just then Angus walked in.

"Yes that's right, but I had to marry this less intelligent Scot to get her to leave home"

Speak about me like that, laddie, and you might be lucky to get any dinner tonight," she retorted with a smile in her eyes.

A servant dressed in an immaculate white uniform then approached with what Patrick later came to know as 'the sundowner tray'.

"Good evening, sirs," he said politely. Without thinking, Patrick automatically answered the greeting in Zulu.

"Good evening and thank you."

The man hesitated then quickly replied in Zulu, "Welcome, sir, I can hear you are one of us."

"What was that all about, Benate?" Angus asked.

"Just a Zulu greeting, Boss," replied Benate before he returned to the kitchen.

Angus poured the drinks and raised his glass saying, "Here's to Pat, for a safe journey back to Newcastle and may we meet again sometime." Jeannie sipped her sherry, but soon excused herself and went off to check how things were doing in the kitchen.

Patrick then took the opportunity to express his sincere thanks to Angus for the hospitality he had experienced throughout the four days and for the privilege of seeing around the whole of the colliery.

"It was only a pleasure," Angus replied. "But of course there's a price to pay. I would like to know, not what you liked, but what you found wrong here."

Patrick had of course realised that there was more to the visit than a sightseeing trip so he had made copious notes of his impressions, in preparation for such a question. Angus was pleased, but not surprised, when Patrick pulled from his suit pocket several handwritten pages dealing mainly with his speciality, the African workers' welfare, housing and the significance these had on worker/management relations. Angus thanked him then dropped the papers straight into the briefcase next to his chair, obviously planning to study them later

After pouring second whiskies for them, Angus decided he should confide in Patrick.

"I want to tell you something, Pat, but please, it must be treated in the strictest confidence. What is only known to me at the present time is that the colliery directors have taken the decision to develop a new shaft at Number Two Colliery. This will double the mine's output and naturally will also mean a large increase in staff, particularly miners and unskilled underground workers. These new employees will need houses, training programmes as well as recreational facilities and so forth. We will need someone to oversee all that new development. I'm sure you are enjoying your work at Newcastle and obviously I cannot offer you employment, but at this stage I would just like to know if you could be interested in the possibility of joining us in the future. It would be a senior staff position. Salaries are not grand here but we consider them adequate; with free housing, generous leave conditions and all of the usual mine perks."

Just at that moment Jeannie came back and saying, "Drink up, you old soaks, dinner is ready."

Patrick nodded his head to Angus but in fact he was grateful for her interruption as he didn't really know how best to answer the question.

"Good," said Angus, assuming his acceptance of the offer.

They went through to a traditional dining room and enjoyed a sumptuous meal, served with choice South African wines and spiced with delightful conversation.

After dinner Patrick told them how much he had enjoyed his visit to Wankie, thanking them both most sincerely for their kindness and hospitality. As he was taking the 6am train back to Bulawayo the next day he would not be seeing them again.

Deep in thought Patrick strolled down Victoria Road to the mine guest house. The cool night air, coupled with the chirping of the cicadas created a perfect ending to one of the most enlightening and stimulating evenings of his life. The following morning the company driver took him to the station in good time for the journey home.

There were not many passengers on the train and he had the whole compartment to himself, which pleased him as he had a lot to think about. The questions uppermost in his mind were: would he be offered the position at Wankie and if so, should he take it? While the impressions were still fresh in his mind he pondered on them again and again, the main one being the good atmosphere on the mine. The staff he had spoken to had been willing to talk openly to him about their jobs, their working conditions, their suggestions for improvements and also their frustrations. He had learnt a great deal from them, and about them. Their loyalty and admiration for Angus came as no surprise and he noted that they all referred to him as 'the Boss'. However, there was one notable exception and, interestingly, he was the only one who had referred to Angus as 'The Manager'. This person, Mr Powys P. Davies, was the mine accountant and his was also the only office to have a large polished brass nameplate on his closed office door. Patrick was told by one member of staff that the unfortunate man was inevitably nicknamed 'Penny Pincher Davies' and his department was referred to as the PPD.

The tour of the African housing proved to be an eye-opener as there had been no long term planning and the township had been allowed to just grow randomly as workers were engaged.

The design of the houses had changed little from those built in 1901, while even those currently being built, twenty-one years later, were only a little better than the traditional round thatched huts (known as pole and dagga kias). Fresh water was supplied via a number standpipes resulting in queues of people collecting water in buckets for washing and cooking purposes. In his opinion, the toilet facilities and the communal cookers were also shockingly inadequate. The only sign of any real development was a new mine hospital which was nearing completion, plus a row of houses for the hospital staff. A thought which unexpected came into Patrick's mind was 'preparation for accidents, perhaps'. He quickly dismissed that in favour of the more positive motive of 'improved facilities for African mine workers and their families'.

Patrick was also surprised by the fact that none of the accepted fire precautions were taken underground. Open arc electric welding was being carried out; men were carrying matches and smoking cigarettes with absolutely no regard to the risk of fires or explosions. When he queried this he had been told that Wankie was "not a fiery mine and there was no methane at all underground"

Angus had not exaggerated when he said there would be challenges; of that there was no doubt but Patrick wondered if sufficient funds would be provided to achieve the results which he envisaged. He also wondered how much influence and control Mr Powys Davies would have over the allocation of funds. There could well be potential problems there, he forecast.

Patrick's final thoughts were of envy for the happy relationship in the Mackay family and this made him realise just how much he had neglected his own private life by his dedication to work in Newcastle.

The journey to Bulawayo and then on to Johannesburg was comfortable enough, with good food served in the Rhodesian Railways dining car. On arriving at Plumtree, Patrick was delighted to see Theo on the station platform to greet him, having completely forgotten that he had told him of the date of his return to Johannesburg.

"I am settling down well, Patrick," he said. "Even in this short time I have no regrets about moving to Rhodesia. It is a vibrant and promising country. I hope an offer to move to Wankie does come your way and of course I would like to think that we were within visiting distance."

Arriving at the family home in the afternoon, Patrick had time to discuss the details of his Rhodesian trip with his mother. She listened intently until he had finished.

"Pat, I hate the thought of you being even further away than Newcastle, but I have the feeling that this would be a good opportunity for you. From what you have told me the people seem easier to work with, and I feel you would be happier there than in Newcastle. Perhaps, in time you could even find an opening for young Shaun. I would really like to get him away from his present friends, especially that empty-headed Miss he is going out with now."

A moment later Shaun blew in like a whirlwind and greeted Pat and his mother. Without pausing for breath he went on to tell them he was off to a dance and wouldn't be in for dinner. Pat followed him upstairs and tried to talk to him as he scurried through drawers looking for various items of suitable clothing.

"I can tell you have been talking to Mother. She thinks Mariette is a bad influence. She may be right on that score, but boy, is she pretty, and pretty hot too"

Pat quickly realised he was wasting his time. He stood up and grabbed Shaun firmly by the front of his smart dinner jacket and in slow measured tones said, "You, boy, are not only spoilt and selfish, you really are a bloody idiot Try thinking for a change. You had better change your ways or you will find yourself in BIG trouble." With that, Pat released his grip on the jacket, pushed Shaun out of his way, leaving behind a rather shaken but unrepentant young man.

Pat and his mother sat down to a quiet dinner together. As usual, his father spent the evening at the Rand Club in Commissioner Street. He wondered for how long his mother would put up with being alone night after night, but had yet to learn about the strength and loyalty of Victorian women; and of course he had no idea of the strength of the woman who was destined to come into his own life one day. By nine o'clock there was still no sign of his father, so Patrick said goodbye to his mother, walked down to Park Street station just in time to board the over-night train back to Newcastle.

Patrick spent the remaining few days of his leave in the Drakensberg Mountains, reliving the experiences of his youth, and, in those idyllic surroundings, he pondered deeply about what the future may hold for him.

Feeling thoroughly refreshed at the end of his leave, he went back to work. He had only just arrived in his office when Kumbula came in to see him. Unusually for him, Kumbula was looking agitated and most unhappy. He didn't even exchange their traditional greetings nor did he enquire about his holiday break.

"Boss Pat, the personnel manager is causing big trouble. Yesterday there was an argument between two underground workers, a Zulu and a Basotho. It was nothing too serious, but the personnel manager's important visitors saw them being treated in the first aid station and now he plans to fire the one who started it. The other Zulu miners claim the Basuto was at fault and don't want their man to be punished, and of course, the Basotho are threatening to strike if the Zulu is not found guilty. It is a stupid thing and there will be trouble either way. I asked the personnel manager please to wait until you returned. I think he did not like me advising him. He wants to see you straight away, now"

Patrick had come to work with a light heart and full of enthusiasm but this news blew all of that away in an instant. He had no great liking for the personnel manager at the best of times for although born in South Africa, he had little understanding of the African workers. His whole attitude was coloured by the fact that the Zulus had murdered the Boer leader, Piet Retief and his associates, back in 1836. His approach was that the Africans should consider themselves lucky to have jobs on the mine and they should be aware that they could easily be replaced.

The personnel manager's door was generally kept closed. He believed it helped to keep out those people who disrupted his routine with their complaints and trivial problems. Patrick knocked on the door and waited. When he heard the booming voice of Daniel van der Waldt shouting in Afrikaans, "Kom binner" (come in), Patrick took a deep breath before walking into the office. He was not invited to sit down so he remained standing in front of Daniel's huge polished mahogany desk. He knew from past experience that this was a tactic designed to make people feel inferior; something he had obviously learnt from his headmaster when he was a schoolboy.

"There was trouble underground yesterday." After pausing for a moment he added the rhetorical question, "O'Connor, why is it that you are always away when we have troubles?" Patrick smiled inwardly knowing that Daniel did not realise he was actually paying him an unintended compliment, but deeming the question as unworthy of a reply, he enquired as to what had actually happened underground. "I was taking important government officials on an inspection tour of the underground workings and they saw two blacks being patched up at the first aid station. The stupid bastards had been fighting but the visiting officials thought that there had been an accident and they started asking me a whole lot of awkward questions. I had to call the shift boss to explain what had happened. It was very embarrassing. I've instructed the shift boss to suspend them both and I'm going to fire the one who started the fight."

"Mr van der Walt," said Patrick, still standing in front of the massive desk, "why were they fighting and what nationality were they?"

How the hell should I know what they were fighting about or where they came from? They are from the bush somewhere and it is their nature to fight. You should know that by now. It was probably woman trouble. They had been dondering (thumping) each other with shovels."

"I think they would probably be a Zulu and a Basotho," said Patrick with conviction. "There is still considerable rivalry here between those ethnic groups, and most likely some insult or comment was taken too seriously, or the wrong way. They have their own ways of settling their problems. Would you like me to interview them and settle the matter for you, Mr van der Walt?"

"No, I have already written a report for management."

"I might be mistaken, Mr van der Waldt, but firing one of them would indicate your preference for the other's nationality. This could possibly trigger serious unrest, or even strikes. It would take a very brave man to propose such a step, knowing the General Manager's concerns over labour relations and not forgetting the good price we are getting for our coal at present."

"Perhaps you are right, O'Connor. I think you should sort this out. It will be good 'labour relations' experience for you." Dismissing Patrick with a wave of his hand he added, "Just see to it that this sort of thing doesn't happen again."

At the door Patrick paused, turned back and said, "By the way, Mr van der Waldt, please don't forget to withdraw your report. It would not look good for you if the General Manager received your report at the same time as mine." Patrick turned and walked out, deliberately leaving the door wide open. He was hurt and angered by the man's attitude but resisted the temptation to slam the door.

Once back in his own office he calmed down, then phoned Kumbula and asked him to send in the two belligerents. After asking some pertinent questions he gave them both stern words of warning and pointed out that the reason he had installed a proper boxing ring at the sports stadium was for settling silly argument such as theirs. He fined them each three days' wages and told them they were very lucky to not lose their jobs. As they walked away down the passage he heard them happily congratulating each other on their narrow escape and good fortune.

When Kumbula saw the workers leave the office he came over to talk to Patrick about his 'holiday'. They spoke for a long time, covering the trip in some detail, but Patrick made no hint of the possibility of employment in Wankie. When he stood up to leave the office Kumbula laughed and said, "Boss Pat, when are we leaving for Wankie?"

"Kumbula, I haven't been offered a job and what makes you think I would take a lazy, chattering old woman like you with me anyway?"

CHAPTER 4

୧୭ 1924 ୧୭

Kumbula had not been joking. It had been two painful years since his young wife and their daughter had died during her childbirth. He felt a desperate urge to get away and leave those dreadful memories behind. Wankie might give him the chance to rebuild his life and perhaps satisfy his heartfelt longing for a family of his own.

Patrick had written his 'thank you' letter to the Mackays within the first few days of returning to Newcastle, but a month went by before he received a three line personal note from Angus Mackay. It read:

A vacancy is coming up. Advise if you are interested and when you could be released by Newcastle. Reply soonest and, if favourable, a detailed offer will follow. We would really like you to come. Angus.

Although he had half expected it, Patrick was rather thrown by the letter. He had no close friends with whom to discuss it, and although his mother had assured him she could manage without him, he wanted to be certain so he sent her a telegram. Later that day he had her telegraphic reply:

YOU FORTUNATE YOUNG MAN. GO WITH MY BLESSINGS. DON'T WORRY I CAN COPE.
    LOVE MOTHER.

Kumbula wasn't in his office so Patrick left a note on his desk asking him to come to see him at his quarters after work that evening. When he arrived, Patrick handed him the letter from Angus. He read it and passed it back saying, "Boss Pat, you must accept! You are well liked by the workers here but there are some who don't like the way you seem to favour us black people. There are those too who resent you because you have succeeded where Boss Daniel has failed and that rankles with them. They watch for you to make just one mistake."

"Yes, Kumbula, I know that but I have started schemes for training and improvements to the sporting facilities for our workers. I feel I would be letting them down if I pulled out now. I know you would be capable of carrying on with my plans but I also know the colliery's policy and you would not be allowed to take over my position. Were you serious about coming to Wankie if I get the job?"

"Boss Pat, I am very serious. I want to start building a new family. I must have sons and daughters to care for me in my old age. I want grandchildren to play with and teach. I know I will not find that chance here. The local women are 'town people' and lack our traditional upbringing; not people I would trust to look after my children."

"Then we must talk seriously, Kumbula. I have some cold beers in the fridge. There is much to talk about and our throats could become very dry."

Patrick filled their beer tankards several times during the next two hours while they went through every aspect of the possible move. Finally they reached the conclusion that it would be the right thing to do. It was nearly the end of May so they could both be ready to start work at the end of June. It would now depend on the Wankie Colliery Company conditions and if they could be persuaded to offer Kumbula a position as his assistant.

Patrick sent a personal telegram to Angus saying:

INTERESTED AND AVAILABLE FIRST JULY. WOULD LIKE TO BRING MY VERY CAPABLE PRESENT ASSISTANT KUMBULA ZULU IF POSSIBLE.

Angus's typically staccato style reply came that afternoon:

GOOD. BOTH COME. CONDITIONS ALREADY POSTED.

The conditions were better than expected so Patrick and Kumbula put in their resignation notices and waited for a summons from Mr van der Walt; but none came. Instead the General Manager's secretary phoned asking them both to come and see him. In the four years Patrick had worked for the colliery he had never spoken one word to the GM so didn't know what to expect. He was therefore pleasantly surprised to find the GM showed a genuine interest in knowing where they were going and why they were making the move. Patrick was very careful in his replies. Kumbula was rather more direct. He said he was very happy in his work but told the GM that he foresaw serious problems in the near future because of the racial tensions between the African workers and the lower grades of white workers. He also feared that the attitude of the personnel manager would aggravate things further because he had little understanding of the black workers and yet he was unwilling to listen to or learn from people like Mr O'Connor.

The GM thanked them sincerely for the service they had

given to the colliery and wished them well in their new jobs in Rhodesia. With a knowing smile he thanked Kumbula for his frankness.

"I already know of the difficulties and we have plans for changes, but these will take some time still." He shook Patrick's hand firmly.

"I regret that we have not met until now. The work you have done here has not gone unnoticed and I am personally very sorry to see you both going. I wish you everything of the best in your new positions. I have authorised funds for a farewell party for you two at the sports stadium on the last Saturday of this month."

The 'send-off' party was a wild but touching function. Patrick and Kumbula were quite overwhelmed by the warmth and sincerity of the good wishes that were showered on them both.

CHAPTER 5

◇ 1924 ◇

As Lisa Khumalo had yet to meet Mr O'Connor, she was naturally curious as to what kind of man she would be working for. She was eighteen years old and had been employed as a learner housemaid in the Wankie Mine guest house for only a few months. On that July morning in 1924 her supervisor had told to report for work at number 16 Victoria Road, where she would be working for the new African Personnel Manager. The house was a fairly large bungalow built in the Rhodesian style with verandas on three sides, all gauzed-in to limit the mosquito and malaria problems. It stood on the hill overlooking the mine township, but not as well elevated as the general manager's mansion; number 1 Victoria Road. It was newly built but she immediately set about dusting and cleaning in preparation for the arrival of her new boss.

Lisa came from the Binga district, a remote area about seventy-five miles to the north-east of Wankie, bounded by the Zambezi and Binga rivers. Apart from her schooling at the Jesuit mission at Lupane, she had experienced only limited contact with any other Europeans. She was extremely apprehensive about her new employer especially when she was told that he came from South Africa. She had heard that those people could be very harsh and unkind to their employees.

Eric, the guest house driver, was at the railway station to meet Patrick and Kumbula. He drove them straight to Patrick's new home. Leaving Kumbula in the car, he carried Patrick's suitcases up onto the veranda where he introduced Patrick to Lisa. She curtseyed shyly then apologised for her poor knowledge of English. Recognising her accent, Patrick smiled kindly and switched to Zulu, saying how pleased he was to meet her and asked her full name.

"I am Jabulisa Khumalo," she answered lifting her head slightly as pride replaced her nervousness. "But I am called Lisa by the European people here."

"That is a pity," said Patrick. "They obviously don't know that Jabulisa means 'happiness'. If you live up to your name I'm sure we will get on well together. If you don't mind I will have to call you Lisa to avoid confusion."

She was very relieved and taking an instant liking to him offered to show him around his new home. It comprised three good bedrooms, a reasonably sized dining room and a large lounge, plus kitchen, pantry and laundry. On the kitchen table they found an enormous cardboard box filled with groceries. A note on the top of the box was addressed to him. Lisa said it had been delivered earlier that morning. The note was unsigned but he immediately recognised it must be from Jennie Mackay.

Welcome to Wankie Pat, I have opened an account for you at the 'best' store in town and bought these few groceries just to get you started. You can order by telephone and they will deliver whatever you want. They bill you at the end of each month. Let me know if you need anything.

Eric drove Kumbula past the African Administration Building and on to the African township. As they entered the township he pointed out the beer hall, the canteen and shopping centre before stopping at the 'house' which had been allocated to Kumbula. Eric helped him offload his luggage then handed him the key saying, "It is best to lock up when you go out, even though we don't have many skelems (thieves) here."

Before leaving, Eric told him that he could spend the rest of that day settling in, but he should report for work at the administration office by seven o'clock the following morning. Kumbula thanked him and went into his single quarters 'room'.

Kumbula was not in the least impressed by the mine's accommodation. The room measured eight feet by nine feet and was equipped with a narrow iron bedstead with a thin coir-filled mattress on it, a bedside cupboard, a small table and an upright chair. There was no toilet, shower or wash basin so he presumed there must be a communal ablution block somewhere nearby. Behind the door there was one solitary four-inch nail which served as a coat hook, but the enterprising previous occupant had strung a length of fencing wire diagonally across one corner of the room for extra hanging space. On the bedside cupboard the remains of a candle stood in a white enamel holder. Along the back wall of the room was a wide high window which provided the possibility of some through ventilation. He was surprised and disappointed. Although Patrick had warned him that conditions were primitive, this was far worse than he had expected. He couldn't help but compare it with Patrick's house at number 16 Victoria Road.

He unrolled his blankets and made up the bed but left his suitcase at the foot of the bed and went outside to find the men's ablution block. This was modern, clean and well kept, with hand basins, hot showers and numerous toilets. About fifty yards beyond it there was a communal cooking area with an enormous coal fired stove; about twelve feet long and three feet wide. The top was made of a single thick sheet of cast iron on which several pots of meat were already stewing, in preparation for the midday meal. Across the road was the mine's store and butchery; full of morning shoppers. He felt rather conspicuous in his suit, but was warmly greeted by the busy shopkeepers, all eager to serve him. For less than a shilling he was able to buy enough meat, vegetables and mealie meal for a good lunch. To these purchases he added sugar and a packet of Five Roses tea. He took the food back to his room and unpacked his two pots and an enamel plate from the suitcase. Lying down on the bed he couldn't help wondering if he had made a grave mistake in moving from Newcastle, but at the same time felt ashamed about doubting Boss Pat's judgement. This was the first time he had ever done so and he sincerely hoped he was wrong about it.

After a restless night in the strange surroundings he was up early and decided to walk around the township to familiarise himself with the layout and the general conditions. He soon realised that his accommodation certainly looked much better than the majority of thatched roofed rondavels. However, on speaking to several people during his walk he was assured that their thatched huts were far better than his brick built house with its corrugated iron roofing.

"Our traditional houses are much cooler in the summer. Being new to the area you don't know just how hot it gets here in October and November; and that iron roof on your house will be as hot as the top of a cooking stove."

In contrast to the rest of the buildings, the new hospital was a fine structure, situated on higher ground. A short distance away was a row of new houses for the doctors and nursing staff. Proper roads had been built to serve the area and each house had a picket fence enclosing a small garden. All the indigenous trees had been retained giving welcoming shade to the area. At the end of the road was a new sign indicating that the road had been named 'Albert Griese Road' after the founding geologist. Patrick will be pleased to hear this name, thought Kumbula, making a mental note to tell him, in case he didn't already know about it.

After a light breakfast of toast and tea, Kumbula made his way across to the African administration building where he found Patrick already in his office. They exchanged greetings and Patrick asked how he was settling in. Kumbula did not want to cause any offence so replied, a little unenthusiastically, "Fine thank you." Patrick immediately picked up that the housing was not good and assured him that this problem would be dealt with. The General Manager had agreed that Kumbula's position would be that of 'Assistant African Personnel Manager', not assistant to him, so he had to be patient in waiting for better houses to be built in the township once the contractors had finished all the work on the hospital. In reply to Kumbula's further enquiry, Patrick had to tell him that the houses under construction were just for the medical staff so it would not be one of those.

Patrick spent the next hour discussing the programme of improvements and changes which he had in mind for the department. He then asked Kumbula to inform the office staff that he would like them to gather in the conference room for an introductory meeting at ten o'clock.

All conversation ceased and the fifteen members of staff, twelve men and three women, stood up the moment Patrick entered the room. He asked them to be seated and as soon as they had settled down, he looked at each one of them briefly without saying a word. Then, speaking in Zulu he said, "I am happy to meet you all. My name is Patrick O'Connor your new personnel manager. I don't believe in formality but in the presence of outside visitors or senior mine staff you should call me Mr O'Connor. At all other times I will answer to Bwana Pat if you are from Nyasaland or Northern Rhodesia, Boss Pat if you are N'debele or from South Africa; I don't mind which. However, if you choose a bad nick-name for me I will certainly find those concerned and move them to the worst houses in the township." When the general laughter subsided, Patrick instructed each person in turn to stand up and give their full names, their home language and to explain briefly what their routine work for the company entailed. As they answered Kumbula made some notes but Patrick simply filed all the information in his phenomenal memory bank.

When they had finished, Patrick introduced Kumbula saying, "You have already met Kumbula Zulu but let me tell you about him. He has worked with me for four years in South Africa and he is the first African assistant personnel manager to be appointed here in Wankie. He has taught me most of what I know about handling staff matters. He has my full confidence and he acts with my authority, so listen when he speaks to you and please obey his instructions. Beware of him; he has a short fuse and easily explodes if he is given wrong information, or if you are late for work. If you have any problems you must bring them straight to him or to me; such things can fester if they are not dealt with promptly. I put my full trust in each of you and I expect you to do your utmost to make our department the best on the mine. If you do this ours will also be the happiest."

From the back of the room someone started clapping. It was Angus Mackay. All the staff immediately looked around, stood up then joined in the clapping, as the general manager walked up to the front to address them. Patrick hadn't seen him come in and had no idea how long he had been there at the back of the hall. He indicated for the staff to be seated.

"You have been given some good advice. These are good people. You support them and it will be in your best interests. I have seen what changes Mr O'Connor made in South Africa and with your help and total cooperation he will make the much needed improvements to our mine. There will be proper sporting facilities and, quite soon a school for your children. There are also plans for improved housing and as you have seen, the mine's own hospital is nearing completion. So it will now be up to every one of you to play your part."

There was excited chatter and broad smiles on the faces of all of the staff as Mr Mackay and Patrick left the room.

As they walked back to Patrick's office Angus said to him, "Good work, Pat. I am very pleased we met and that you decided to join us. I wish we had more like you. How is your assistant settling in? I expect that he's rather disappointed with his housing but I would like to hear your thoughts on the subject as I think he should get the same benefits as other assistant heads of departments, regardless of their ethnicity."

"I agree but I suspect the average miner from South Africa will not. A compromise might be possible, but I'd like to think about it and come back to you later if I may. Meanwhile, would it be in order for me to mention the possibility to Kumbula?"

"Sure, go ahead if you wish but don't raise his expectations too high or too soon. I must be away now. I've got one of those damn finance meetings to attend."

Patrick had a great deal to think about but decided that a walk around the existing African township with Kumbula would help to clarify some of the development plans he had in mind. Knowing what he wanted, he also knew that for the next three months the whole department would be turned upside down in a hive of activity.

Patrick had a seven point plan involving vast amounts of data for submission to the GM before any construction work could be started. He desperately wanted these, his first proposals, to be accepted. He had discussed the broad outlines with Angus and obtained his approval in principle, but they had to be backed up by facts before they could be put before the board for approval.

*

After five months of long hours and hard work, Patrick had the information he needed. However, what he had not appreciated, or made allowance for, was the close scrutiny of his figures by the mine's accountant, Mr Powys Davies. Within days of submitting the documents to Mr Mackay, all beautifully typed by Ethel, his best typist, they came back to Patrick from the mine's accountant. There were numerous figures circled in red ink, plus question marks alongside, or notes saying something like, 'justify' or 'where does this come from?'. Patrick was furious and it took all of his self-control to resist phoning Mr Davies. When he had calmed down sufficiently, he called Kumbula to come through and discuss the documents with him. They spent the rest of the day going through them, adding explanatory notes and rechecking all of their figures. Impatient for completion, Patrick suggested to Kumbula that they take all the papers back to his house in the hope of finishing the work that night so that it would be ready for retyping the next day. He phoned Lisa telling her that there would be two of them for dinner. That afternoon they walked back together to Pat's house, carrying a heavy briefcase full of the relevant papers.

Lisa met them on the veranda, telling them that she would clear one end of the large dining table for their paperwork, while setting the other end for their meal. Patrick then realised that he had not introduced Kumbula. When he did, she smiled, then dropped her eyes, put out her hand to him and did a respectful little curtsey. Kumbula seemed to suddenly come to his senses and hesitantly shook her hand, at the same time greeting her in Zulu. It is said that black skinned people don't blush, but this is not true and Patrick, the keen observer, noticed the tell-tale signs immediately. They went through to the dining room and spread out the offending papers on the table.

"Could we have some drinks please, Lisa?"

She answered, "I have already put them on the veranda, Boss Pat." So, they walked out and sat on the easy chairs, relaxing and admiring the soft light of the setting sun, while drinking their ice cold Castle lagers. Patrick knew Kumbula desperately wanted to know more about Lisa but he deliberately let him suffer for a while before commenting that his housemaid was very satisfactory and he was very pleased with her. The subject having been opened, there flowed a torrent of questions from Kumbula. Patrick mischievously tormented him a little further by saying that he didn't really know very much about her but eventually did relent.

"No she is not married but she might be promised. Her family name was Khumalo. Yes, she is of royal blood. No, she does not have living parents. She is from the Binga district and her parents had come there from Bulawayo on the last journey north with King Lobengula's wagons and the remnants of his warriors. Just you remember this though, she is my housemaid and you cannot steal her. She's too good for you anyway, you old skabenga (bad man)."

"Aikona (No) Boss Pat, how can you say such things?"

Patrick laughed and said, "Come on, Kumbula, finish up your drink and then we must get some work done before dinner time."

Lisa gave them a hearty dinner and Kumbula tried desperately to avoid staring at her while she served them, and again afterwards as she cleared away their empty plates. She too avoided any eye contact; Patrick noted.

They worked on until midnight completing the rest of the bulky report, ready for retyping the following morning. Kumbula made his way back to his room and eventually went to sleep with the picture of the lovely Lisa foremost in his mind.

Arising early the next morning, Patrick collected up all the papers they had worked on; sorted them into their correct order, ate his breakfast, then walked happily down to his office.

He found Ethel busily dusting her Remington typewriter and handed her the edited pages of the report. Immediately distressed, she asked, "Oh no, Boss Pat, have I mistyped something?"

Smiling, Patrick replied, "Ethel, you typed it perfectly but unfortunately there have been a number of changes so a lot of it will need to be done again. It is very urgent, so do you think you can finish it today?"

"I will try my hardest," she said, "and maybe it could even be ready by lunchtime."

"Thank you, Ethel, I know you will do your best."

Mr Powys Davies was surprised and more than usually irritated when the office messenger put the bulky freshly typed report into his in-tray; just when he was in the middle of signing a pile of requisitions. In his mind he had reckoned it would take several days, or even a week, for that slow-witted Irishman to make the corrections; and that would have ensured it would miss the September board meeting. Now, to his annoyance he was being pressed into rechecking the revised document. He hated being rushed, especially on papers for the board. That there might be any changes or additions to the general text in the report never occurred to him. This, coupled with the fact that the wily Irishman had deliberately failed to return the original draft, which was marked up with his comments in red ink, were things which would come back to haunt him later.

CHAPTER 6

❧ 1925 ❧

The following day the General Manager's secretary phoned Patrick and advised that he was required to attend the board meeting for discussions on staffing of the mine's new hospital. She told him that the mine's doctor and the two government doctors would also be attending. For Patrick this was welcome news as the new buildings and staff accommodation were nearing completion so a start should also be made on his own special projects.

As chairman, Angus thanked the three doctors for making time to attend the meeting then detailed the agenda:

1. Arrange terms and conditions for the mine and government doctors to cover for each other's responsibilities when one was away on leave or in the event of work overloading.
2. Discuss and agree on the recruitment of additional nursing staff for both hospitals.
3. Approve the allocation of accommodation for the new staff.
4. Approve the employment of a hygiene and sanitation inspector for the mine's townships.

The meeting went very well and, following a good deal of detailed discussion, items 1 to 3 were all agreed and resolved. However, when they reached item 4, the mine accountant pompously announced that he had not been consulted about the appointment of a sanitation inspector and it would be quite impossible as there was no allowance in the annual budget for salaries for such a post. Angus turned to Patrick and asked, "Is that correct, Mr O'Connor? I thought you had covered that point in your report."

"Yes indeed it was, Mr Mackay. If my memory serves me correctly, I recall stating that my deputy would be prepared to undertake the extra duties of sanitation and hygiene inspections with no addition to his salary; the only requirement was that his appointment should be classified as a medical one, as far as accommodation was concerned."

"That's settled then," said Mr Mackay. "Good work, O'Connor." Then turning to the accountant he added, "I'm sure you will agree and be happy to avoid any extra costs, Mr Davies?"

"Yes, of course I am, Mr Mackay." He then gave Patrick a venomous glance but not yet appreciating the full implications of his consent.

Patrick could barely conceal his delight. His plan had succeeded. The post of Sanitation and Hygiene Inspector had been approved and as a new medical appointee Kumbula would qualify for the last house presently being built in Albert Griese Road. Kumbula was also highly amused by his fancy new title of 'Sanitation Inspector'. Each day from then on he checked the builder's progress.

CHAPTER 7

Patrick went home after the meeting and on the small table where he always put his keys was a letter from South Africa. Recognising his mother's handwriting, he wondered why she had written again so soon after her recent letter. Suspecting it must contain something important, he decided to read it before showering and changing into casual clothes. So he sat down, poured the cold beer which Lisa had brought, and opened his mother's letter.

102 Claim Street,
Hillbrow,
Johannesburg.
Friday, 22nd November 1925

My dearest Boy,

It pains me greatly to have to burden you with my problems, yet again, but I truly have no one else to turn to at present. You may recall that I was concerned about young Shaun's developing relationship with a local girl living not far down the road from us. Well, this morning I had a visit from the girl's two elder brothers demanding to know the whereabouts of young Shaun. It would appear the girl is with child and the two men believe he could be responsible.

To protect my errant son I told them an untruth, saying that he was away in Benoni on some job but would be back by about 6.30 in the evening. I assured them that it was highly unlikely that Shaun was involved in any way, as Shaun would easily convince them.

They left saying they would return this evening. Desperately worried, I telephoned your father and asked him to get a message to Shaun at his work. He said that he would try but added that getting a message to anyone on the mine was extremely difficult. He went on to say that he had already advised Shaun not to get involved with the girl anyway, because she was a Catholic

The two young men were back on their motorcycles shortly before 6.30. I then I heard the unmistakable roar of Shaun's own powerful machine approaching so I went out onto the veranda. There was some heated discussion and Shaun suddenly rode off at high speed. The two young men leapt onto their motorcycles and gave chase. However, they were unable to catch up. I have never liked Shaun's great big beast of an engine but I gave thanks to God today for its speed, for he left them far behind.

About half an hour later the brothers returned and, using the most uncouth language, told me that they would find him and they would ensure that he never sired any further babies.

I am at my wits' end as to what we should do

Your ever loving Mother.

Disappointed but not really surprised, Patrick thought carefully through the whole sordid business and then decided on a possible solution to the problem. A contract had recently been awarded to a Bulawayo based firm of electrical contractors for the installation of street lighting in the government town of Wankie which adjoined the mine's own township, but was separate from it by about a mile. Patrick had recently met Mr Taylor, the contractor's engineer, for discussions on the likely costs if the mine were to install similar lighting in the African township.

So, wasting no time, Patrick phoned through to Bulawayo the following morning and asked Mr Taylor if his firm had any vacancies for electricians; saying that his younger brother had completed his apprenticeship the previous year and had worked as a journeyman on the mines in South Africa since then.

Mr Taylor's reply was encouraging. "I'm recruiting staff for the government contract now and I would certainly be willing to interview him." Patrick thanked him saying that he would get his brother to call in as soon as possible.

He then sent the following telegram to his mother:

TELL HIM COME SOONEST TO BULAWAYO FOR INTERVIEW BY MR TAYLOR OF POWER CONTRACTORS IN LOBENGULA STREET FOR JOB IN WANKIE. LOVE PAT.

In the meantime Kumbula had been visiting Lisa when she was off duty over weekends. He was desperately in love and had agonised over the problem of accommodation. Now, quite out of the blue, the 'miracle house' had materialised. He felt it was a sign from his ancestral spirits that good things do happen and there was a possibility she might accept him; in spite of his 'lowly birth' and the fact that he was several years older than her.

He had tried to keep his liaisons with Lisa secret from Patrick but having no one else to confide in he plucked up courage and told Patrick the great news. Enjoying his discomfort Patrick put on his sternest expression.

"I suspected something was up and now I can see that I am right. You want to steal my housemaid. I would remind you that you promised me you would not do that." Kumbula squirmed with embarrassment and couldn't look directly at Patrick.

"No, no, Boss Pat, I would not break my promise but I must tell you that I really only want your permission." Patrick burst out laughing, then congratulated him and wished him every success.

"She is a fine young woman. I'm sure she would make you very happy and be proud to bear your children." Kumbula was greatly relieved and supremely happy to have 'official approval'.

Patrick was truly pleased for them both but couldn't help a twinge of envy when he considered his own situation. He had met most of the mine's female staff plus a number of ladies from the government township of Wankie, but had yet to meet anyone special. The majority were married, generally happily and unavailable, or unmarried, available but undesirable. In spite of Jeannie Mackay's best efforts to find a suitable partner for him, he remained unattached and more than a trifle lonely.

In this contemplative mood, he reviewed what he had achieved since his arrival in Wankie. Following the pattern established down in Newcastle, he had introduced classes in Fanika Lo for the European workers as well as for the foreign Africans. He had also started a school for the African miners' children and taken on the full responsibility as Principal. A start had been made on the development of good sporting facilities; the football field had been levelled and proper goal posts had been made using piping from the mine scrapyard. To cut costs the netting for the goal posts had been skilfully made by the 'African Women's Group'. A portable boxing ring had been made by the mine's carpentry apprentices, and this was proving very popular. Besides providing a safe place for settling minor disputes, Kumbula suggested a novel way in which anyone could enter the ring and issue a general challenge to others of approximately the same weight. There was a five shilling prize for the winner of three rounds. For the loser there was a sixpence which he had to accept. This always caused great hilarity amongst the crowd who all called out "Shame!" and laughed as he was forced to take the sixpenny coin.

Patrick was very pleased to learn that the designs for new houses incorporated kitchens, solar heated showers and a sitting room had been approved. Electric street lighting was being considered but this installation was still being evaluated. Discussions had been held about the introduction of full apprenticeships for Africans, but this too was still subject to approval by the Chamber of Mines. Unfortunately there seemed to be considerable opposition from the European artisans.

Patrick leaned back in his chair and decided the satisfaction of doing a good job was reason enough to be quite pleased with life.

The next morning, the office messenger came in with a telegram from Johannesburg reading:

SHAUN LEFT FOR BULAWAYO THIS MORNING. GRATEFUL THANKS FOR YOUR EFFORTS. LOVE MOTHER.

Whilst the telegram relieved some of Patrick's worries, he was still uncertain how best to handle the whole messy business. He and Shaun had never been close friends and of course being away fighting for the British in the Great War, followed by the years working in Newcastle, he had only known Shaun as a young, rather spoilt teenager. So, after deliberating over the situation for a while he decided the only course would be to try to get to know his brother better before making any judgement. He didn't relish the idea of having him to stay for any length of time, but could hardly refuse him accommodation.

He spoke in confidence to both Jeannie Mackay and Kumbula and felt a good deal better for doing so. He didn't go into detail about Mariette, but just mentioned that there was 'a bit of a problem over a girl'. From the way they had gently nodded their heads Patrick knew they had both understood the problem and would be quite willing to help him to cope, if needed.

Four full days passed before Patrick heard the familiar sound of the big Aerial Four Square motorbike coming up Victoria Road. From the front veranda he watched a very dusty and dirty Shaun parking his bike in the driveway, then slowly and stiffly dismounting before taking off his goggles and rubbing his eyes. Patrick walked down and greeted him warmly. Shaun replied saying, "This must be the end of the bloody earth. I've been in the saddle for nearly three days; in this heat it's not much fun, but thanks a lot for helping. I've accepted the job and will be starting early in the new year."

"Come on in and have a shower while I organise something to drink. I'm sure you could manage a cold beer. You will find the bathroom at the end of the passage. Dump your kit in the first bedroom on the left."

Twenty minutes later a barely recognisable Shaun returned; clean and immaculately dressed, looking like a tennis player about to go onto the court in a major competition. Patrick encouraged him to talk about the arduous journey from Johannesburg as well as the details of the interview in Bulawayo. The salary sounded high to Patrick, compared to his own, but he suspected that the contractors would make quite sure he earned every penny of it. The completion period for the project was twelve to sixteen weeks from the starting date of 2nd January, and there was no guarantee of being kept on afterwards.

Patrick had started eating his main meal at midday and Lisa always saw to it that there were the makings of a cold supper before she went off duty in the afternoon. After a few beers he excused himself and shared out a meal that had been left for them. There was some tension because they both knew that there were serious issues to be discussed and plans to be made for the future.

Patrick gave Shaun time to relax. From experience he had gained in his years dealing with a wide range of employees personal problems, he was able to judge the best moment to ask questions. That moment came after supper when they were sitting on the veranda in the semi-darkness, enjoying a cup of coffee. Patrick said quietly, "I think we should talk about Mariette. Tell me from the beginning." Shaun readily agreed, anxious to state his side of the case to the one person he knew would listen to him.

"Well, she was a popular girl and had many fellows after her. She was vivacious and pretty, but maybe 'not the brightest button in the box'. She thought I was terrific, which of course did my ego no harm. Initially I was tempted but resisted her open invitations, mainly because I knew what our parents' attitude, being Presbyterians, would be. She was a Catholic and I think she may have confessed her sins too fully or, maybe, too often, because one Saturday afternoon when I was visiting her, the local parish priest pitched up. On seeing me he jumped to the conclusion that I was the one she had mentioned in her confessions and he virtually accused me of seducing the girl. At that stage I was in fact completely innocent. As you can imagine, I was very angry but I held my tongue for a while, not admitting nor denying the accusation. This seemed to infuriate the priest and he started preaching to me about the sanctity of marriage, the sins of contraception and so forth. At that point I nearly lost my temper. I truly wanted to punch the pompous bugger, but thought better of it. Instead, I told him I was not of his faith and he had no right to tell me what I could or could not do. Foolishly perhaps, I went on and said, 'If you want every one of your fornicating flock to enter into forced marriages then you are going the right way about it.' He stormed out of the house cursing me as a wicked Protestant seducer of innocent young Catholic girls. Mariette, laughing at the exchange of words, clapped her hands saying, 'Shaun, come into the bedroom now! We'll show him.' Prophetic words indeed, as they turned out to be. Clearly I was not the first nor the only one, so I cannot be sure if I was responsible for her pregnancy."

Patrick sat silent for a while then asked, "How do you feel about it now? Would you marry the lass if her family and ours would allow it?"

"I truly am ashamed of myself for being so foolish and reckless, but I definitely wouldn't want to become entangled for the rest of my life with her, her family and Father Luke. I knew full well that she was a tart and that she slept around, and for all I know she may have seen me as an eligible father for her child, and led me on with that in mind."

"Well, you've been very frank about it all but one thing I notice is that you made no mention of Mariette's situation and feelings?"

"Pat, before I left Joburg I promised her that if she ever needs help of any kind I would do my best to provide it, but I also made it clear that I would never marry her, and actually, to my astonishment and relief she accepted what I had to say."

That is at least something, thought Patrick. He hoped that his brother had learnt a worthwhile lesson; only time would tell.

Shaun's first priority the following morning was to go to the local post office and send a telegram to his mother. He was also very conscious of his lack of clothing as he had only been able to carry a few items strapped in the saddle bags of his motorbike. Realising how ill-equipped he was for the coming Christmas festivities, and without a thought for the transport costs involved, he sent his mother the following telegram:

ARRIVED SAFELY BUT DESPERATE FOR CLOTHING. PLEASE PACK ALL MY SUITS JACKETS SHIRTS AND SHOES IN A PACKING CASE OR TIN TRUNK AND SEND BY TRAIN TO PATRICK'S ADDRESS. LOVE SHAUN.

Within two weeks there was a notification from the Rhodesia Railways office of the arrival of a packing case. Shaun's delight was short lived because the goods attendant at the station pointed out that the goods had been sent 'carriage forward' and there was a bill of seven pounds six shillings and eight pence to pay before the goods could be released. He didn't have that much money and was a little peeved that his parents hadn't thought of that.

When Patrick came home for lunch, Shaun told him about the money required by Rhodesia Railways, and wondered why his parents hadn't paid the transport charges. Patrick was irritated and pointed out that his parents might have also been unable to pay. Patrick didn't offer to pay and Shaun's pride prevented him from raising the question again. However, that evening after sundowners, Patrick said, "I think it is time we set some ground rules and talked seriously about your future plans." Shaun eagerly agreed.

"Shaun, you will be starting work on the 2nd of January and will be earning a very good salary. I am prepared to lend you £25 for your expenses until then; but no more. You must repay it, in full, from your first and second month's salaries. Next, you are to pay Lisa for any washing and ironing she does for you and you must always let her know if you will be away for any meals. You are welcome to stay here at no cost until you start work but I do not want you to entertain any friends or acquaintances here. I will sign you in as a guest member at the Mine Club where you can have meals and entertain friends but you will have to pay in cash at the bar. You cannot charge anything on my club account. Remember also that this is a small community and any bad behaviour on your part would affect my position and reputation. Do you fully understand what I've said?" Shaun readily agreed, thankfully pocketing the cash.

The next morning Shaun went down to the railway station, paid the charges then found two men who were willing to carry his box back to 16 Victoria Road for a shilling each. Opening the box on the veranda, he felt a surge of pleasure on seeing his precious clothing and the new dancing shoes; his pride and joy. These things had arrived just in time for him to make a noteworthy appearance at the anticipated Christmas festivities. He hung up his suits and jackets in the spacious wardrobe, put aside any creased shirts for Lisa to wash and iron, then cleaned and polished his dancing shoes.

For Patrick, it was a very busy time of the year. As principal of the African school, he had to sign and comment on every pupil's test examination as well as seeing to and attending the organisation of the year-end sporting events. He enjoyed the challenges but, quite frankly, he was looking forward to settling back into his normal routine. Although they got along well enough, he found Shaun was not the easiest of guests because they shared so few common interests.

At the Christmas party Shaun excelled, outshining all competition in his latest Joburg suit and his dancing skills. He had a very good line of chatter, and the ladies loved his charm and subtle flattery. He had no hesitation in asking Jeannie, the General Manager's wife, to dance. Within minutes she was laughing and joking with him. He has definitely 'kissed the Blarney Stone', she later commented to Patrick.

Christmas Day was a relatively quiet affair but it was a highlight for Lisa. Patrick had bought her a brand new bicycle; a Raleigh, the best money could buy. She had no idea it was coming and her delight was beyond words. She clapped her hands, jumped up and down, danced around Patrick and

Shaun, and then, with tears streaming down her cheeks, kissed the bicycle's saddle.

"Oh, thank you, Boss Pat, it is beautiful, but I don't know how to drive it."

"Don't worry about that, Lisa, Kumbula knows all about bicycles and I feel sure he would be willing to teach you. He has also been given a bicycle to use for his sanitation and hygiene inspection work, so allow him to teach you to ride and I hope you will teach him a few things too! He probably hasn't told you, but I know that in many ways he has had a rather sad and lonely life. I'm certain that you will bring him the happiness he deserves."

CHAPTER 8

By the end of January the new hospital buildings were finally completed and ready for occupation. The new European and African nursing staff arrived from Salisbury, plus some from South Africa. Patrick and his helpers saw to their transport, luggage collection and generally helped them to get settled into their new accommodation. The senior white sister, a kindly faced middle aged woman, was appointed as Matron and the four young nurses were designated as Staff Sisters. They would be responsible for the supervision and training of the African orderlies, who tended the patients.

Patrick's impression of them all was very favourable. Having travelled together on the train journey from Bulawayo to Wankie, they had got to know each other and he felt confident that they would settle down well. There was a good deal of laughter and general fun between the younger ones. They were all attractive girls and he noticed that none of them wore engagement or wedding rings so they would be a welcome addition to the mining community. He was pleased to find that Mary, a South African nurse from the Eastern Cape was reasonably fluent in Xhosa, while the other South African understood basic Zulu. The Salisbury girls spoke passable Fanika Lo, the universal mining language. These abilities would make a great difference to their patients' confidence and trust, as well as helping when giving instructions to the orderlies.

The two South African nurses had trained together at Boksburg hospital near Johannesburg and were close friends. In appearance they were very different; Wendy being blonde and of slim build, while Mary was about five feet seven inches tall, nicely rounded with soft dark hair and an olive complexion. Both were good looking and shared an equally wicked sense of humour, and mischief. Patrick was instantly smitten by both of them and he immediately resolved to protect them from his young brother at all costs! The Salisbury girls, Rhoda and Francis, were very pleasant but quieter, and in Patrick's inexperienced opinion, less vivacious; but no doubt they would all be good nurses.

He gave them a fortnight to settle in, by which time Shaun had moved to the electrical contractor's temporary chalets in town. Patrick felt it would be safe to invite the matron and the four new nurses over for sundowners and to meet the general manager, the departmental heads and their wives.

There had been an inch of rain on the morning of the sundowner party, cooling the evening for the occasion. Lisa had spent the day making sausage rolls, roasting monkey nuts and preparing a huge selection of delicious snacks for the guests. Patrick was in his element introducing the new arrivals. As was his way, he had already found out all he could about their interests and backgrounds, so within minutes the nurses were chatting to the other guests and feeling completely at ease. New blood in a small community is always welcome and a most enjoyable evening followed. Just before leaving, Jeannie

Mackay took Patrick to one side and, in a conspiratorial whisper said, "I think the dark one is the one for you." Patrick felt embarrassed; his face flushing guiltily.

"I hope you are right, Jeannie, but we will just have to wait and see."

"Don't wait too long, laddie," she cautioned. "Good women are in short supply and we have a surplus of males here. It's a characteristic of mining towns"

The government street lighting contract was finally completed and as expected, Shaun came to visit him. Patrick had seen little of Shaun since his arrival in Wankie but the staff at the hospital had informed him that his brother was often seen with the two South African nurses. This news concerned and worried Patrick considerably.

After a little idle chatter Shaun came out with the reason for his visit. It involved the setting up of an electrical contracting business in Wankie. He felt sure he could assist the mine by rewinding burnt out electric motors, and also undertaking the electrical maintenance of the mine's staff houses. The icing on the cake he said, was the prospect of tendering for the street lighting contract in the mine's African township. Patrick did nothing to sway or encourage him but allowed him to ramble on until he came to the inevitable question.

"I don't suppose you could help with some initial capital could you, Pat, either as a loan or to become a partner in the venture? I estimate that £250 would get me started and your influence in the township would be very useful."

Patrick sat silent for a while, as if giving the matter serious thought before answering.

"Shaun, I have no doubt you are a hard worker and an excellent electrician but I must tell you that I have serious misgivings over your handling of financial matters, as well as your ignorance of the ethics of business and contracts." Shaun looked shocked.

"Really, Pat, I don't know what gives you that impression. I know I was a little extravagant buying good clothing when I was younger but that was in the past; and surely you know that everyone uses friends and relatives in business today? Father certainly told me that the Freemasons and the Catholics did so"

"For a start, Shaun, what you suggest would be absolutely impossible. I would be obliged to tell the colliery company if I had any interest on your business affairs. Just think about it for a moment; how could I take any part in the adjudication of a tender from your company? But tell me about this sudden resurgence of brotherly love. How often have you bothered to even visit me since you started work? What happened to our agreement in which you undertook to repay that trivial loan of £25 from your first two salaries?"

Shaun squirmed in his chair in genuine embarrassment but couldn't think of any suitable reply, other than to say he was sorry and he had brought the £25 with him now. Using a more conciliatory approach, Patrick asked him what he thought he might do if his contracting scheme fell through.

"I've heard of a vacancy on the copper mines up north and I've been thinking of applying. There is one problem though; I have been taking out, on a friendly basis so far, two of the nurses at your hospital and I don't know which of them I prefer, or more importantly which one would be prepared to join me on the mine in Luanshya. They are both lovely girls and I am sure either would accept my suggestion of a move north, but I simply don't know which one to choose. I think Wendy is more my type but Mary would make a wonderful wife and mother one day."

"Shaun, for goodness' sake, man, you are speaking about a major life commitment not just choosing a potted plant at a florist or a puppy at a pet shop. This is a serious matter and I would strongly advise you to think things through like an adult, and at the very least get a permanent job first. Learn how to save some money and get to know your prospective wife before making a horrible mess of her life and yours"

Thoroughly shaken, Shaun apologised then genuinely thanked Patrick for his advice. He put a £5 note on the table for Lisa, picked up his jacket and the motorbike keys and said, "I'll be off then, but do come up north and see me some time. Meanwhile, I will do my best to improve.' Patrick realised he must forget about Shaun but he needed to take action soon or he might miss the boat and lose Mary.

CHAPTER 9

❧ 1927 ❧

During the Christmas/New Year break Kumbula spent most of his spare time in the garden of his new home. He cleared the builder's rubble and prepared beds for his vegetables. He still had great difficulty accepting the fact that this house was shortly going to be his own. Boss Pat was truly a miracle worker as well as valued friend. Kumbula spent many hours thinking about the new world which could possibly open up for him; the most important factor was that Lisa might now consider him worthy of her affections. The house had three bedrooms and his mind raced at the thought of his own sons and daughters being in them one day. He wanted to run through the township shouting for joy, but he had to hold in his feelings. Instead he lay back on his rickety old iron bedstead thinking of the comparative luxury of his new home and sending grateful thanks to his ancestors, Boss Pat and to the creator of all good things.

Kumbula had not seen Lisa since Boxing Day when she brought her new bicycle to show him. Her first lesson was hilarious; so much so that little real progress was made. However, he was thrilled just to hear her happy laughter and the mixed squeals of fear and delight as she tried to keep her balance. He suggested that she leave the bike at his house for safe keeping and arranged for further lessons the following weekend.

Kumbula's appointment as Sanitation Inspector had come as a surprise, and initially he had thought it was a rather demeaning task but he now realised that it was a vital step in the allocation of the house. An unexpected bonus was that the task required him to travel all over the township on the new bicycle provided by the mine. It would be lovely, he thought, once Lisa mastered her bicycle, as they could then go riding together in the surrounding countryside. His office work entailed dealing daily with dozens of people and their problems, so at the weekends he craved solitude. Having a bicycle enabled him to get away from the mine to explore the local hardwood forests and the streams which fed into the mighty Zambezi river. Although there were no roads the numerous well-worn footpaths made reasonably good cycle tracks, provided one was careful of what lay ahead. He soon became familiar with the area and relished being able to hear again those unforgettable sounds of the bird calls and animals which are so typical of Rhodesia. He wondered how soon it would be that he might be able to experience them in the company of a beautiful girl like Lisa; 'The bringer of happiness' indeed.

A week later Lisa achieved the seemingly impossible. She learnt to ride her new bicycle, only occasionally losing control when lack of concentration caused her to wander off the road. Kumbula suggested that, on her next off duty Sunday, they should go for a picnic to a place he had found. She thought it would be good to get away from the mine and readily agreed. Kumbula made all of the necessary plans for the following Sunday's picnic. On the day he was up early and packed some sausages, two pieces of fillet steak, several sandwiches, a couple of enamel plates and two bottles of cool drinks for their picnic lunch. They rode out about four miles from Wankie then turned off along a little used dusty footpath to a stream which he had found while exploring previously. It was an idyllic picnic spot on the banks of a small tributary of the Gwaai river. The bush had overgrown the pathway so they had to dismount and push their bikes. After about ten minutes they came to a grassy bank overlooking a beautiful crystal clear pool. Having learnt from Boss Pat about Lisa's father having been taken by a croc, Kumbula went straight down to the pool and checked very thoroughly for crocodiles. Finding none, he returned and sat down on the soft green grass with Lisa, and they ate the sandwiches and sipped the welcome cool drinks.

For the first time in their relationship she spoke of her childhood and family background. She confirmed that she was a direct descendent of King Lobengula.

"My father was the son of one of the King's lesser wives, so I am not very royal. He had however grown up to be one of Lobengula's younger Indunas and was chosen to accompany the King in 1893 when fleeing from Cecil Rhodes' soldiers. As a reward for their loyalty, he and the other Indunas were each given a small leather pouch containing twenty-five gold sovereigns. These were a very small part of the payment made to Lobengula in terms of the Rudd Concession. Shortly after this gift was made, the King contracted malaria and died. Disaster then struck in the form of the dreaded Rhinderpest, a cattle disease which had swept down from Somalia in the north right down to the border of Natal in South Africa. It killed hundreds of thousands of cattle, zebras and numerous other cloven hoofed wild animals as well. Finally it spread westwards into Matabeleland. All of the cattle and most of the game animals in the area died, leading to dreadful starvation which decimated the Matabele people. Lisa's parents survived by catching fish in the Binga river. Traditionally, such food was never eaten by the Matabele people. They believed fish to be unclean and closely related to snakes."

The gold sovereigns were of no value at that time but when Lisa reached the age of nine years, a Jesuit mission had established a boarding school at Lupane, about 120 miles south of Binga and they were willing to teach and board her for one golden sovereign per term; three sovereigns per year. At the age of twelve her father was taken by a crocodile while fishing near Binga village, which forced her mother to find work as an office cleaner at Wankie Colliery. Sadly her mother had recently died, leaving her the one remaining coin, which she always believed was for buying her wedding dress. Kumbula was almost in tears hearing her sad story but Lisa put her arms around him.

"Don't be sad for me, I have learnt a lot and I've been very fortunate. I think I might have found a man who would love me and treat me kindly." She leant over and kissed him lightly on his cheek.

"I love you more than anything in the world, little girl. I will look after you always and I kill any man who is ever unkind to you."

They cooked their steaks and sausages on the open fire and, when they finished eating, they lay back on the soft grass and slept, shaded from the midday sun by a small acacia tree. Later they were woken; feeling very hot, as the afternoon sun had moved over and they were no longer shaded. Lisa stripped off her outer clothes and jumped into the pool, squealing with delight as her body hit the cool water. Kumbula followed her after another hasty look for crocodiles. Lisa was a powerful swimmer, having grown up in Binga where the Shangani and Gwaai rivers joined and spilt into the Zambezi. Kumbula on the other hand could keep afloat but made little progress, just dog paddling. She enjoyed teasing him, then swimming underwater and ducking him. Finally they staggered out of the water exhausted but happy. She walked over to some small bushes, stripped off her underwear and hung the skimpy items over bushes to dry in the afternoon sunshine. Kumbula stood, transfixed by her beauty. Her slim youthful body was covered with water droplets which glistened on her dark skin like small diamonds in the sun. He went over to her and they stood together feeling the warmth of the sun and each other's bodies. When they were dry they lay down on the soft grass then tenderly and exquisitely made love.

As the evening started to close in they hastily tidied up their picnic site, pushed their bikes back through the bush then silently rode back to the mine; neither of them wishing to break the spell of their love making. They arrived home just as the sun set and gently kissed before going their separate ways to their homes.

Three months later Lisa told Kumbula she was sure she was pregnant. He was absolutely delighted and immediately proposed marriage, which she happily accepted. In the Zulu and Matabele traditions, she had now proved that she was not barren and therefore was fit to become a wife.

She told Patrick that Kumbula had proposed and he congratulated her warmly.

"I am delighted. As soon as I met you I hoped you two would get together. He is a fine man and deserves the best possible wife to love and look after him. I am sure you will have a long and happy life together. Don't you forget to put my name on your wedding invitation list, or you will not be given 'time off' to get married."

Knowing the tradition Patrick added, "I am friendly with the new nurses in charge of the hospital's maternity ward so I will see to it that you get the best of treatment when your time comes."

Lisa felt that the assistance and advice of the white nurses may well be a great help when her time came, but it also brought home to her the sadness and loneliness of not having a mother to be with her sharing the joy of a first grandchild.

In the course of his normal duties Patrick generally called in at the African hospital once a week to check that everything was running smoothly. He had built up a good working relationship with all of the medical staff but he found himself making additional visits when he knew Sister Mary Brown was on duty. The next time he saw her he mentioned Lisa's pregnancy and asked her if she would be prepared to advise and help her later on. Mary readily agreed but added that the majority of African women coped remarkably well, usually with the some help from their mothers and their traditional midwives. Mary put this down to the fact that in the rural areas the women worked hard, tilling the lands, carrying water, grinding meal as well as cooking for the whole family. However, she had noticed in

South Africa that urbanised women exercised infrequently and, as a result, problem births were on the increase.

"I was wondering if antenatal classes would be worthwhile and helpful. I could quite easily fit them in once a week, during my 'off duty' afternoons."

Patrick was pleased he had spoken to her and said he would put the idea forward at the next heads of department meeting and asked what remuneration she would require.

"Don't be silly Pat, I wouldn't dream of charging for my time. All I would need is the use of a room in the admin block for about an hour, once a week." Patrick noticed, with some pleasure, the use of his name for the first time.

Patrick scheduled Mary's scheme for discussion at the next meeting. He hoped that, being a 'no cost' service, it would put Mr Powys Davies in a more amenable frame of mind when discussing the next item; the latest ideas for improving the conditions for the foreign mine workers who were recruited for the colliery through an agency called Wanela.

Presently the agency did little other than sourcing workers for the mine. However, Patrick felt a good deal more could be done by Wanela and that their efforts would go a long way towards improving welfare and labour relations generally. He had in mind a system which would ensure that all workers could send a percentage of their monthly earnings back home to their wives and dependants. He also wanted to put forward the idea that the workers' transportation fares should be paid by the colliery for an annual trip home. Many of the men had to return home in time to do the ploughing and planting of their crops before the rains set in, and Patrick wanted to ensure that they were given priority for re-engagement as it was to the mine's advantage to have them back rather than training raw recruits. He also knew that often the men couldn't afford the return train or bus fares at the end of their leave. In spite of the proposed advantages, Patrick knew that he would have trouble convincing Mr Powys Davies who disliked anything to do with change, especially if it meant extra work for him or expenditure by the mine. Patrick and Kumbula spent many hours working on the figures and had a number of worthwhile meetings with the Wanela staff who welcomed their ideas wholeheartedly. After studying the figures, the agency even offered to operate a fleet of buses for transporting the Nyasalanders and Northern Rhodesians home and back, thus minimising the costs and avoiding days of tedious train travel.

At the meeting, Mr Powys Davies readily agreed to the no cost antenatal classes but bitterly opposed the arrangement with Wenela. Fortunately after considerable pressure from Angus Mackay, the accountant had to withdraw his objections and, to Patrick's delight, the proposed scheme was put into practice. He was to learn later that the bus scheme was the start of an excellent road service, which Wanela soon introduced to the Southern Rhodesian gold, copper and asbestos mines, with great success.

A major task, also undertaken by Wanela, was the actual delivery of the workers' money to their dependants. In Southern Rhodesia it wasn't needed as a simple, reliable and safe system already existed; all the workers had to do was to open Post Office Savings accounts in the names of their dependants and pay into those accounts at the Wankie post office. The dependants could then withdraw funds at their local district post offices. However, Northern Rhodesia and Nyasaland, being governed by the British via their Colonial Service, did not have dependable post offices due to corruption, inefficiency and unreliability. Wanela found that the only safe way was to undertake door to door deliveries once every two months. This was a remarkably generous and much appreciated service for which the agency made only a small charge.

CHAPTER 10

⟨⟩ 1928 ⟨⟩

The marriage of Lisa Khumalo and Kumbula Zulu took place in Wankie in mid-May. The bride had requested that she retain her maiden name, not for her own sake but because she felt that recognition of her royal lineage could be important for her children in the future. Patrick wholeheartedly endorsed the idea but nevertheless teased Kumbula unmercifully at his readiness to do whatever she wanted.

"She's got you where she wants you. I can see already who will be wearing the trousers in that household"

"Boss Pat, that is not so, and you know it. But I would do anything for that girl. Isn't she going to be the most beautiful bride you've ever seen in your life?"

They married in the afternoon; a simple ceremony in the local church. Having no family or relatives, Lisa took the unconventional step of asking Patrick if he would give her away. He assured her that he would consider it a great honour. The ceremony was followed by a reception held in the township hall for their many friends. Patrick proposed the toast to the bride and groom in a light-hearted speech, delivered in fluent Zulu with occasional amusing anecdotes in English and Fanika Lo. It was a joyous celebration greatly appreciated by all. After the main reception the newly-weds invited six of their best friends, including Sister Mary and Patrick, to join them at their home for a special private dinner which they had prepared.

*

Patrick was not a naturally introspective person but Shaun's revelations had really upset him. He badly needed help so he phoned Jeannie Mackay and invited her over for tea. He had a special regard for this gracious lady, who from their first meeting had shown a motherly interest in him.

He left his office early that afternoon, having asked Lisa to make special scones as the GM's wife was coming for tea and he would like it to be served in the garden. It was peaceful in the shade of the acacia trees. Jeannie arrived a little earlier than expected but after a general chat he mentioned his concerns about Mary. Jeannie listened intently until he had finished. Then, she leant over and took his hand gently in hers saying, "Oh you poor boy! I'm so pleased you have woken up at last. I was getting quite worried for you. My assessment is that Mary is a strong sensible lass; not a gambler. The ball is actually in your court, but don't wait too long or she might think you lack the will to play the game."

"Oh Jeannie, I knew that you would understand and I truly value your help and advice. My inexperience and Victorian upbringing must be quite amusing to you." They laughed together and then sampled Lisa's delicious scones, with her homemade strawberry jam topped by a generous peak of cream.

Patrick thanked Jeannie once again for her advice while seeing her to the gate. He then sat back in his chair, thinking. Her words produced a warm glow of self-confidence in him, plus a thrill of anticipation at the prospect of Mary possibly returning his affection. Being cautious by nature, however, he decided to sleep on it before making any specific plans.

After a day of tormenting indecision, he phoned the hospital and spoke to Jacob, the switchboard operator. He was the one person who knew everybody and everything that went on at the hospital. Jacob was instantly able to tell him that Sister Mary was on day duty for the rest of the week and would be teaching at the antenatal clinic on Wednesday afternoon.

"I can call her to the phone if you want to speak to her," Jacob offered.

No, thanks, Jacob, I will speak to her later on. How are things there?"

"They are going well, Boss Pat. I've heard that Lisa is attending those classes for pregnant ladies. Can you tell me why do they now need classes on producing babies?"

Patrick laughed and replied lightly, "Jacob, there are many things on this earth that you and I don't understand; women and babies are two of those mysteries. If you want to learn more I can easily arrange for you to attend the classes."

Jacob laughed and said, "Boss Pat, neither of us is married, so I don't think we should bother with those classes yet"

*

On Wednesday morning Lisa came into the dining room and asked Patrick if she could take the whole afternoon off as she needed to do some shopping after her antenatal class. Patrick readily agreed and later in the morning phoned Mary and invited her to come and have tea after the classes. She hesitated for a moment then asked, "Is it something official?"

"No, no it is purely social."

"That is fine then; I can be with you shortly after three o'clock."

Patrick didn't return to his office after lunch. He prepared the tea tray with the best china, cleaned the circular outside table and chairs, and then moved them into the shaded area under the large acacia tree. Satisfied that everything was in order he showered and changed into his smartest casual wear, then paced up and down the veranda until he caught sight of Mary walking briskly along the pavement, shaded by the line of mature jacaranda trees. He walked quickly across the lawn, opened the garden gate and went down the road to meet her. Patrick felt his heart beating faster as the gap between them closed.

"Welcome, Mary! You are looking lovely." She smiled, flushing slightly at the unexpected compliment.

"Thank you, Pat, it's good to be out of uniform and visiting this upper class area of yours"

"I'm pleased that you think that but you might have noticed that mine is the sixteenth out of a total of sixteen senior staff houses and it has the rockiest garden."

She laughed and said, "You probably need some gardening tuition and I would be pleased to advise you."

Mary sat down at the garden table on which Patrick had already placed the tea tray, covered with a light 'tea shower' to keep the acacia leaves from falling into the tea cups. This was the first time that they had been alone together and he found her very relaxed and easy to talk to. She asked him many questions about his family and their history, then suddenly apologised for being so inquisitive.

"I just like to know about people I meet. I got very little out of Shaun as he was always joking about your ancestors and it was difficult to extract facts from the comedy. Before he went north, he tried to teach Wendy and me to play golf, and we spent many hilarious hours 'learning' the game. I think Shaun missed his vocation; he is a born actor and should have gone on the stage. It concerns me that he may treat life itself as an act."

Patrick was surprised and extremely interested at Mary's assessment of his brother, and laughingly added that when he was younger his parents thought the circus might be Shaun's best bet. To change the subject, Patrick asked her what else apart from golf she did for entertainment, as Wankie must be very dull after South Africa. She became serious and told him that her social life was largely dictated by hospital's duty roster, which changed each month, so that the unpopular shifts, such as night duty, were shared fairly.

"When we can synchronise our duties, Wendy and I play golf, and now Rhoda Long, who you will remember as one of the Salisbury nurses, is starting up a table tennis team to compete with other mining towns like Shabani and Filabusi. She is getting good support from the men at the club, as well as from Wendy, but I feel sure that I won't ever be good enough, especially as I keep referring to the game as ping-pong. Apart from the activities at the club, there are quite a few things going on, I read a lot, mainly historical novels and biographies. Our local library is very good. What about you, Pat?"

"Actually much the same, except I don't have time for golf or club activities at the moment, but I certainly hope to social- ize in the future. I also read a lot, and have a fair selection of books, so when you have out-read the library please come and rummage through my lot."

They were enjoying each other's company and the time passed unnoticed. Darkness comes rapidly in Africa. After apologising for talking too much Patrick offered to run Mary home in his recently acquired, second-hand 1924 Ford, but she politely declined.

"I've nothing against your car, Pat, but I do enjoy walking, especially under this spectacular evening sky. I can't tell you how impressed I am with the brightness of the stars in Wankie and I get tremendous joy at looking up at them each night."

"I can well believe that, Mary; and I agree that the southern skies are certainly magnificent. I'll walk you safely home now and perhaps my little car will come in handy another time. It is such a pleasure for me to have your company, for as I've said, most of my time so far has been devoted to work." Patrick left the tea tray on the garden table and shyly took her arm while they walked along the hard gravel road leading to the nurses' home.

The following morning he was wakened by Lisa who scolded him saying, "Boss Pat, you will be late for work. Your early morning tea is already cold, and you left our china tea set outside all night"

Patrick had slept like a happy and contented child, dreaming of the future.

*

In the next few weeks Mary and Patrick met frequently. However he noted with some concern how often Shaun's name came up in their discussions. Although Patrick was incredibly naïve when it came to women, he was wise enough to refrain from making any adverse comments about his brother. On the whole their discussions were wide ranging and they learnt a great deal about each other's backgrounds, likes, dislikes and ambitions for the future.

Mary came from a large family who farmed in the Eastern Cape Province of South Africa. They were descended from the settlers who emigrated from Devon in the year 1820. She was the eldest girl in a family of six children. Her mother suffered from poor health but this did not prevent her from adopting two other boys who had been orphaned. From the age of twelve Mary had undertaken the care of the whole family whenever her mother was unwell. She told Patrick that it was not an easy task but it was just expected and accepted that she should do so.

"I was fortunate in that I was a quick learner and I had an excellent dedicated teacher at the local village school. Also, I had my own horse so I was able to gallop to school after seeing to the small ones every morning"

It surprised Patrick that the experiences had not put her off children or nursing.

Her father had been conscripted into the British Army to fight against the Boers in the Anglo Boer War. The Boers were mostly South African farmers whose parents had emigrated from Holland and settled there after Jan van Riebeeck established the first white colony named 'The Cape of Good Hope', in the year 1652 (well before it was taken by the British as reparation in terms of the Treaty of Utrecht in 1713). Mary's father had proudly told her, "We saw no good reasons for fighting against our Afrikaans and German speaking neighbours. In fact, we actually spent most of our time avoiding any confrontations with them. When we sighted them, or they us, we rode off in opposite directions, frequently meeting up again as a result! In two years of warfare we never fired a single shot at each other. The Boers wanted their independence and the right to farm the unoccupied lands they had developed following the 'Great Trek' into the African interior, without interference from the British Colonial government. For the country the war was absolutely devastating, and the fighting seemed to go on for ever. The British generals eventually realised that the Boer commandos could not be defeated as they chose not to engage in the static British style battles, so a change in tactics was necessary. A decision was made to cut off the Boers' supplies and safe havens. To achieve this they invented a new measure which became known as 'concentration camps'. These were barbed wire enclosures in which thousands of tents were erected and the Boer women and their children were detained as prisoners. Troops were then sent out with orders to destroy the Boers' homesteads and their crops. The farm labourers no longer had any work or food and thousands of them perished as a result. Many of these Black workers sided with their former employers and they too were herded into separate camps where a great number of them also perished. The living conditions in the various concentration camps were absolutely appalling; bitterly cold in the high veldt winters and unbearably hot in the tents in summer. Diseases inevitably broke out and up to twenty thousand white women and children died there. An interesting statistic was that the number of deaths in the camps was approximately the same as the final count of British troops killed in their battles with the Boer commandos. Only one Boer soldier was killed for every ten British troops; a clear indication of their relative fighting skills." Patrick was absolutely sickened on hearing Mary's father's accounts and inwardly questioned his own service in France in the 1914/18 war.

Mary completed her village school education, then following a series of crop failures due to drought in the Eastern Cape Province, their farm was abandoned and their whole family moved up to Johannesburg, seeking a better living on the Witwatersrand Goldfields. She was accepted by Boksburg hospital for training; a four year probation, to finally qualify as a state registered nurse.

Patrick compared his own relatively unexceptional upbringing and his early life with hers. It amazed him that she was such a bright, happy and outgoing person after what he considered a very difficult life.

As his friendship with Mary continued and while he personally received no mail from Shaun, he gathered from the odd comments she made, that he was now working on the Roan Antelope Copper Mine in northern Rhodesia, and that he was still single. Patrick resisted the temptation to comment that there must be a dreadful shortage of eligible women in Northern Rhodesia.

*

Lisa's pregnancy proceded satisfactorily, her baby being due early in the new year. By the end of December she had put on a lot of weight and was finding the mid-summer heat very trying. In spite of this she insisted on continuing to work, refusing help from a part-time maid.

CHAPTER 11

❧ 1930 ❧

Three weeks before Christmas Patrick received a telegram from his mother asking him to return to Johannesburg urgently as his father was seriously ill. The doctors suspected a liver problem and that his condition was critical. So, Patrick decided to take his annual leave. This would also enable Lisa to be at home for the last stages of her pregnancy. He informed Shaun of his father's situation but an answer came back saying he was unable to get away at that time.

The train journey to Johannesburg was hot, dusty and very tedious so arriving in the cool high veldt in the early morning was a great relief. Patrick's mother was comforted to see him, but as was to be expected, she was looking very anxious and drawn. She made him a good breakfast and then told him about his father. She knew that Patrick was aware that the last few years had been very unhappy ones. The Rand Club had become his father's second home where he spent most evenings, drinking heavily. Eventually, he had developed cirrhosis of the liver and it was now only a matter of days before he was expected to die. He was in the Johannesburg general hospital, only a few blocks away from the family home in Claim Street. Straight after breakfast Patrick walked across to the hospital where he was given special permission to visit out of normal visiting hours.

He barely recognised his father; instead he saw a shrunken, gaunt old man lying in the hospital bed. Patrick was deeply shocked to see how this once tall, proud man had allowed himself to degenerate to this state, all because he wanted to be liked and respected by his associates. Patrick had never been really close to his father but at this point in time he felt deeply and sincerely sorry that he had not been around when his father might have benefitted from his support. He simply could not find adequate words to express these feelings so instead he gently took his father's hand to let him know that he was there. The sick man's eyes opened, and then filled with tears.

"Pat, my boy, I am so sorry. I have let the whole family down. Please look after your mother and try to help young Shaun to keep on the straight and narrow."

Patrick nodded saying, "I will do my best, Dad. You just lay back and rest now. I will come and see you again at visiting time tonight, and I'll bring Mother." That was not to be, however, as shortly after he arrived back home, there was a telephone call from the hospital to say that his father had passed away just after his visit. His mother took the news philosophically, saying how relieved she was that his suffering was now over. Patrick sent a brief telegram to Shaun giving him the details and recommending that he did not travel down for the funeral as it was scheduled to take place within the next few days. There was no response from Shaun and the burial took place at the Brixton cemetery. A number of family friends attended, but Patrick noted how few of his father's 'important drinking friends' from the Rand Club made the effort to attend.

Patrick saw to all of the formalities. He was deeply distressed to find that although the family home was mortgage free and bequeathed to his mother, there was practically nothing left in his father's bank account. His mother's position was precarious to say the least, and a heavy financial burden would undoubtedly now fall on his shoulders. She had barely sufficient money to meet her next month's normal living expenses.

When sorting through his father's papers Patrick came across a number of Newcastle Colliery share certificates in his father's name, dating back to the period prior to his marriage, as well as others from his early years of employment with the colliery. Patrick immediately contacted a firm of brokers in Commissioner Street and arranged a meeting with them on behalf of his mother. They were extremely helpful and explained that not only had the value of the shares doubled several times over in the past twenty-five years, but an attached document showed that the colliery was holding additional certificates, paid for from the annual dividends and which had never been claimed. The brokers undertook to collect these and offered to look after his mother's portfolio if she was agreeable, and assured him that once his late father's will was processed, his mother would in fact be left quite comfortably off. Patrick was greatly relieved and, for a special treat, took his mother out for celebratory lunch at one of Johannesburg's finest restaurants.

In high spirits after their lunch they went home and found the following telegram waiting in their post box:

O'CONNORS,

102 CLAIM STREET JOHANNESBURG.

ECSTATIC MARRYING THE MOST BEAUTIFUL NURSE IN WANKIE NEXT WEEK SORRY BOTH OF YOU WILL NOT BE HERE TO CELEBRATE WITH US LOVE SHAUN

At first Patrick was angry that there was no mention of their late father but as he read further his anger turned to distress, and seeing this, his mother said, "Calm down, Pat, it can't be that bad. I'll make us some tea then you must tell me what is upsetting you so." She returned with the tea tray about ten minutes later to find that he had regained his composure.

"I know from your letters, Pat, you were becoming fond of Mary, but tell me how and why Shaun comes into this." Patrick poured his heart out to her; leaving nothing out. Finally his hurt and anger came to the fore.

"Mum, this is the cruellest and most thoughtless thing anyone has ever done to me! Surely he could at least have had the decency to end with: 'LOVE MARY AND SHAUN, or LOVE WENDY AND SHAUN.' Has he, in my absence, married the girl I love?"

"Patrick, it's not like you to jump to conclusions. If Mary loves you she would not marry another, and if she doesn't then you are better off finding someone who does. You deserve the best and I feel sure that is what you will get."

The next morning the postman delivered a letter for him from Wankie. Recognising Mary's hand writing, but trembling with apprehension, Patrick slowly opened the envelope and read the following:

21st December

My dear friend,

I was so sorry to hear of your father's illness. I suspect it must be something quite serious for you to have had to dash off so suddenly. Being so far from one's family is a high price we pay for living in Wankie, but your presence at home will be a great comfort for your mother.

Shaun will be here shortly to pick up his bride for the wedding in Luanshya on the 29th. I shall miss Wendy very much, but you will shortly gain a 'sister-in-law' as a happy addition to your family.

Please write and tell me when you expect to be back so that I can ensure that Lisa has everything spick and span for your return.

With best wishes for Christmas, and a happy New Year.

Love, Mary.

PS Wendy's wedding list grows by the day and in case you want to buy something useful for them in Johannesburg, may I suggest a six-place canteen of cutlery would be very welcome.

Uncharacteristically he let out a yell and ran through the house looking for his mother. He gave her a huge hug and thrust the letter into her hand. His throat had closed up with emotion and he couldn't say a word. When she finished reading, she knew that she would soon have two new daughters-in-law, and was delighted at the prospect as she had always wanted a daughter since losing her first one at birth. She quietly vowed to herself that she would be the best mother-in-law in the land! It was just such a shame that her sons chose to live so far away.

"Patrick, why don't you telephone Mary? She took the trouble to write to you and I'm sure she would appreciate hearing from you and would want to know about Dad."

It hadn't occurred to him but, on reflection, he realised how slow males are about such things. He knew it would be quite expensive but putting that thought aside he called the Johannesburg telephone exchange and asked for a 'person to person, fixed time, trunk call' to be booked to Mary. This service had only recently been introduced internationally by Rhodesia and South Africa and was proving very popular, in spite of the charges. The telephone operator at the exchange was most helpful and phoned him back confirming that the call would be taken by Mary Brown at the nurses' home, Wankie hospital, at 6pm that day.

To pass the time and help relieve his anxiety, Patrick walked into the city and bought the cutlery that Mary had suggested from John Orr's, one of Johannesburg's best stores. After going from one department to another looking for a gift for Mary, he finally made up his mind, settling on a necklace of small perfectly matched natural pearls, contained in a pink presentation box. It was the first gift he had ever bought for a girl and he hoped that she would like it.

Rather shyly, he showed the necklace to his mother and asked her if she thought it was alright. She told him it was lovely and assured him it would be greatly appreciated as it was a sign of his genuine affection without being mistaken as a down payment for her affection such as a diamond necklace might have been. Satisfied, he waited impatiently at home for six o'clock and wondered what it would be like talking to her on the phone.

On the dot of six, the Joburg exchange operator rang and asked him to hold on for his booked call, then he heard her speaking to Wankie exchange who replied, "I am calling Mary Brown, please hold," and then, "I'm putting you through, Joburg." "Mr O'Connor, I have your call to Wankie on the line and you have three minutes. Please speak up." He then heard Mary's anxious voice saying, "Hello Pat, is there a problem?"

His heart raced and he was glad he was sitting down as he felt quite overcome by the sheer joy of hearing her voice. Firstly he thanked her for her letter and told her that his father had passed on peacefully. She responded sympathetically assuring him that in her experience dying was a quick and relatively painless business.

He then told her that he had almost completed all the family business and was planning to return earlier than originally planned, and was thinking of spending the remainder of his leave at Victoria Falls. Summoning all of his courage he asked if she would like to join him there for a short break from Wankie. She hesitated for a moment then answered, "I would like that, Pat, but unfortunately we are short staffed here until Wendy's replacement starts. When do you expect to be back?"

"Next Friday morning," Patrick replied.

"Well I am due for some leave," she answered, "so I'll try to get off for that weekend, but I'll only be able to let you know when you get back." Three bleeps sounded on the phone and the operator announced that their time was up. Patrick thanked her and regretfully said goodbye.

He was astounded that he had actually asked her to spend time away with him, but what really thrilled him was her cautious but positive reply. When he told his mother, she primly reminded him that he must book two single rooms at the Victoria Falls Hotel. He felt the colour rising on his face and quickly answered, "Of course I will, Mum, and that goes without saying." After the long distance phone call, Patrick felt that the time was right to discuss his mother's future in some detail. He went through her assets, most of which she now knew about, and they both agreed that she should stay on in the family home, at least until the estate was settled. She enjoyed and truly appreciated him spending the whole of the following week with her.

Catching the train at Johannesburg's Park station was actually quite a relief for Patrick; so much had changed since his arrival, and strangely enough he suddenly felt that he was going home. December was not the best time to travel so he was pleased that he had booked a coupe, hoping that he would have it to himself, which turned out to be the case. He was able to catch up on his thoughts, as well as reading the two interesting travel books that he had bought in Hillbrow. When the train stopped at Francistown in the Bechuanaland Protectorate he was surrounded by sellers offering small wooden animals, and for amusement he bought a tiny, beautifully carved tortoise, which he hoped to offer to Mary one day, saying that it represented him – very slow but getting there in the end.

As the train pulled into Plumtree station he was astounded to see Theo Odendaal on the platform, obviously ready to board the train as he had a suitcase at his side. Patrick lent out of the carriage window and called to Theo but could not attract his attention. Knowing that the train would be stationary for some time while taking on water, he jumped down on the platform and eventually found Theo in a compartment at the other end of the train. In no time at all the two men had settled in Patrick's empty coupe, and then to each other's delight, they caught up on what was happening in their lives. Theo simply could not believe that once again they were travelling together, but accepted that in Africa these coincidences do frequently happen.

Because Theo was bubbling over with enjoyment at their meeting, Patrick encouraged him to talk about himself as there obviously were some changes in his life.

"Oh Pat, my good news is that I am engaged to be married in May, during the school holidays. My fiancée is the music teacher at the school, and from the moment we met we knew that we were meant to be together. Her name is Joanna van Niekerk. I am on my way to Bulawayo to stay with her family who have a smallholding a few miles up the Vic Falls road. I have already met them once, and am accepted as a suitable husband for Jo, their only daughter. Originally they owned a sugar cane farm in Natal, but Mr van Niekerk always wanted something small that he could run entirely on his own. He did well out of the sale of the sugar plantation, so he could now follow his hobby of growing fruit and vegetables. Leaving his wife and Joanna in Durban, he trekked alone by ox wagon to Rhodesia. He had read about the Moodie Trek to Melsetter, and thought he may travel as far as the eastern districts, but once he reached Bulawayo, he felt that he should go no further. Farms were reasonably priced here and he found exactly what he wanted; a small farm on the banks of the Umgusa River, ensuring that water would never be a future problem. Once Joanna had gained her music degree at Natal University, she and her mother came up by train to Bulawayo, by which time her husband had built a substantial home, and this is where I am now heading. My future father-in-law is a hardworking man and the property is now well established, and really very beautiful. He is concentrating on growing avocado pears, paw paws, naartjies and strangely enough brinjals, which are in great demand at Vic Falls Hotel. So, now I have told you all my news, how are you doing in Wankie?"

Patrick, with his reticent nature, was reluctant to say too much about his hopes for the future, but simply told Theo that he was very interested in one of the nurses at the mine hospital, and hoped to shortly ask her to marry him. This was the first time he had verbalised his thoughts of Mary, and to a comparative stranger at that, but somehow in speaking to Theo, he suddenly felt exhilarated by the real possibility of major changes in his life.

As they pulled into Bulawayo, Joanna was waiting for Theo on the station platform – eagerly searching the carriages for sight of him. Patrick was introduced to her, and fully appreciated why Theo had fallen for this attractive young lady. Saying their goodbyes, and feeling sure that their paths would cross again, the young couple left the station arm in arm, obviously delighted at the prospect of a holiday on the family farm.

CHAPTER 12

O n arrival at Wankie, feeling very hot and soot covered from the long steam train journey, Patrick went straight home and after a well needed bath phoned Jacob, the hospital switchboard operator, and asked him if the new nurse, Wendy's replacement, had started work yet. "Yes, Boss Pat, she started work yesterday. Should I call her to the phone for you?"

"No thanks, Jacob, but please ask Sister Brown to call me as soon as she goes off duty today."

Next, he phoned the Vic Falls Hotel and made a provisional reservation for two single rooms for the weekend. For some unknown reason this brought back to him the excited guilty feeling he had experienced as an eight-year-old, when he and a friend bunked out of school and stole ripe peaches from a neighbour's garden.

At four that afternoon Mary phoned and said, "Hurrah, I've got next weekend off. I've swapped my duties with Rhoda, but unfortunately I will have to be back for duty on Monday morning."

"Don't worry, Mary, I will get you back in time. It is great news that you can come. I suggest we make an early start. Could I pick you up at 7.30 on Saturday?"

Next he took his car to Duly's workshop for a service, oil change and general check over. He wanted nothing to go wrong and spoil this trip.

It was an unexpectedly cool morning for April following a light drizzle during the night. The Ford, unkindly named Blitzen (meaning lightning or the devil) started first time and Patrick let the engine warm up as he carefully checked that he had packed everything they needed. Mary was standing at the gate of the nurses' home, in a sky blue summer dress, with a small suitcase at her side. She smiled and waved as he drove up; while Patrick, overcoming his normal shyness and caution, walked up to her giving her a tender hug saying, "Mary, you're looking absolutely gorgeous." He opened the car door for her and put her case on the back seat. He was so distracted by her sitting next to him that for the beginning of their journey he found it difficult to keep his eyes on the un-tarred dirt road, the condition of which had fortunately improved as a result of the previous night's light rain.

The journey took just over three and a half hours which included a break for coffee at a lay-by, under one of the monstrous ancient 'upside down' baobab trees on the side of the road. They had so much to talk about that the time flew by, and were suddenly amazed to find they had arrived at the front of the hotel, located only a short walk from the world famous Victoria Falls. This elegant building of Edwardian colonial styling was built on the instructions of Cecil John Rhodes, just prior to his death in 1902 and was opened in 1904. Initially it was owned and very successfully operated by the Rhodesia Railways, who had the foresight to run reduced fare excursion trips from Bulawayo. These attracted numerous international and local tourists.

On their arrival Patrick was directed to a garage from where their luggage was whisked away by a uniformed porter who led them to the reception desk where they individually signed the guest register. A waiter then offered them a choice of complimentary drinks; wine, champagne, beer or fruit juice. After accepting and drinking the juice they followed the porter down several long, thickly carpeted corridors, to their elegantly appointed rooms. Patrick had considered the mine guest house to be the height of luxury but compared with this, it was almost under furnished. He began to be concerned as to whether he had brought suitable evening attire to wear in the lavish dining room they had passed on the way to their rooms. He had brought a dark suit but not his seldom worn, black tie dress-suit. Knowing that nothing could now be done about his clothing concern, he forgot about the problem, had a good wash to get rid of the road dust and joined Mary on the veranda. Wanting to lose no time for viewing the promised splendour of the Falls, they set out along a well-worn path with signposts indicating that they were going in the right direction.

The thundering sound of falling water filled the air and with great anticipation they hurried through the dense vegetation that initially obscured their view of the falls itself. Above the trees huge clouds of spray billowed hundreds of feet into the sky, indicating that these were indeed mighty falls. Although they knew that they were about to gaze upon one of the Natural Wonders of the World, they had little idea of the magnificence of the sight that lay ahead, nor of the drenching they would receive while walking through the so-called 'rain forest'. The spray from the water tumbling more than 300 feet down into the chasm below created a thick mist, or, if the wind was in the right direction, quite heavy rainfall, which was the case on that morning. Concerned for Mary, Patrick suggested that they turn back but she just laughed and wouldn't hear of it. She held out her hand and said, "Come on, run with me, a little water never did anyone any harm!" So off they ran laughing like children in the rain. However, a few steps along the grassy pathway Patrick lost his footing and fell full length down onto the muddy grass. He got up unharmed but was faced by Mary doubled over with laughter.

"Oh Patrick, I will remember this moment to the end of my days"

"I'll teach you to laugh at me, and vengeance is mine said the almighty one." With that he took her face between his two muddy hands and kissed her as she struggled to get away. He was thrilled by his spontaneous and unexpected gesture, which Mary accepted amid further peals of laughter.

At the viewing point an elderly vicar was busily photographing the falls from different angles. They didn't disturb him but when he finished he turned around and looked them over saying, "Goodness me. Whatever happened to you two?"

Mischievously, Mary replied, "Nothing much, Vicar; we were suddenly overcome by a moment of unbridled passion"

Adding to the gentleman's astonishment Mary then handed him her Kodak box camera and asked him if he would mind taking a snapshot of the pair of them; just for their family records. He obliged, but they were well aware that he thought them an extremely foolish young couple and would no doubt have noticed that Mary wore no wedding ring.

Mary took two pictures of the magnificent scene, capturing the first section of the one mile wide falls, while saving the rest of her precious film for other viewing angles. The muddy pair then made their way back to the hotel to bath and change for lunch.

The dining room was surprisingly full and included the elderly vicar who spent most of the mealtime trying to avoid making eye contact, as if reluctant to witness their debauchery or guilty secrets. They had a sumptuous meal then rested on the long veranda before exploring the rest of the sights. Very happy with events thus far, it confirmed for Patrick the start of a wonderful relationship with this very special and adorable person. Whilst not wishing to compare, he sincerely hoped that Shaun felt for Wendy what he was now feeling for Mary.

They spent the remainder of the afternoon walking, talking and sightseeing; there was so much they each wanted to know about the other. What was soon clear to them both was that they were very independent and self-sufficient people. They spoke openly about their strengths and weaknesses, finally concluding that they were very similar and yet in many respects complementary. In their work it was plain that Mary was loved for her friendliness, compassion and strict discipline while Patrick was respected and liked for his quiet, unhurried, common sense and his way of getting things done. They were both hard workers and more importantly enjoyed a similar sense of humour.

Returning to the hotel just as the sun was setting; they chose to sit on the spacious veranda while ordering sun-downers; a gin and tonic and an ice cold Castle lager. Having spoken at length about their lives, Patrick now asked what news she had from Wendy, adding that Shaun was a typically male non-communicator.

"You are quite wrong there," she said firmly. "Shaun kept up a steady stream of letters to me from the time he left Wankie until their marriage. The poor boy was so besotted with Wendy that he found it very difficult to write to her about his feelings, so instead he wrote to me to find out more about her and how best to understand her." Patrick was greatly relieved, and Mary went up even higher in his estimation.

After sitting silently for a while, Mary said, "Poor Shaun, he was a very troubled young man. I think I might be the only person he ever had to confide in. He admired his father and wanted desperately to please him, yet his father never praised him or acknowledged his abilities. Then later Shaun lost all respect for him. He actually broke down and cried when he told me how ashamed he was for punching your father when he came home drunk one night and started abusing your mother. You were away by then and there was nobody he could talk to. Please don't ever let on that I have told you about this, Pat. I felt so sorry for him but I believe he is a young man with delayed potential and Wendy will look after him. She is a strong person and she will keep him on the right track, so there is no need for you to worry about him now."

Seeing their glasses were empty and as they didn't re-order, the waiter asked which restaurant they would prefer to dine in. Patrick hadn't realised that there was more than one so he asked him which was best.

"They are both very good, sir, but I will fetch their menus so you and the madam can choose."

"There is no need to do that. If you were a poor person like me where would you like to dine?"

With candour and conviction the waiter replied, "Even if I was very wealthy I would go to the large one, sir. You get more food there and you pay less money. In the small one the names for all the dishes are written in a foreign language, so people cannot tell what food they will be eating; and it is all much more expensive."

"Thank you. You are an honest man. Please reserve a table for us in the large dining room. You can keep the change from the drinks; you have earned it and I am grateful for your sensible advice."

They went to their rooms and changed into their evening clothes. Patrick slipped the pearl necklace into the inner pocket of his suit and waited in the corridor for Mary to join him. She emerged looking stunning in a deep red evening dress and was obviously delighted when he enthusiastically complimented her. The meal was excellent and they finished a whole bottle of very fine wine, from one of the best Stellenbosch vineyards in the Cape Provence. It had been a memorable day and a perfectly delightful evening. However, Patrick decided he should not give her the necklace yet.

After dinner they strolled around the gardens which surrounded the hotel enjoying the refreshingly cool evening and the wonder of the stars above them. Pat put his arm around her as they walked their meal down. She snuggled up to him and, when they turned to come back, they exchanged their first really serious kiss. Feeling her lovely soft body pressed against his, Patrick knew he had found his perfect partner.

They went up to their bedrooms and, pausing at her door, Mary asked at what time he wanted to start back home in the morning. Patrick sensed a slight tension in her, which he felt too, so he kissed her good night.

"Thank you for a wonderful evening. We should have an early breakfast so let's meet at seven tomorrow. Good night and sleep well, you beautiful girl." She smiled and closed the door. He turned and went to his own room.

The reason for the early start the next morning was in order to take a detour through Robins Farm to see the wild animals. Mr Robins had started what he called a 'game farm' on a vast tract of land he had bought several years earlier. He had converted his original homestead into accommodation for local and overseas tourists. The visitors paid good money for game viewing trips along the rough roads which Mr Robins had cut through the bush. Mary was very excited about seeing animals in the wild for she had never had a chance to visit game parks in South Africa.

After a hearty breakfast, they collected the packed lunch they had pre-ordered, thanked the hotel staff for the excellent service, paid the bill and set off. As it was not the ideal time of day for game viewing, Patrick had warned Mary that they may only see an occasional giraffe plus a few impala and zebras. However, because of the recent rains, Mr Robins felt differently, and cautioned them saying that they must not at any time get out of the car as there were many lions about and that the elephants with young ones could be aggressive. They were not disappointed. After driving for only a few miles they came across a small herd of elephants, many of whom had babies walking alongside. Mary was like a small child at the circus and couldn't contain her excitement at the majestic giraffes browsing the tall acacia trees. They saw herds of graceful impala grazing on the new green shoots, ever watchful for lions in the open grasslands. Quite unexpectedly they came upon a small pride lying lazily in the shade of a tree near the road. The lions paid little attention to them, other than an occasional glance and a weary yawn in their direction. Patrick stopped the car and they had their tea, still hot in the thermos flask. At the next water hole there was an enormous herd of buffalos jostling each other, trying to get to the water to drink, while others chose to wallow in the muddy pools.

Reluctantly they headed south for home and after two hours of driving stopped and parked under a huge baobab tree, where they ate their packed lunch. Mary was deep in thought and after being silent for some time she said, "I was just thinking how lucky we are and how much I have enjoyed these last two days. I will never forget them."

"Nor will I," said Patrick. "As a reminder I have a small memento which I hope you will accept with my love." He handed her a package.

"What is it? Can I open it now?"

"Of course you can, it's something small I brought for you from Johannesburg."

Eagerly she pulled off the paper wrappings then slowly opened the oval pink case, her eyes sparkling with anticipation.

"Oh Pat, I cannot believe that this is for me" She gently lifted the string of pearls and held them up to her throat. "How did you know I loved pearls? You are naughty spending money on me, especially at a time when you had so many family commitments. I will always treasure this gorgeous present. Thank you so very much."

She leant over and kissed him, and he knew that the timing of the gift had been correct.

CHAPTER 13

L isa's pregnancy had proceeded quite normally but she was now three weeks overdue and rather worried. After discussing the delay Mary advised her to go to the hospital, as a precautionary measure. The doctor examined her and decided it would be best to induce labour as she was carrying a very big and highly active baby. He commented on the unusual movements of the child. Instead of kicking occasionally, like most babies do, this one appeared to be running. On hearing the news, Kumbula was desperately worried having lost his first wife and baby in childbirth. As it turned out, his concern was justified. Lisa produced a fine eight pound ten ounce baby boy, but only after an extremely difficult delivery. The doctor later indicated that she would probably be unable to have any further children. This was a dreadful blow to Kumbula as he had always wanted a large family, but was nevertheless overjoyed at becoming a father and extremely proud of Lisa.

The two of them spent hours trying to decide on a name for their son. Mary finally solved their problem to everyone's satisfaction. She reminded them that their baby had not kicked like most babies do; he had a running action before he was born. "Why don't you call him Gajima?" (Meaning 'to run swiftly'.) This turned out to be somewhat prophetic as he started running soon after he learnt to walk. Running was to earn him many prizes and great praise when he went to school. His birth certificate name was quite a mouthful; Gajima Khumalo Zulu, but his friends tended to use the Anglicised abbreviation of 'Jim'.

CHAPTER 14

ࣾ 1931 ࣾ

During the following months Mary and Patrick met frequently and their good relationship blossomed into deep understanding, friendship and love. They became engaged in July and started making plans for a September 'spring' wedding when the jacaranda trees would be in full bloom. Their friends were relieved to hear the news and didn't hesitate to ask why such an obvious step had taken them both so long. Mary just laughed at their teasing and said, "I was born by the sea and my grandfather taught me about fishing. He told me there were many fish in the sea so it's not hard to catch one. However, to catch and land a particular fish, takes skill and patience. I wasn't in a hurry and I wanted to be sure of landing this one."

Patrick wrote to his mother regularly every fortnight, and from his letters she guessed that a wedding was being planned. What she had not expected was that he would arrange for her to travel up to Wankie and have three weeks' holiday with them prior to the wedding. She was delighted by this prospect as it gave her the opportunity to see her sons again, and to meet her two new daughters-in-law. From Patrick's letters she felt she already knew Mary and was sure she would like her. Wendy on the other hand was a total mystery and, although she hoped for the best, she couldn't help wondering about her, knowing

Shaun's former preferences. Although not relishing the thought of the long train journey on her own, she was interested in visiting Rhodesia and learning why so many young people were now settling there. The excitement of the coming wedding was, of course, upmost in her mind, and she kept imagining how she could be of help in the preparations. She was surprised to hear that although Wendy was expecting her first baby she would still be Mary's matron of honour, and that Shaun would be Patrick's best man at the wedding. It promised to be a great family celebration.

Mary's parents were very pleased by her news but, as they had only just returned to the Eastern Cape Province after a holiday in Natal they felt they couldn't leave their farm at planting time to make the long journey north. However, Mary's eldest brother Paul, now a lawyer in Pretoria, enthusiastically agreed to come up to Wankie to give his sister away. There was no question of the Brown family paying for the wedding. Mary and Patrick had agreed to share all the costs. In a small mining community it was very difficult to limit the number of invitations so it would inevitably be a large affair. On the plus side however, the mine would make no charge for hiring out the club hall for the reception. This included the full use of their kitchens for catering, but stressed that all the drinks, other than wines and champagne, were bought from the club's bar. This was fair enough, even though the arrangement didn't meet with Mr Powys Davies's approval. He felt that the mine staff earned good salaries and it would not hurt them to pay a proper hire charge for the facilities. Luckily he was overruled by long standing precedent and tradition.

A month before the wedding Mary suddenly realised that time was slipping by and she had done nothing about her dress. So taking Rhoda with her, the two young women caught the train down to Bulawayo to see what was available in the shops there. Although Rhoda came from Salisbury, she knew that at least three of the large department stores had branches in Bulawayo and these would provide the start of their search for Mary's wedding dress. They had booked into the Carlton Hotel in Abercorn Street, an ideal position in the centre of town from where they could come and go as they pleased, offloading parcels as their purchases increased. After a morning of trying on a selection of dresses Mary was delighted to find exactly what she wanted at Sanders store, just a block away from the hotel. She bought a flattering Edwardian style gown with a sweetheart neckline and butterfly sleeves, which Rhoda assured her, would be perfect for September in Wankie. With the wedding dress bought and safely delivered to the hotel, the two young friends began buying other items of clothing as shopping in a town was very different to shopping in Wankie. Mary also bought a length of lilac silk taffeta for Wendy's dress which was to be made for her by an experienced dressmaker in Luanshya.

On their return to Wankie, Patrick picked them up from the station and they told him how they had felt like teenaged girls who had bunked off school and were now being checked in by their teacher.

"Punishment is coming," said Patrick. "You are to be examined and inspected by the great dragon from South Africa; your future mother-in-law. She will be arriving soon on the mail train"

Three days later Patrick met his mother at the station, and was immediately aware of how well she was looking; a different woman to the one he had left in Johannesburg after his father's death.

"Oh Pat, how stupid I was to be concerned about making this journey. I felt that I would be going off into darkest Africa, and it turned out to be quite the most wonderful adventure of my life. Now I want to introduce you to my travelling companion who made my journey such a pleasure." Patrick was then introduced to Mrs Marjory Moir, a good-looking woman slightly younger than his mother, who he later found out was going up to Ndola to help her engineer husband open a mining supplies store in the town.

"Marjory and I had a full compartment to ourselves, so we could talk our heads off and really get to know each other. With two hours wait until the north train took off, we hired a taxi for a ride around Bulawayo, and that town, with its very wide streets was really an eye opener. I'll tell you all about it later."

The two ladies then hugged each other like old friends, promising to keep in touch as they had obviously exchanged addresses. It gave Patrick great satisfaction to feel that the beginning of her holiday had started so well, and he had no doubt that the two ladies would see each other again. He was reminded once again that it was often through these chance meetings in Africa that lasting friendships were made.

That evening Patrick drove to the nurses' home to collect Mary. Mrs O'Connor and Lisa both went out onto the veranda when they heard the car coming up the driveway. Mrs O'Connor was nervously fingering her necklace as if counting the beads on a rosary, while Lisa ran down to the car to meet them. Patrick put his arm around Mary as he guided her up the steps on to the veranda.

"Mum," he said proudly, "here is your future daughter-in-law."

Unfamiliar with the ways of the younger generation, his mother put her hand out to shake Mary's, but was delighted to feel the girl's arms around her and a soft kiss on her cheek. Mrs O'Connor was overwhelmed by the warmth and informality of the greeting and could only say, rather shyly, "Oh what a lovely girl you are, Mary. I am so looking forward to getting to know you, and of course Wendy too when she arrives for the wedding. I was blest with two fine sons, and now I'll also have the daughters I always longed for."

Left alone with Lisa, Mrs O'Connor had had time to talk to her and realised how friendly and open she was, very unlike the sometimes surly housemaid she had had in South Africa. She also spent time playing with baby Gajima who came to the house every day with his mother. This was the first time she had had such close contact with an African baby, and she enjoyed the novelty of looking after this bright little boy while his mother worked in the house. Lisa was as delighted as everyone else about the coming wedding but added, as an afterthought, that a tribal fortune teller had long ago foretold of this marriage, and as his predictions were mostly correct, the wedding was no great surprise to her. "How wonderful to have this gift, Lisa, does he only foretell good news?"

"Not always, madam, he tells of crop failures from drought as well as from heavy rains. Some time ago he told of something very bad that would happen at Wankie, but as it is far into the future nobody is worrying about it yet."

"Well, if it's far away, I'm not going to be worrying about it either, so let's get on with our lives and our present happiness. I am so lucky to be here and I simply cannot tell you how much I am looking forward to the wedding."

With his mother being successfully looked after by Lisa, Patrick realised that he had to now devote more time to the numerous wedding related details. The problem that troubled him the most concerned the reception arrangements. The local rules dictated that the club was for the use of the mine's European staff who were free to entertain their friends there, but African guests were definitely not allowed. In his work as African Personnel Manager, Patrick had made a number of African friends, yet he was not able to invite them to the reception. They were in his opinion very respectable men and women, in fact often better behaved than many from the white community. Fortunately the prohibition did not apply to the local church; for although most Africans preferred to attend their own traditional places of worship, none were barred from the two Christian churches in Wankie. After dinner on the second evening of her stay, Patrick brought up the problem with his mother and was completely taken aback by her Victorian reaction.

"Of course not, Patrick, you cannot mix the races. It would create all sorts of problems for them. You would find that the black waiters would not be prepared to serve their fellow blacks. It would be beneath them to be subservient to their own race."

"Yes, Mother, what you say is true but somehow we have to make an alternative plan. These people are not just my work colleagues, they are also our genuine friends and they would be deeply hurt if we excluded them."

Mary felt the same way as Patrick and she wanted three of her staff from the hospital to come to the reception. However, Kumbula unexpectedly sided with Mrs O'Connor and suggested an interesting compromise.

"Your mother is right, Boss Pat, it would be unwise to mix the races so I have thought of a way around this problem. I know that your friends and Miss Mary's would be very sad if they couldn't share in the celebrations; it is a big event and you are both well-liked and respected by us all. We have been watching and hoping for your wedding for a long time now. Many of us will be coming to the church but I was wondering if you could spare us some of your time after your reception at the club? Would you allow me to organise a small separate party? I know our wives would like to see your bride in her fine wedding dress, and many of us want to show our respects to both of you and to wish you good fortune in your marriage. When the time comes for your bride to go and change into her ordinary clothes, couldn't you bring her first to the assembly hall at the school where we can have our own short celebration with you and Miss Mary?"

"Kumbula, you are a genius. I will put your plan to Miss Mary and I know she will agree. You really are a wily old boozer. You will go to endless lengths for some free beer"

*

On the Friday before the wedding Shaun and Wendy arrived from Luanshya. Mrs O'Connor was immediately impressed at how well her son had matured under Wendy's gentle but firm influence, but what pleased her most was the young couple's devotion to each other. Ever since Shaun's hasty departure from

Johannesburg she had worried about his future and the possible mischief he might get up to on his own in Northern Rhodesia. Now her fears were laid to rest and she gave Wendy full credit for the changes in her son.

On Saturday morning Patrick took the three women to see the African school hall. The junior school pupils had been given the task of making the decorations and their parents and teachers had helped to put them up. There were coloured paper streamers, flowers in empty jam jars and ivy vine creepers strung across the windows. Drawings and bright paintings adorned the walls, while chairs and desks had been set out for the teachers and the invited guests. The room was full of colour and reflected the appreciation felt by them all for Patrick's work in starting and running the school and for Mary's help with the expectant mothers.

The Mine Club had also been decorated to their approval, and was ready to receive all the wedding guests. They dropped Wendy off at the nurses' quarters where she was to assist Mary. Satisfied that everything necessary had been taken care of, Patrick and Shaun made their way back home.

Mary's brother, Paul, had driven up from Pretoria and after spending the night at the Wankie Hotel, called in first at the nurses' home to see Mary. A hive of activity greeted him there, so after confirming the time he was required to take his sister to the church, he escaped and made his way over to Patrick's home to introduce himself to his future brothers-in-law. There he found a much calmer atmosphere with Patrick and Shaun busy washing and polishing his old Ford car in readiness for the couple's honeymoon journey. After introducing himself, it didn't take long for Paul to realise what a good choice his sister had made. The three of them finished working on Patrick's car and then started on Paul's Chev. After agreeing to disagree over the relative merits of Fords and Chevrolets, they washed and polished Paul's car in readiness for transporting the bride to the church.

Lisa had prepared a light lunch for them. While they were eating, Mrs O'Connor said once again, "Oh how fortunate I am to be at the heart of all these preparations; to think I could have missed them through my reluctance to travel on my own. I am absolutely overjoyed to be here with my entire family."

The wedding ceremony was well attended and Mary looked exquisite in her elegant white dress, complemented by Wendy's lilac outfit. Patrick's adoration of his bride shone out like the sun after a rainstorm. It was also touching to observe Mrs O'Connor's pride and admiration of her two sons and their delightful wives. She shed joyful tears throughout the marriage ceremony and several times again when being congratulated by many of the guests.

The reception at the Mine Club went according to plan and Paul proved to be an excellent master of ceremonies. His light-hearted speech and sense of humour set the tone for the celebration of the marriage of these two popular people. While thanking him, Patrick welcomed newly married Theo and Joanna Odendaal who were among the guests and whose recent wedding he had unfortunately not been able to attend.

Unexpectedly, Mr Angus Mackay stood up to speak, and after apologising for 'pushing himself without being formally asked', told of his delight that once again his wife had excelled in her matchmaking. "She's a witch at the art of getting the right people together, so you young nurses better look out; you are her next targets."

At about six o'clock Mary and Patrick quietly slipped away for their appearance at the African school. They met with thunderous applause from between two and three hundred enthusiastic pupils and parents. Patrick made a short speech thanking them for their congratulations and good wishes and commented on how well they had decorated the school hall. He apologised for not being able to spend a long time with them and caused great laughter when he told them how he and his bride had slipped out of the Mine Club without the guests even realising that they had gone. He explained that he had been quite a bad boy when he was at school and had learnt how to disappear without the teacher knowing. "Now don't any of you try those tricks because I have told your teachers what to watch out for." Two of the young children then presented them with a large basket full of hand crafted gifts made by the children and grateful parents. Kumbula thanked the couple for all that they had done for the African community and for taking the time to share their happy occasion with them; adding that in the thirty year history of the mine such a thing had never happened before.

At the nurses' quarters, Mary quickly changed from her wedding dress into a tailored linen outfit and Patrick drove them back to the reception at the club. From the noise level it was apparent that the guests were all still enjoying themselves and had not even noticed the pair's absence from the reception. The party went on late into the night.

*

The family members all met up at number 16 late on Sunday morning, having taken some time to recuperate from the festivities. Paul had offered to drive Patrick's mother back to Johannesburg but she refused as she had been invited to stay with her friend Marjory Moir in Ndola for a couple of weeks. However, he then realised that he could save Theo and Joanna a train journey back to Plumtree School. This was gratefully accepted as the school term was about to begin. Wendy and Shaun drove back to Luanshya to be in time for work the following morning. In this way the wedding guests scattered.

Mary and Patrick had mapped out an interesting sightseeing trip for their honeymoon and even by Rhodesian standards it would be a long journey. Wankie lies in the north-western corner of the country but their final destination was near the eastern border; a total round trip of approximately 1700 miles. However, they were in no hurry and were keen to explore their adopted homeland, simply stopping wherever they fancied. Mary was only due to be back at the hospital in the beginning of December and, as Patrick had not taken long leave since joining the mine; he was in no hurry to get back.

They stopped at the Gwaai River Hotel for lunch, before arriving in Bulawayo in the late afternoon. The town had grown noticeably since Patrick's previous visit; enhanced by an imposing post office and library as well as several fine shops and municipal buildings. The wide streets indicated good planning for the future, following Cecil Rhodes' decree that the main streets should be wide enough for a wagon, with a full team of oxen, to be able to make a 180 degree U-turn.

With Patrick driving, Mary started reading from a travel brochure they had bought before setting out.

"It says here that tarred roads are only laid in the towns, as the Roads Department's finances didn't stretch to building full width tar macadam surfaces throughout the country. That's interesting isn't it, Pat?" She then continued reading from the brochure. "However, unique to Rhodesia, strip roads are constructed by laying down two narrow ribbons of tar, twenty-four inches wide, set a distance apart to match the wheel spacing of cars. These roads are known as 'the strips'."

"Oh how amusing, darling, what else could they have called them?" They both laughed at this obvious information and wondered what other descriptive jewels lay ahead.

Mary continued with her reading. "The strips are far cheaper to build but of course it is necessary to move over onto a single strip when passing or overtaking another vehicle and when meeting an oncoming vehicle. You will remember that won't you, Patrick, just in case I doze off? We are nearly at the end of this information so don't give up on me. Now I'm on to the last page where it says only the country's main roads enjoyed the luxury of strips; the remainder are constructed of compacted earth cleared of bushes and with drainage ditches on the sides. These are known as 'dirt roads'. Continuous traffic along some of these dirt roads causes surface ridges to develop, known as 'corrugations'. Caution is advised. Slow speed makes for an uncomfortable ride but high speed can cause bad wear and tear on the vehicle's suspension. Select the best speed."

"It is all a matter of knowing what lies ahead; we are learning as we go along," said Patrick. "One day our grandchildren may well think of us as pioneers braving these conditions which to them will seem very harsh. Mary, isn't it amazing to think that we will have grandchildren one day? I can't help but wonder if there will be a good future for them in Rhodesia."

On the recommendation of the proprietor of a petrol filling station they decided to spend a night at the Matopos Hotel. It overlooked a large recently completed dam which had been built to provide water to the Rhodes Estate Research Farm and a proposed junior boys' boarding school nearby. They arrived just as the sun was setting behind the hills on the far side of the dam; a memorable sight indeed, and a fitting honeymoon memory. They were shown to a spacious well-appointed bedroom with its own bathroom. After a wash to remove some of the dust from their journey, an attentive waiter seated them at a table on the broad veranda and brought them ice cold Castle lagers to clear the dust of the first leg of their epic journey.

At dinner, the hotel manager joined them briefly, recognising them instantly as a honeymoon couple he congratulated them and instructed the waiter to bring them a bottle champagne. He suggested that they visit the burial sites of Cecil Rhodes and the Shangani Patrol at World's View, a solid granite mountain about seven miles away. He assured them it was an easy climb for fit young-looking people like them. Rhodes himself had regarded it as one of the best views in the world and that name was adopted. Rhodes was quoted as saying that looking out from there at the vastness of the country one realises just how insignificant mankind really is by comparison; a strangely profound statement, coming as it did from one who was not noted for humility or modesty.

With a picnic lunch supplied by the hotel, they drove along a winding dirt road to the mountain, parking in a flat cleared area which was signposted as the Outspan. The initial climb was relatively easy going, followed by a fairly steep section, at the end of which they paused to rest and marvel at the scenery. Beautifully wooded areas with hundreds of small kopjies stretched as far as the eye could see. The final section of the climb really tested their fitness; about fifty yards of smooth granite rising at an angle of approximately twenty degrees. At the top was a cluster of three huge granite boulders, companionably grouped together. Just in front of the largest one was Cecil John Rhodes' grave, carved into the solid granite rock and enclosed by a simple heavy bronze plate inset between four nine by nine inch blocks of granite. It was the final resting place of the man whose drive, energy and money had opened up the country which was named Rhodesia in his honour.

At the grave the couple stood together; firstly out of respect but then in order to take in the magnificence of the 360 degree view. It seemed to go on forever, with no signs of any habitation nor anything man-made; just undisturbed nature at its best. It was beyond words. Mary and Patrick just held hands, happily sharing and storing these moments together.

Patrick spoke to the elderly African security guard on duty at the grave. He informed them that the lead coffin containing the body of Cecil Rhodes had been brought to the burial site on a gun carriage drawn by a team of twelve oxen. He assured them that the oxen had pulled it all the way up the mountain. He had witnessed it himself in 1902. It was a truly remarkable feat considering the slippery surface combined with the steep gradient. Teams of soldiers and BSA policemen had attached long ropes to the gun carriage just in case any of the oxen stumbled on their way up. Fortunately, the oxen made it, as in the opinion of the guard; the men would have had little chance of holding it on their own.

On a fairly level area beyond Rhodes' grave was a spectacular new memorial housing the bodies of the forty men of the Shangani Patrol. These bodies had recently been exhumed from their original memorial site in Fort Victoria and interred at World's View. This was of particular interest to Patrick as he knew that Lisa's parents had been guarding King Lobengula only three miles from the place where the forty men of Allan Wilson's patrol had fought and been killed by the stabbing spears and 'knob kerries' (clubs) of Lobengula's soldiers near the Shangani river, in 1893. The four sides of the memorial bore large bronze panels with sculptures depicting likenesses and the names of each of the forty troopers killed in that action.

Feeling overwhelmed by the history of the area they were relieved to return to the car and made their way to Maleme Dam and spent hours watching a herd of impalas quenching their thirsts drinking its cool water. Finally they spent an hour viewing the so-called 'bushman paintings' in a vast natural rock cave. The paintings, mainly of animals and people hunting with bows and arrows, were thought to be painted by the original inhabitants of both Matabeleland and Mashonaland. These people, more accurately known as the San People, were driven westwards, out into the Kalahari Desert by the later invaders of the country. Their art work is of excellent quality and can still be seen in caves throughout the country.

Hot and tired, Mary and Patrick returned to the Matopos Dam Hotel for dinner, after which they ordered an early breakfast for the following morning; the start of a new travelling day.

The onward journey from Bulawayo was uneventful; at Gwelo they saw the Jean Boggie Clock Tower, recently erected in memory of her famous husband, an early pioneer in the country. They made steady progress although the road was becoming busier, which meant going off and then back onto the strips quite frequently. They arrived in Salisbury at precisely five o'clock and were stunned by the number of cars on the roads. They realised that they had arrived at precisely 'knocking off time' for the hundreds of civil servants who, like other civil servants worldwide, were heading home, not a minute later nor a minute earlier.

They were very favourably impressed by Salisbury. The tarred suburban streets were lined with jacaranda trees and the majority of houses had colourful gardens filled with shrubs and beautiful flowers. Being in a higher rainfall area with adequate water supplies was indeed a great advantage, compared with Wankie. The building of Salisbury's cathedral had just been completed so the town was looking forward to claiming 'city' status. Also noticeable was the milder climate as it was 5000 feet above sea level, compared with Bulawayo; a thousand feet lower. They spent the night at Meikles Hotel in a good room overlooking the lawns and gardens in Cecil Square. At the reception desk Patrick noticed a leaflet advertising the Automobile Association and decided it would be a good idea to join them before continuing their journey. While signing up as a member, he asked the lady assistant about the condition of the road to Inyanga and was told that it was rough but passable. She then warned Patrick that as they would be journeying into an area whose altitude was more than 1000 feet higher than Salisbury's they should be prepared for much colder weather conditions. She recommended warm clothing, plus raincoats and good walking shoes if they wanted to explore the countryside. Grateful for this advice, Patrick waited for Mary to return from her shopping, then together returned to the nearest departmental store and purchased jerseys and raincoats.

Mary being enchanted by the shops, returned to Meikles store the next morning for things she had noticed were missing from Patrick's bachelor home. She was back at ten o'clock; in good time for departure to Inyanga and the beginning of their real honeymoon.

Travelling along the Umtali road, which had strips all the way to Rusape, they caught their first view of the Inyangani mountain range, approximately eighty miles away. It reminded Patrick of his boyhood, much of which was spent exploring the Drakensberg mountains to the south of Newcastle. At Rusape they turned left onto the dirt road leading to Inyanga. Progress was now slow as the road had been churned up by local farmers' lorries and ox wagons. However, once they were out of the farming area, they began to enjoy the remarkable scenery around them as well as having the pleasure of travelling for miles without seeing any signs of human habitation. It was late afternoon when they approached the foot hills of the Inyanga mountain range, from where they had their first sighting of Msasa trees in the light of the setting sun. In the travel guide they had read that unlike most other trees, the Msasa's new leaves come out in autumn colours, ranging from pale pinks to deep orange. Only later do the leaves turn to green. They are indigenous trees and seeing them at this time of year, under these lighting conditions, created a deep impression which they would remember as a honeymoon introduction to the region.

It was beginning to get dark by the time they reached the junction of the roads to Inyanga village and the Rhodes Hotel which meant that they had to negotiate the mountain road in darkness. This required extreme caution as the road was not only steep; it was deeply rutted and eroded by early rains. As they stepped out of the car they immediately felt the change in temperature and were grateful for the warm clothing purchased in Salisbury. Porters carried their cases, guiding them up onto the broad veranda and through to the reception desk. After signing in they paused for a few minutes in the lounge where a very welcome log fire was blazing and then walked through to their room where they found their suitcases had already been placed on wooden stools at the foot of each bed. A fireplace stacked with logs and kindling was ready to be lit if needed during the night. To warm up they chose the better option; a steaming hot bath. The bath water was very near to boiling point, so the room rapidly filled with steam. After debating who should bath first, they decided, a little shyly on Patrick's part, to go in together as the huge old fashioned Victorian bath tub could easily accommodate them both.

The next ten days were blissfully happy ones. They walked for miles, climbed three-quarters of the way up mount Inyangani, 8504 feet above sea level; caught fresh trout in one of the numerous mountain streams, sampled delicious apples, ripe plums and pears at the Rhodes Experimental Fruit Farm, studied the ancient pit dwellings, played tennis on the hotel's courts, and enjoyed the hotel's excellent food. They really got to know each other, and together experienced the exquisite intimacy and intensity of true love.

After dinner one evening, Simon, a dining room waiter, came through to the lounge in a highly agitated state and told them he had heard that Patrick's wife was a nurse and begged him to allow her to come and assist his wife who was having major problems giving birth. He said their house was quite nearby but there was no road for motor cars; so would they be prepared to walk? Mary immediately agreed to go. They put on their warmest clothing, collected Mary's emergency first aid box and the three of them hurried out into the darkness with Simon leading the way and Patrick following at the rear. Fortunately they were both fit, because the African interpretation of 'nearby' can be anything from one to ten miles. It was a clear night and although the moon was not yet up the brilliance of the stars gave them sufficient light for following the narrow footpath. They walked for nearly half an hour, with Simon constantly assuring them that it was 'very near'. They finally arrived at a group of five or six round thatched huts and Mary was led into one of them. She was introduced to the grandmother (gogo in the Shona language) who was the acting midwife. With only limited light coming from a small oil lamp, Mary examined the distressed woman and quickly established the cause of the problem and what needed to be done. At this point Gogo objected strongly, shouting, "What could this young white girl possibly know about such things?" Overhearing the argument, Patrick quickly went into the hut and explained to Gogo in Shona that Mary was a very knowledgeable young woman who had delivered many hundreds of babies already; black ones and white ones.

"Watch what she does, Gogo. It could be very useful to you in the future and it will add to your importance in the community when they hear that you helped save the life of this mother and her baby. You know, even the cleverest of us can still learn new things; even from the young people."

A baby boy was successfully delivered much to the delight of his parents. The occupants of the surrounding huts all came out singing and dancing, to celebrate the safe birth and to express their thanks to Mary and Gogo. Amongst them was a wizen and very elderly great-grandmother. She hobbled slowly up to Mary, took her two hands in her own and thanked her. Then looking deeply into Mary's face for a few moments, she said in Shona, "You are a wise and kind woman. You will be rewarded with two girl babies. I will be sending you something to protect you and all of your children." Before Mary could ask the old woman what she meant, she had disappeared into the darkness. Simon, being intoxicated with excitement over the safe arrival of his first born son, chattered ceaselessly all the way back to the hotel. Mary asked him how he knew she was a nurse.

"Oh madam, Lazarus who works in the lounge heard you telling two of our other guests that you were a nurse at Wankie. So that is how I knew."

Patrick and Mary should have remembered that Africans are always intrigued by what white people talk about, and of course are always keen to learn new English words.

At breakfast the next morning Simon came again to thank them and, apologising for the fact that he was not a rich man and could not buy her a gift, he handed Mary a small leather pouch, which he explained came from his great-grandmother whom they had met the night before. Mary opened the little pouch and carefully examined the contents. Inside were two beautifully polished, pitch black round stones, probably having been tumble polished in one of the mountain streams for hundreds of years. A third stone in the pouch was similar but oval and completely flat. Mary laughed.

"I know what she meant; I will have two plump rounded daughters plus a scrawny boy like you were, if the family photos your mum brought are anything to go by."

At the end of their stay at the Rhodes Hotel, they were given a great send-off; the entire staff turned out to wish them well. It was the perfect end to their honeymoon. They naturally felt very nostalgic about leaving as they drove away along the road lined with English oak trees which Cecil Rhodes had himself planted as saplings thirty or more years earlier. As they drove away they agreed that one of their aims for the future would be to come back one day to spend more time exploring the Eastern Highlands.

The return journey to Wankie was leisurely but uneventful and they were pleased to be home again; excited by the thought of starting married life in earnest and the opening of some of their wedding presents.

Lisa had made good use of the time they had been away and everything was spotless. Her friends had warned her that working for a 'madam' was very different from working for a 'boss'. Madams, she was warned, noticed little things like dust, cobwebs and marks on the carpet. However, as she knew and liked Mary, she really had few fears of their future relationship.

Mary knew that she would not be allowed to continue working at the mine's African hospital now that they were married.

It was a long standing company rule that husbands and wives could not both work in the same department; namely African Personnel in their case. Prior to the wedding she had submitted an application for a position in Wankie's government hospital and had been told that she was almost certain to be successful as they were short staffed.

Mary gathered up the pile of mail from the telephone table in the hallway and decided to read her letters before unpacking. She put aside the bills and 'official' letters for Patrick to deal with, and started on her personal mail. Wendy had written saying that she was huge and uncomfortable and expected to 'pop' soon. The other news from Northern Rhodesia was that Shaun was doing well and had been promoted. They had moved and he was now the underground electrical foreman at the Mufulira Copper Mine; the most recently developed of the Rhodesian Selection Trust mines.

Several of her unmarried friends had also written saying how much they had enjoyed the wedding and how envious they were of her marrying Patrick. She knew it was true and thought it would give his ego a well-earned boost if she showed him those letters later. Last of all there was a typewritten letter with no stamp and OHMS (On His Majesty's Service) printed across the top. This meant that it was a government letter. With some apprehension, she opened it and found it was from the Ministry of Health in Salisbury. In essence what it said was that their employment policy had recently changed and preference was now being given to unmarried nurses. Regrettably, they had to withdraw their offer of employment. She felt completely devastated and went to Patrick in tears. She loved her work and firmly believed that it was the only thing she was really good at. He consoled her as best he could but her disappointment was painful for both of them. This was the first of a series of developments and changes which would affect their lives and those of many other people.

CHAPTER 15

1932

Good news soon came from Shaun and Wendy. She had produced a fine and healthy eight pound boy who was to be named David, after Wendy's favourite grandfather. Wendy's letter went on to say:

Luckily, he takes after me, good looking and smart, but there is a look of Shaun in his eyes and shape of his head. I am not at my best at the 2am feed time but he certainly brightens my day by taking all I have to offer. Shaun is quite besotted and at the Mine Club the other day I caught him very knowledgeably discussing babies with one of his electricians. I had difficulty controlling my mirth. As soon as we can get a few days off we would love to come down to see you both and show you our little treasure.

On a rather sombre note, we have been warned of the possible effects of the worldwide depression seriously dropping the price of copper. However, at this stage we are not unduly worried and continue to be optimistic as always.

CHAPTER 16

❦ 1933/4 ❦

Wankie Colliery's coal production had reached an all-time record of one million tons for the year, but the bad news was that their two biggest customers, the Rhodesia Railways and the thermal power stations in northern Rhodesia were beginning to feel the effects of the developing worldwide financial crisis.

By early 1934 it became clear that the proposed opening of Wankie's number two colliery would have to be postponed. All the paperwork and planning Patrick and Kumbula had done in preparation for the increase in labour force would not only be wasted but a good deal of it had to be unscrambled. Thousands of migrant workers had already been offered jobs and this was of major concern to the department. The new housing and other facilities were nearing completion and about half of the existing workforce had been relocated to those houses which were ready. They couldn't move back to Number One Colliery because the old houses had already been demolished. It was a total mess and a major headache for Patrick and his whole organisation.

Three months later, in her usual weekly letter to Wendy, Mary wrote giving her the great news that she was expecting a baby sometime in June/July. She told her also how delighted Patrick was, and that he was already fussing over her and not allowing her to drink wine or lift anything heavier than a tea pot. "I wonder what the poor darling will do when I go into labour." Lisa on the other hand insisted that Mary should take long walks and keep on working in the vegetable garden. The African people had always done so and claimed that this kept them strong and fit for delivering babies. It amused and amazed Mary that after her years of nursing, she was only too pleased to go along with Lisa's traditional ideas; they simply seemed so obvious.

Mary's pregnancy was proceeding well and she was thankful for the cooler winter weather as she was already becoming very uncomfortable with the extra weight that she was carrying.

A letter then arrived from Wendy asking if they could spend a few days with them on their way through to Bulawayo. The copper mine had been on reduced production for some time due to the depression, but now it had been decided to close the mine down altogether and put it onto a 'care and maintenance' basis only, with all production ceasing at the end of the month.

Everyone, other than a small maintenance team, had been given one month's notice to leave the mine. They would receive a month's extra pay for travelling expenses. It was a dreadful blow to all of the miners and their families. It was even worse for the African workers as there was no other work for them in the whole of northern Rhodesia and little prospect of any in the neighbouring countries.

Shaun had put in an application to the Electricity Supply Commission in Bulawayo, for any vacancy, but had not yet had a reply from them. Fortunately, with Wendy's firm hand controlling the finances, they had built up sufficient capital to meet their living costs for two to three months and they had just finished paying off their new Chevrolet car. Shaun had given his monstrous motorbike to a young South African couple with a small baby. They hadn't enough money for their train fares back to South Africa plus their living costs until they found work there. Resolutely they had decided that the three of them would ride home on the motorbike. It would be a very long arduous trip but they had little choice without borrowing money, which they couldn't be sure of repaying.

Many of the white miners from the mines decided that it was not practical or worthwhile taking their household possessions with them when they left; having simply no idea where they might find work in the depth of the depression. After eating their last meals in their mine houses they just walked out, leaving everything that wouldn't fit into their suitcases. The mine's maintenance crews were left with the task of clearing up hundreds of houses and securing them to prevent vandalism. The abandoned possessions were donated to local charities for distribution to the out of work Northern Rhodesian workers.

CHAPTER 17

ℰℐ 1934 ℰℐ

The Wankie Colliery Company was more fortunate than the copper mining companies in that there was still a demand for coal for the railways and the power stations in Southern Rhodesia; plus a growing demand for export coal. However, they were forced to introduce various economy measures which brought Mr Powys Davies' cost cutting skills back to life with a vengeance not seen in recent years. He immediately focussed his attention on his old enemy, the African Personnel Department. This became a source of constant irritation to Patrick and Kumbula. It stalled their extension plans for the school and their proposed African apprentice training facilities.

Patrick appreciated the need to economise but was deeply concerned when he learnt that substandard equipment was being installed underground. Added to this a reduction in the number of good technical staff had begun to affect safety underground. A case had recently arisen where an electrician had reported to his foreman that his semi-skilled black worker had refused to obey his instructions. The worker contended that he had been told to do certain electrical work for which he was untrained and unqualified. The electrical foreman then applied to the personnel department for the man to be fired, and for a more obedient worker to be found to replace him. Kumbula interviewed the man concerned and concluded that he had actually been very sensible in refusing to do what he considered to be the electrician's work. Unfortunately, the accounts department had become involved and Mr Powys Davies saw the opportunity of further cost cutting by getting rid of the electrician's helper and not replacing him.

Patrick, sensing that this might become a serious issue, asked Kumbula to establish the full facts of the case.

"Boss Pat, this electrician's helper, Steven Jongwe, is a bit of a hot-head; a 'trade union' type of person, but he is no fool. We should tread carefully or there could be big trouble. He didn't tell me this, but I know that many of the European artisans expect their helpers to do a lot of their work. It is dangerous yet it is common practice throughout the mine. The helpers don't generally complain because they want to learn so that one day they can do all the work themselves and get better pay. Boss Pat, you know that I am frightened of electricity. Working with it is like playing games with a wild animal. You really need to know what you are doing or you can easily get killed by it. If only our young men could become apprenticed and serve time learning the necessary skills then these problems wouldn't arise."

"You are quite right, Kumbula, and I agree with you, but the problem goes further back than that. To be taken on as an apprentice a full secondary education is required, and although I have repeatedly pressed for this, the mine has not reached that level yet."

"Boss Pat, I hope we will succeed because I look to the future for my son, and you may do the same too when Sister Mary gives you a son."

"Kumbula, I have the start of an idea; perhaps we could look at this upset as an opportunity rather than a problem. Please call Steven Jongwe in for interview. I would like to talk to him."

Patrick quickly put Steven at ease with the traditional greetings and enquired about his family and home. Patrick learned that he came from the Zvimba district in the north-west of the country and ascertained that Steven, who was a Shona, had been educated at the Jesuit mission near Kutama where he had met and studied with political agitators Steven asked Patrick if they could speak in English rather than Shona, as he himself would prefer to practise his English, if that was acceptable to them. Patrick readily agreed and listened intently as Steven explained in detail what had happened underground.

"I was assisting the electrician in an older section of the mine where we were recovering power cables and switchgear for reuse elsewhere. I had been told by the electrician to cut the main incoming cable. Before doing so I took the precaution of asking the electrician if he was sure the power supply to the cable had been switched off. 'Of course the cable is not alive,' the electrician had said. 'Do you think I would tell you to cut it if it wasn't dead?' I explained to the electrician that I had come on shift at the same time as he did and I had not seen him checking that the power supply switch was still off, and for this reason I was not happy to cut the cable without first testing it at the switchboard. The electrician then shouted at me. 'Are you trying to teach me my job? I know it's off because I put it off myself yesterday, before we went off shift.' I politely asked if he was sure that somebody on the night shift hadn't put the power back on again. He didn't answer so I told him I would only cut the cable when he proved to me that it was dead. He became very angry and abusive and a formal report was put in to the electrical foreman stating that I had disobeyed instructions and had refused to do my work."

Patrick and Kumbula had listened in silence and were both shocked by what they heard. Patrick nodded his head but instead of discussing it any further, he asked Steven what kind of work really interested him.

Steven was rather taken aback by the apparent lack of interest in his immediate problem.

"I would like to use my brain, not my hands. I am an organiser of people. I can read and write and I was good at arithmetic at school. I would like to use these skills as I have visions of a better future for us Africans."

"Thank you, Steven. I want to see if we can help you to resolve this present matter but before I do so, is there anything else that worries you?"

"Well there is one thing you might not know about; it concerns the reporting of accidents. There are many small explosions underground now, but they don't get reported because it would look bad in the mine's safety records."

Patrick thanked him and said, "You may go now but please come back and see me first thing tomorrow morning."

Kumbula and Patrick spent the next hour discussing Steven Jongwe's character, strengths and weaknesses. They both agreed that he had the potential for causing major labour problems over this issue and perhaps others in the future. Kumbula told Patrick about Steven's aspirations in the field of the Black Nationalist politics. However, weighing heavily in his favour was his value in gaining support for their other plans and for extending the secondary school for the African miners' children.

Patrick then took the unusual step of phoning Angus Mackay and very briefly told him that an incident had occurred which could trigger labour problems.

"Come and see me now, Pat. This matter needs to be discussed privately, not on the phone."

Patrick immediately went up to the GM's office and outlined the salient points of the case. Angus listened carefully and finally said, "This is a nasty one, shocking in many respects. It's tricky, no matter which line we take. Firing Steven Jongwe is not an option and hauling the electrician over the coals would be difficult without witnesses."

"I agree with you completely, Angus, and for this reason I would like to transfer Steven to a clerical job in my department. I will have a vacancy for a statistics clerk at the end of this month as one of my staff is about to retire because of ill health. I would be able to keep a close eye on Steven. He is a 'bush lawyer' and a political troublemaker but I would rather spend time educating him and monitoring what he gets up to, than to be fighting with him and the trade unions. I think he could be useful as a source of information and I believe he trusts me enough to pass on details to me."

Angus asked a few more questions then finally agreed saying, "OK, Solomon, you win; but understand that the baby will be in your lap."

When Steven returned, Patrick said to him, "I am going to put my trust in you, Steven. For your part you will have to abide by my instructions without question. Know also that I have the power to dismiss you if you fail me." Without a moment's hesitation Steven agreed.

"That's fine, Steven. Now firstly you will be questioned by the mine accountant and the electrical foreman and it is essential that you keep your temper under control. Secondly, you must admit that you made a bad mistake by not obeying orders from the electrician. I know this is untrue but it is part of my plan that you do this. Say you are very sorry, but explain how frightened you are of the electricity. Tell them that you would rather leave the mine than continue working on electrical things. Tell them how much you would like to continue working on the mine, if there is a vacancy in another department. If they follow the normal procedure they will then refer your case to me for disciplinary action and processing. I will recommend a punishment for you of two weeks' suspension with loss of pay. After that I will find a position for you. I will do this for you only if I have your promise, on your mother's life, that you will never tell anybody about my assistance, because that would be very bad for me. Now tell me, what you would like to do?"

Very puzzled, Steven asked what kind of work he would have to do, but Patrick laughed and said, "Knowledge is power and I need you to get facts and figures for me in order to achieve my plans for more classes for our workers' children in the secondary schools." Steven's face lit up.

"Mazvita, Boss Pat (a very big thank you). I will do whatever you require and I will work hard, to the best of my ability. If it is possible I would like to be employed in your department"

It all went according to plan. Steven's abject apology was a little overdone but the foreman and electrician readily accepted it. They were grateful to be spared the trouble of a full scale enquiry, which might have exposed the shortcomings of their safety measures plus the amount of work which was being done, illegally, by the electricians' helpers. They were also pleased to be so easily shot of 'that bloody troublemaker'. The mine accountant was relieved to have successfully averted a potential strike by the African mine workers and relished the opportunity of off-loading a burden onto Patrick's shoulders.

Steven joined Patrick's staff as a junior statistics clerk; his first job being the preparation of forecasts of the numbers and ages of the children of the mine's entire African labour force. From these figures he established the future projected needs for their secondary education. Unexpectedly he stumbled over certain figures in the accounts department, and this confidential information interested him greatly as he was then able to covertly extract full details of rates of pay for all grades of workers. Steven fully realised the truth of Patrick's words, 'knowledge is power'.

Patrick and Kumbula never really got to like Steven as a person, but the information he extracted from various sources proved to be of considerable value to them then; and his gratitude proved to be of even greater value many years later.

CHAPTER 18

❧ 1934 ❧

Wendy and Shaun arrived late in the afternoon, with their smart new Chev packed full of household goods plus their very active two-year-old son David. It was a lovely reunion. David was the centre of interest and he thoroughly enjoyed all the attention. He was a sturdy good-looking child, with his father's impish smile and his mother's blonde hair and bright blue eyes. As soon as he saw Mary he ran up to her with his arms outstretched which really was the best possible introduction. She picked him up and hugged him. It was love at first sight for both of them. Wendy looked on with pride and pleasure. She had not coached David to greet Mary in this manner but had naturally hoped that her best friend would love her son.

The two girls went through to the bedrooms, chatting non-stop, catching up on each other's news while Lisa brought beers out onto the veranda for the men. They had very good news to drink to as Shaun had received a telegram just prior to leaving the mine; this being the offer of employment with the Electricity Supply Commission in Bulawayo, subject to a successful interview. It was fortunate that Southern Rhodesia had been granted self-government ten years earlier because the country's solid agricultural base and its financial separation from the British economy minimised the effects of the Great Depression. The brothers talked at length and Patrick was impressed and pleased to find how much Shaun had matured. He was disappointed that the family weren't able to spend more time in Wankie as he would have liked to get to know his 'totally reformed' young brother. Marriage to Wendy and parenthood had certainly brought about remarkable changes.

Lisa brought four-year-old Gajima to play with David and in spite of the two-year age difference they got along marvellously. Lisa put them into the fenced-in back yard and left them to it; shrieks of delight confirmed that they enjoyed each other's company. It was in fact the start of a bonding which was destined to last a lifetime. Lisa proudly called Wendy and Mary to come and see the fun the boys were having.

"All we need now is for your son to join them, Sister Mary, then the first stage of our families will be complete."

This, however, was not to be.

Wendy noticed that Mary had put on more than normal weight and with her nurse's knowledge and intuition suggested that perhaps Mary was carrying twins; a possibility that Mary had not thought of. Wendy checked and was reasonably sure she could hear two heart beats. When they joined their husbands for sundowners they announced the possibility amidst much hilarity all around. Poor Patrick was completely bowled over by the news and insisted on an extra round of drinks before dinner. Lisa overheard the news and was immediately concerned as it was thought by her people that having twins was against nature and could be a sign of bad things to come. However, she knew better than to express these feelings, especially with Mary obviously so pleased about the possibility of twins.

The visiting family left for Bulawayo after breakfast, with the sincere good wishes of everyone at number 16 Victoria Street.

By the end of the week Wendy wrote with the news that Shaun had been successful at the interview and had been appointed assistant to the ESC's District Engineer for Matabeleland.

Shaun's first assignment involved the supervision and building a 33,000 volt overhead power line from Bulawayo to the Lonely Mine; a rich gold mine about twenty-five miles to the north of the town. It was going to be a challenging project as time was limited. A new ore body had just been identified and mining it would double the electrical load which couldn't be met by the existing diesel generator sets.

Two weeks later the morning's post brought a letter from Wendy saying that they were busy moving into a house in Pauling Road in a good area which was known as 'The Suburbs'. She said it was not the grandest house in town, but being an older property, it was on a one and a half acres and it already had a flourishing vegetable garden and several avocado and pawpaw trees. A major blessing was a good well and windmill in the back garden and this provided clear fresh water for the front and back gardens. They were renting the property with the option to purchase within a year and Shaun had already started sorting out some minor defects in the house, in anticipation of their future purchase. For the present their plan was that Wendy would stay at home and care for David, but she intended to go back to nursing part-time once he had finished pre school.

Up at Wankie things appeared to be going well with Mary's pregnancy. She had gained more weight than she would have liked but fortunately, being winter, she didn't have to contend with the very high temperatures common in Wankie's summers. Her doctor had confirmed Wendy's diagnosis of twins and warned her to expect the birth to be earlier than normal. Three weeks before the due date of 24th July, in the early hours of the morning, she went into labour. Patrick, in a state of considerable anxiety, rushed her into the maternity ward of the local hospital. Having helped hundreds of mothers through the birthing process, Mary was reasonably confident that she would cope and did her best to reassure poor Patrick, then sent him home to wait for news.

After twenty-four hours of difficult labour she produced the first baby, a six pound girl. An hour later the doctor and maternity staff became seriously concerned that they might lose both the mother and the second baby. Fearing that a Caesarean section operation might be needed, the doctor went to scrub up, leaving the night duty nurse and Caroline, the midwife, who was attending Mary. Caroline had been born and raised on a Yorkshire sheep farm where she had delivered hundreds of lambs. This had prepared her well for her maternity training. Once the doctor was away, Caroline told Mary that she was certain that she could deliver the second baby and warned against having surgery. Mary readily agreed as she also was not keen to have the operation. Caroline was slightly built and had what sheep farmers called 'mid-wife's tiny hands'. She quickly got to work and within minutes had freed the umbilical cord and successfully delivered the baby. By the time the doctor returned both babies had been cleaned, weighed and wrapped ready for Patrick's arrival. The second baby, also a girl, was smaller than the first, but other than that, she looked identical to her sister. In accordance with the nurses' private code of ethics, which is strictly observed worldwide, nothing was mentioned to the doctor about the steps they had taken in his absence. He was naturally very relieved at not having to operate.

Patrick's joy and relief were unbelievably touching to witness. His first concern was for Mary who was lying back in the bed, exhausted but very happy. He gently stroked her hair and kissed her forehead saying, "You wonderful girl! I love you more than anything in the world. Am I allowed to pick them up?"

Mary just smiled and said, "You will do plenty of that over the next couple of years, I can promise you. Just bring them to me one at a time. I would like to hold them both and tell them I forgive them for all the pain and anxiety they gave me."

Very carefully Patrick placed them on either side of Mary then he gazed at the three of them, totally enraptured; implanting the beautiful picture into his storehouse of unforgettable memories.

Mary spent the next week recovering in the hospital before being allowed to take her precious daughters home. They had gained weight and she had mastered the technique of feeding them both at the same time. Initially there was no problem in identifying them because the first born was noticeably heavier, but within days the second appeared to be catching up. As their parents hadn't been able to decide on names, the nurses marked their wrist bands with the numbers one and two, which helped Patrick tell them apart.

After much discussion and many totally unhelpful suggestions from friends, they decided to name baby number two Caroline after the nurse who had delivered her, and finally settled on the Irish family name of Brigid for their first born.

While in the home Mary wrote to Patrick's mother, telling her in detail about her new granddaughters and inviting her to visit them before the warm weather arrives. As expected, Mrs O'Connor was overjoyed at hearing their news, and there and then decided that it was high time for her to make a train trip to meet the new babies, as well as staying with the Bulawayo family on her way. Earlier in the year Shaun, Wendy and David had motored down to Johannesburg to stay with her, but another short holiday with them would be perfect before going on to Wankie. Mrs Moir, her friend in Ndola, was also pressing her to stay for a few weeks, so she eagerly planned a round trip away from home where she was often lonely living on her own.

After leaving the Wankie family, where she had enjoyed every moment of her baby grandchildren, she carried on by train to Ndola in order to spend three weeks there. However, when she arrived she found that Marjory's brother from South Africa was also visiting, but as the house was large and well-staffed, Marjory begged her not to cut her visit short. Three weeks later the following letter arrived at Wankie.

Dearest Children,

I trust that all is well with you. You will be surprised to hear that I have been pressed to stay for longer with the Moirs, and this I am going to do as there is little for me to do in Johannesburg. Marjory's brother Desmond Wood, a recently retired chief buyer for Brakpan Mine, is also spending a holiday with her. Desmond is planning on starting up a mail order needlework delivery business in Johannesburg and Marjory and I are being asked to give womanly advice. His late wife was highly skilled in the art of needlework, but often found that she had to travel to the city in order to replenish unusual embroidery threads. He feels that a small home-based delivery service would be an ideal retirement business and Marjory and her husband are in full agreement with his ideas. By advertising in magazines like The Outspan, which is read by farming communities, he feels that he could be kept busy with mail orders from women unable to get into the main towns. I have a feeling that he will be successful as he just has the right attitude to business, being of course in that line all his life.

Please continue to keep me in touch with the development of 'my babies' as Wendy does with David. I look forward to seeing all members of my precious family on my way home, but at this stage I don't know exactly when that will be.

With much love, Mother.

Mary's parents were also due to visit their new granddaughters, but this was planned for early the following year to fit in with farm schedules. Patrick had become efficient with his camera, so the Browns were kept well supplied with photos of Brigid and Caroline, but of course even their parents found it difficult to distinguish which was which once the photos were developed.

Patrick proved to be a devoted father and a very competent helper for Mary. He was a light sleeper and wakened quickly if one of the babies cried at night; so he took on the night shift of changing nappies and bringing the twins through to Mary for feeding. The system worked well and later, when the babes went onto bottle feeding, Patrick continued with the night shift. He had the ability to drop off to sleep again as soon as he got back to his bed. Mary counted her blessings for this service, while Patrick found it helped him to bond with his girls, gaining their love and trust.

Mrs O'Connor's extended holiday was greatly appreciated by both her young families, as was Mary's parents visit early the following year; this being the first time they had met Patrick; other than on wedding photos. It was decided there and then that once the twins were walking, Patrick and Mary would motor down to the Eastern Cape to spend a holiday at the seaside and introduce the girls to their young aunts, uncles and other members of their extended family.

Then one morning a letter arrived from Mrs O'Connor, containing totally unexpected news.

My dearest family,

This letter will come as a surprise, but I sincerely hope not as a shock. I am very happy to tell you that Desmond Wood and I were married yesterday in the Magistrates Court in the city centre.

I sincerely hope that you don't think that I rushed into this marriage, because I have to tell you that from the first time we met in Ndola, Des and I began to have fond feelings for each other. I now know that my friend Marjory had arranged this meeting from the start, feeling that I would be a very suitable wife for her brother, and with this in mind she made sure that Desmond was in Ndola when I was due to visit.

We didn't want any fuss made, so for this reason we simply went ahead with the marriage ceremony. After all, we are both in our late 50s and although Des doesn't have children

he is more than happy to take on mine. I told you in my last
letter that he is on the point of opening a small mail order
business and the 102 Claim Street house will be perfectly
situated for our home as well as for our office. I am very
excited at the prospect of working at something worthwhile,
and I know that you will support us in our new venture.
The last years have been very lonely and suddenly I feel that
a whole new life is opening up to me. Please send us your
blessings.

I am writing to Shaun and Wendy so that the letters will
hopefully arrive on the same date.

God bless you my dearest little family, with love from
Mum and Des.

PS Des asks that you should please call him by his name.

*

The next two years were very happy and contented ones;
watching the girls learning to walk and talk and simply enjoying every minute of their development. Patrick continued to
take numerous photographs which Mary posted on to Wendy,
her parents and to Granny Wood in Johannesburg. In return,
Wendy wrote every week with news of David's progress and
Shaun's work. They had been granted their mortgage and were
now the proud owners of their own home in Bulawayo.

CHAPTER 19

◌ 1937 ◌

The effects of the Great Depression were easing and the copper mines had reopened but Wendy and Shaun had no thoughts of returning to Northern Rhodesia. After completing the construction of a 33000 volt power line to the Lonely Mine, promotion had been rapid, together with an appropriate rise in salary for the added responsibility. Plans were being made for building a new power station in the small town of Gwanda about sixty miles south of Bulawayo. It was centrally located for supplying electricity to the Antelope and Filabusi gold mines, plus the Liebigs meat canning factory at West Nicholson, thirty miles south of Gwanda. It became necessary for Shaun to make frequent visits to check on progress there.

Young David had finished pre-school and his teachers reported that he was a 'keen and bright scholar, with good potential'. Wendy and Shaun felt very proud and enclosed a photograph of him aged four and a half, dressed in his 'big school' uniform. He quickly settled down to the daily routine. The school was a bit too far for him to walk, so Wendy bought him a bicycle and one for herself. Initially she rode to the school with him at 7.30 every morning and accompanied him back at lunchtime. It was downhill all the way from Pauling Road to the school, which was a lovely ride at that time of day. Coming back up-hill at 12.30 was less pleasurable, especially during the summer months. With David in school for the whole morning, Wendy found she had spare time on her hands, and after some time she decided to look for a part-time job. She contacted the matron of the Bulawayo Memorial Hospital offering her services for part-time morning duties. After a quick interview, the matron, who was very short staffed in the children's ward, asked if she could possibly start immediately. With her love of children, and without any hesitation, she agreed to report for duty the next morning.

Wendy told Shaun her good news that evening, but surprisingly, he was very annoyed that she had accepted the job without discussing it with him first.

"We don't need the money since my promotion and what about David? Surely you should be at home with him?"

"Shaun," she said sharply, "please don't use that tone with me, nor take me for a fool, I know we don't need the money and you know perfectly well that David is at school for the whole morning. I would never neglect him." She paused for breath, then in a more conciliatory way explained that the hospital was desperately short of trained nurses and she felt that the least she could do was to help out for a few hours in her spare time.

"OK, OK. I'm sorry. I just felt it wasn't necessary and that we should have talked it over together before rushing into it."

Wendy walked over and gave him a hug. "Sorry, love. I didn't think it would all happen so quickly. I know you have our best interests at heart but nursing is what I trained for and it is one of the things which give my life a purpose."

After taking David to school the next day, Wendy cycled to the hospital and reported to Matron who gave her a quick tour of the wards. At the children's ward she was introduced to Sister McIntyre, a large well-rounded, motherly person, who was obviously loved by all of the children. The nurses and children all called her 'Sister Maggie'. She took Wendy around the ward, quietly telling her about her small patients whilst laughing and joking with each of them. Wendy was impressed and took an instant liking to her. Later she learnt that Sister Maggie had served as a nurse in Belgium during the 1914–1918 war and had lost her husband and only son in that dreadful conflict. Wendy looked forward to working with her and the other ward sisters; as well as the added bonus of nursing the children. That evening she told Shaun how much she had enjoyed her morning at the hospital and told him of the deep satisfaction she gained from doing the work which she had chosen. Shaun sympathised and admitted that he too would be very reluctant now to give up his own vocation.

The next few weeks passed rapidly with a steady flow of children recovering from their illnesses and new patients coming in to replace those who had been cured. Later, on one particular day, Wendy found, on arrival that three new patients had been admitted for observation. The children, two sisters aged five and eight, and a boy who lived next door to them who had just turned four. They were all running higher than normal temperatures and complained of pains in their legs plus bad headaches. The doctor had diagnosed a possible viral infection and had ordered appropriate laboratory tests to be done. As a precautionary measure he had recommended transferring them to one of the isolation wards which was in a separate building connected to the main wards by a long glassed-in corridor.

Wendy's task that morning was to move the three children, with the help of one of the staff nurses, to the isolation ward. They decided it would be easiest to wheel their three beds, complete with their young patients and their bedding to the new ward. This would also obviate the need for re-sanitising the beds. They made a game of the move, telling the children that they would race to see who completed the journey the quickest. Wendy then settled them in and stayed with them until the end of her duty period. The elder girl was quite talkative and told her all about her recent overseas holiday in England.

Before going off duty Wendy learnt that the Bulawayo laboratory had been unable to identify the suspected virus and further specimens had been sent to a better equipped lab in Salisbury. The results were expected the following day.

Wendy was a little late arriving the next day because Shaun had phoned just as she was about to leave home, asking if she would drop off some extra clothing for him as he had to go down to Gwanda for two or possibly three days and nights. On arrival at the hospital she noticed some deterioration in her small patients' condition. Everyone was waiting anxiously for the test results. These finally came through just as Wendy was about to go off duty. Matron came into the duty room, followed by Sister Maggie. Wendy saw tears in Matron's eyes and knew then it must be bad news. The other two isolation ward sisters were already there waiting for what was to come.

"I have extremely bad news for you," said Matron. "The analysis in Salisbury has confirmed that the children are suffering from 'infantile paralysis' (poliomyelitis), for which there was no known cure. I have to tell you that it will be necessary for all of the nursing staff who have been in close contact with the children be kept in strict isolation to prevent them spreading the disease. Isolation will have to continue until it can be established that no member of our staff has contracted the dreaded disease." Matron then said, "I will leave you for a while so that firstly you can consider the implications for yourselves and your families of being confined here for at least the next three weeks, and secondly to make the decision whether or not you are prepared to continue nursing our three patients. Please be assured that I am not asking you or telling you what to do. It is entirely up to you and neither I nor the Department of Health will make any judgement on your decisions. I will come back a little later for your answers."

Wendy's immediate thoughts were for David and Shaun. There was also the possibility that she might have already passed the infection on to them. Her next consideration was how Shaun and David would cope if she herself succumbed to the disease. For the first time in her life she felt alone and totally helpless. She left the duty room and went to the toilet, washed her hands and bathed her face in cold water from the hand basin; then sat and asked herself the question, 'who could possibly advise or help me?' Mary was the only one she could think of but she had the twins to look after and there was the risk too that Mary might pick up the disease from David, if he was already carrying the virus, and she might pass it on to the girls.

Wendy phoned Shaun's office on the off chance that he had not yet left for Gwanda, but she had missed him so she asked his secretary to get him to call her at the hospital. Next she made the big decision and contacted Mary in Wankie. Mary's response was immediate and positive.

"I will leave here within the next ten minutes and should be at your house by about four o'clock this afternoon. I will contact you as soon as I arrive." Mary arranged for Lisa to move back to their home and to take care of Patrick, Caroline and Brigid until her return. She phoned Patrick with the news, and then set off in the Ford to Bulawayo.

Wendy contacted her always helpful next door neighbour, asking her to please collect David from school and give him some lunch, explaining briefly that she was being held in isolation at the hospital, but was making arrangements for her sister-in-law to come down to Bulawayo to look after David.

Matron returned to the duty room and silently listened as each of the nurses agreed to stay on and take care of the children. In spite of Matron's normally formal manner, her voice was strained.

"I am very proud of all of you and I will see to it that your bravery and dedication are recognised when this is over. You are truly a credit to our noble profession and I thank you from the bottom of my heart." She then turned and hurriedly left before she lost control of her emotions.

Sister Maggie immediately took over and said, "Right, girls, we are up to our necks in this, but together we must beat the odds. Don't allow a few little viruses to worry you."

At lunchtime the call which Wendy was dreading came through from Shaun in Gwanda. The other two nurses tactfully left the duty room and went to check on the children. Wendy quickly gave him the basic facts of the situation. His spontaneous reaction was one of extreme anger, directed irrationally at the hospital and then it switched to her. She interrupted his tirade.

"Shaun, for God's sake think. I desperately need your support, not your criticism and anger." When he went on and on, she slammed the phone down and burst into tears. Sister Maggie came in at that moment and put her arms around her until her sobbing stopped.

"Don't fret, my girl; men react badly in times of trouble. Many of them are bastards but most of them are just children who will never grow up. He will be all apologies and regrets once he has had time to actually think the situation through."

*

On the journey down to Bulawayo, Mary tried hard to keep a positive outlook but couldn't help pondering on the dreadful possibility of Wendy herself contracting poliomyelitis. She also tried to prepare herself for the encounter with Shaun because she had some experience of his immaturity and volatility. Mary understood Wendy's reasons for going back to nursing and was prepared to defend her dearest friend at all costs.

When Mary drove up the drive of the O'Connor home, she found Wendy's cook, Silas, playing football with David in the back garden. Happy to see her, he ran up to the car and told her that his mummy was at the hospital and he had just scored a goal against Silas.

"Oh, very good, David. Mummy will be proud to hear that. I am going to tell her that I have come to look after you until she can come back home." Silas greeted her warmly and thanked her for coming to look after the picanini boss(small boy).

"I will take sister's suitcase to the guest bedroom. The front door is open, please to just go in."

Mary went through to the bathroom washed the dust from her hands and face, then phoned the isolation block number Wendy had given her. Both of them experienced great difficulty in trying to be cheerful.

"Oh Mary, I simply can't thank you enough for coming to my rescue and for looking after David at such short notice. Please give my love and apologies to Patrick and your girls. I cannot speak now but I will phone you tomorrow and fill you in properly."

Mary was very tired from the journey and decided to have supper with David, then after reading him two stories, she said good night and enjoyed a relaxing hot bath before going to bed. She was wakened at midnight by a bad dream. Unable to get back to sleep she stole quietly through into David's bedroom. The passage lights gave just enough illumination for her to see the sleeping boy's relaxed face and the mop of blonde hair. Her heart was bursting with compassion and her eyes filled with tears as she contemplated the possible changes which might come into his life during the next weeks. Quietly she returned to her room, determined to be strong for whatever the morning might bring.

She was woken early by a bright little voice enquiring, "Auntie Mary, are you going to ride to school with me until Mummy comes back from the hospital?"

"I might ride with you some days, David, but today I'm going to the hospital to see your mum so I will take you to school in my car."

"Oh lovely," he answered. "My friends will be jealous of me coming to school in your car"

Silas served them a hearty breakfast of Quaker oats porridge followed by bacon and eggs, then toast with marmalade. Mary was pleased to see that David ate it all without any prompting and that he had already dressed himself properly for school.

Familiar with a hospital's morning routine, Mary knew that Matron would be 'doing her rounds' checking on any developments during the night, prior to the arrival of the doctors. Therefore Mary went straight through to the offices and introduced herself to the deputy matron, giving her the full details of her relationship to Wendy and their backgrounds. Although it was outside the hospital's normal visiting hours, the deputy matron was very understanding, and immediately phoned through to the isolation ward, giving instructions to Sister Maggie as to what was required for Mary's visit which would have to take place behind the glass partition. She also undertook to arrange an appointment with the doctor responsible for the isolation patients. Mary thanked her sincerely and made her way over to the isolation block.

Later, Mary met Doctor Scott, as arranged, and found him to be a most sincere and kind person. He acknowledged her position as a nurse and as Wendy's close friend, and then told her 'in strictest confidence' about the condition of the three children. The two younger ones were already suffering high temperatures, fevers, severe pains plus the first signs of paralysis in their limbs. In his opinion it was unlikely that they would survive for more than a week to ten days. The eldest child appeared to have a milder infection and with luck might survive. Dealing with the four nurses attending them, he said they were all show-ing signs of fatigue, which was to be expected, but that if they had picked up the virus then they would probably be showing symptoms within the next three to four days.

The disease had come from Britain, Doctor Scott told her, where there had been a poliomyelitis outbreak of epidemic proportions. It had already killed well over two hundred chil-dren. There was no known vaccine but scientists were working frantically to develop an effective one.

Mary collected David from school then called in at Rept-ers, a moderately priced grocery store in Abercorn Street, where she bought a few items which Silas had asked for. She enter-tained David for a while, answering his continuous stream of questions and was struck by their content and depth. He was obviously a bright little boy by any standards, with a splendid vocabulary for his age.

She then had a long telephone discussion with Patrick, in which she told him her concerns over Wendy and the possi-bility of her having contracted the dreaded polio disease. As expected, he advised her to consider only the facts and make no early judgements. Patrick's cool and calm approach helped her to focus her attention on the realities of the various possible outcomes but in spite of this she felt a dreadful foreboding.

Shaun returned from his Gwanda trip the following evening. David was eating supper when Mary heard the car coming up the gravel drive and ran out to meet him. Mary gave him a hug but Shaun was unable to speak. He simply broke into heart-rending sobs of anguish, and perhaps remorse, while Mary did her best to comfort him. They went and sat down on the veranda while Silas fetched his suitcase from the car and, a few minutes later, appeared with the drinks tray, ice cubes, glasses, a soda siphon and a bottle of Johnnie Walker. Shaun poured a drink for Mary then helped himself to a very substantial whisky. David came out onto the veranda in his pyjamas and dressing gown simply delighted to have his dad back home again.

"Do you know what, Daddy? Auntie Mary has come to stay with us until Mum comes out of the hospital. She took me to school in her Ford car. Even our teacher came out to look at it."

After chatting to David for some time Mary suggested that as Shaun was very tired after driving back from Gwanda, it would be a good idea if he read David a story now instead of later. David happily agreed and the pair of them went off to the bedroom. During his absence Mary sorted out in her own mind the best way to handle the coming discussion. She based her approach on the advice Patrick had given her, namely: deal only with the known facts, otherwise you will get lost in an infinite number of possibilities.

Shaun came back half an hour later and helped himself to another hefty whisky then sat with Mary out on the cool, dark veranda, lit only by the street lights shining through the jacaranda trees in the front garden. Shaun sipped his whisky and silently waited for Mary to speak. He knew Mary would not mince her words nor would she scold him any more than he deserved; yet he still dreaded what was surely coming.

"Shaun," she said firmly, "you have behaved shamefully. You have hurt the person you love most in the world. The only reason I can think of for your behaviour is that you acted spontaneously without giving the real issue any thought at all. This has caused great pain and suffering at a time when Wendy was seriously vulnerable; trapped in hospital with sick patients to look after. Try to imagine yourself alone in that situation. Believe me, I feel ashamed for you. Tell me now, have you any valid excuse?"

Choked with emotion he was unable to speak normally but after a while he recovered.

"Oh Mary, I am so sorry; I've let everyone down. What can I do?"

Mary replied, "I've made arrangements for you to visit the hospital tomorrow morning and you will be allowed to see Wendy and talk to her, but to minimise the risk of spreading the disease you will only be permitted to speak to her through the glass panes of the corridor windows at the isolation ward."

"What do you mean, Mary? Is that really necessary? If so then surely Wendy is at risk herself"

"Yes, Shaun; of course she is."

Shaun let out a cry of anguish and said, "Oh my God. No! We must get her out of there immediately"

Quietly Mary told him to calm down and listen because it would be better if he heard the facts from her now, rather than later from a less caring or misinformed person.

"Shaun, please believe me, I have no wish to rub salt into your wounds, but I have to tell you that the time has passed when you could possibly have talked Wendy into leaving the hospital. Now she cannot leave the isolation wards until all of the nursing staff and the patients are proved to be clear of infection. That is the hard fact and we have to accept it." Mary paused to allow Shaun time to fully absorb what she had said, then added, "Knowing Wendy as I do, I am absolutely certain you couldn't have persuaded her to leave her patients, no matter how hard you might have tried. The doctor has told me in confidence that within the next week to ten days he should be able to tell us if any of the nursing sisters were showing symptoms of poliomyelitis."

Shaun simply couldn't accept what he was hearing and burst into floods of tears. All Mary could do was to put her arm around him and try to comfort this poor shattered man.

When he had calmed down he reached for his glass and the whisky bottle but Mary quickly picked up the drinks tray and carried it away to the kitchen. On her return she said. "You will have a busy day tomorrow and a clear head would be a good idea. I've made a light supper so come and eat now, and then we will have an early night."

After the meal, they walked down the corridor, but he stopped at the master bedroom door and put his hand on her shoulder and said, "Please come in, Mary."

She was deeply shocked but not surprised. After pausing to regain her composure, she gripped his wrist and lifted his hand from her shoulder.

"Shaun" she said angrily, "I understand your need and in my nursing career you are not the first one to seek comforting. Don't ever try that on me again. Take my advice and erase those last words of yours from your memory. If you don't do so, you will regret it for the rest of your days. Understand as well that Wendy is my best friend and I would never allow her to be hurt again; not by you or anyone else."

Stunned, he muttered, "Sorry," then turned and went into his bedroom alone.

The following morning Shaun took David to school then called in at his office and told his secretary that he had an appointment at the hospital but would be back later in the day. As he was leaving she called him and said, "Mr O'Connor, there is an important letter for you from Head Office," and handed him a letter marked Private and Confidential. He pocketed it and drove up to the hospital.

Being five minutes early for the appointment, he decided to open the letter. It came from Mr Metcalf, a well-liked and respected electrical engineer; the Chairman of the Electricity Supply Commission. He had served as a pilot in the Great War against Germany and had lost both legs when his bi-plane was shot down. In spite of this disability he was always cheerful and Shaun had marvelled at the fact that he was able to climb a thirty foot long ladder when he wanted to check the workmanship on a high voltage power line. The letter was short and clear. Shaun was required at Head Office as they had news which was likely to have a major effect on the programme for the Gwanda power station. He was required urgently and should plan on spending three to four full days in Salisbury. He was also asked to bring all available information on the construction programme and the scheduled delivery dates for all of the outstanding imported equipment.

Initially Shaun felt that the timing couldn't possibly have been worse and clearly he had no option but to go to Salisbury. However, in a totally selfish way he felt relieved to be removed from the situation that had developed and which he felt he was not strong enough to handle. He put the letter in his pocket and made his way through to the isolation block and spoke to Wendy through the glass partition.

Neither Shaun nor Wendy spoke about the details of that meeting. It was clearly emotional and very personal. Mary would have liked to know how the issues were settled but respecting their privacy, she never enquired.

Once back in the office, Shaun phoned Mary and told her about the summons he had received and asked her if she could possibly stay on and look after David. She readily agreed. Shaun and his office staff spent the next hour and a half gathering up all of the files, letters, programmes and data which referred to the power station project then all of these were loaded into his car. He called in at home, packed the clothing he would need and by midday he was on the road to Salisbury. Fortunately there was now a fully tarred road all the way, so even allowing for a break at Gwelo for a snack lunch and refuelling, barring any problems, he would be checking into Meikles Hotel in time for dinner. The long journey gave him time to think about Wendy and David. He realised just how lucky he was to have Mary's help at this time, but completely refused to even contemplate the problems the future might hold.

Shaun was up early the next morning feeling totally refreshed but anxious to find out what had triggered the need for this urgent meeting. Although the ESC's offices were quite close to the hotel he took the car and parked as close as possible to the office entrance. He carried five loads of files and other paperwork up to the conference room, as directed by Mr Metcalf's secretary, and waited in her office until Mr Met, as he was known to the staff, called him in. Mr Met greeted him warmly and said he had heard about the polio outbreak in Bulawayo and offered his apologies for tearing him away from his family at this difficult time. Shaun thanked him for his concern and said he realised that the problem at Gwanda must be very serious. "Yes, Shaun, it is. But I will tell you all about it when the other senior staff arrive." They walked down to the conference room.

Mr Met thanked them all for coming at such short notice then said, "What I am about to tell you is strictly confidential and no one must speak about it without my personal permission. Is that clearly understood?" There were murmurs of agreement, so he continued. "We have been tipped off by the intelligence services in Britain that another major war with Germany could be on the cards. This would have potentially serious financial and logistical implications for the Gwanda power station project. As you all know, apart from the boilers, which are coming from Babcock & Wilcox in England, the rest of the equipment has been tendered for and is about to be ordered from Siemens in Germany. What we now need to figure out, and decide upon, is whether or not we could get all of the Siemens equipment here, install it and finalise the testing and commissioning before any nonsense starts. If we cancel the Siemens contract and have to call for new tenders we waste the best part of five months and will let our consumers down. Apart from our loss of revenue from sales, Siemens would be entitled to claim vast cancellation charges. I want you to drop all other work and concentrate on this job. You have three days to come up with the full facts, costs and time scales for each of the workable options. Are there any questions?"

"Yes, Mr Met, I have one," said one of the engineers. "Have the intelligence people any estimates for the soonest and latest starting dates for hostilities to commence?"

"Yes. They are nine months and eighteen months. I appreciate this is a wide range, but these are their best guesses and you will just have to work to them."

Shaun was very favourably impressed by the way the staff worked together. There were frequently differences of opinion but by the end of the second day they had reached consensus. The best option was to place the orders with Siemens immediately, and to offer them a negotiable 'penalty/bonus' clause for full completion within nine months. The ESC would have to commence the civil and structural work immediately, based on the detailed schedule which was appended to the full report. Mr Met accepted their report and its recommendations but pointed out that while it was feasible, there would be no room for any errors or unexpected delays.

During Shaun's absence Mary visited the hospital daily and to her trained eye, there was further deterioration in Wendy's appearance. She made an appointment to see Doctor Scott, and she told Wendy she had done so, as it was essential for her to know as early as possible whether or not Wendy had contracted the disease.

Mary saw Doctor Scott the next day and she immediately sensed that there was bad news because he asked her to come to his office. He ordered tea and asked her to sit down.

"Mrs O'Connor, I am extremely sorry to have to tell you we have very bad news. The two younger children are showing signs of breathing problems and the eldest has lost all feeling in her lower limbs. It has been one hell of a night for everyone. The nursing staff were wonderful and I am immensely proud of them." He was silent for a while, drinking his tea and thinking how to tell her about Wendy and the others. "I have just received the test results on our nurses and I'm deeply distressed and sad to have to tell you that all three of the younger nurses have tested positive. It was awful giving them the news this morning, especially after all that they have already been through last night. Wendy O'Connor must have known her condition as she gave me this letter for you early this morning. Only Sister Maggie is clear. Privately she had joked with me some time ago saying, 'No virus would dare to enter my old body; I built up immunity for all the known viruses when I was a young girl in the concentration camps in South Africa during the Anglo/ Boer War.' How amazing it is that one remembers this flippant conversation when one is deep in sorrow and tragedy."

Doctor Scott then handed Mary the duly sterilised letter from Wendy and said, "Wendy O'Connor is a wonderful woman and a totally dedicated nurse. I would urge you, as her trusted friend, to act as soon as possible if her note requires you to do anything for her."

Mary thanked the doctor and gave him her phone number and asked him if he could keep her informed of any changes. She walked slowly back to her car, dreading what might be in Wendy's letter, but she decided it would be best to find out before driving back to the house. It read as follows:

The Rhodesian Government Public Health Department

Bulawayo Memorial Hospital

My dearest friend,

It was wonderful to see you again and a thousand thanks for looking after my boys. As always I knew I could count on you to come up trumps in these unfortunate circumstances. Excuse the hospital paper but I'm writing this in the duty room as I need to have it ready for Doctor Scott to give it to you this afternoon. He's a lovely, kind man and a darn good doctor too. The unmarried nurses here are all doing their best to land him; whoever does will be a very lucky girl. I noticed you casting your professional eye over me this morning and of course we never could hide anything from each other. The sad news is that Doctor Scott seems to agree with your diagnosis and he says the next three to four days will tell us, one way or the other. It is no good saying if only… if only, but I firmly believe that my personal choice of nursing as a profession always meant that I might have to risk my own life for the sake of my patients. My regrets are not for that, but for leaving you all; especially Shaun and my small boy so early in their lives.

I need your help desperately now. There are things that need to be planned for while I am still able. Shaun is a wonderful husband and a devoted father to David but he simply couldn't cope on his own. He is not as strong as your Patrick or even my little David, and he would need a woman to guide him and someone to bring up David. I cannot risk passing our precious son over to any woman other than you for that task.

What I am asking of you is way beyond any reasonable request but, as a mother yourself and my dearest friend, you will understand my dilemma. I have to ask you if you will become the nominated legal guardian of David if I die, or if I become paralysed, and physically or mentally unable to care for him. You are so much better with words than I am so I am also asking you to do the tricky thing of convincing Shaun that I have thought this through most thoroughly. I love him absolutely and would trust him to the end of the earth to do what is best for our beloved son; and yet I feel that you, Mary O'Connor, are the only person I know who will raise him, with Shaun's assistance, in the way Shaun and I had always planned. I just cannot rely on Shaun's choice of a new wife when the time comes.

Next, we will need a competent lawyer to draw up whatever papers would be necessary for the setting up of guardianship and, to be safe, your possible future adoption of David, if anything should happen to Shaun. Perhaps your brother Paul could give you the name of a trustworthy legal colleague here in Bulawayo, one who would be familiar with the Rhodesian laws, and would be competent to draw up whatever papers would be necessary. So sorry, all of this is most presumptuous of me, but I am hoping that you will relieve me of these worries. Please reply as soon as possible if you are able and willing.

Remember, no tears. Think only of the wonderfully happy times which we have enjoyed together. Tons of love, W.

P.S. I will be writing to advise my parents when things are more definite, but will ask them not to come up, as I don't want a big send-off

It took Mary several minutes before she could bring herself to reread Wendy's letter as she had the weird feeling that this was all totally unreal, unbelievable, and it couldn't possibly be happening. She read it again slowly, drawing the full meanings, and the implications for everyone, of each of Wendy's carefully chosen words. This was no time to dwell on the tragedy so, with supreme effort Mary focussed on the things she needed to do for Wendy, Shaun, David, Patrick and herself in preparation for Wendy's possible death.

As soon as she had sorted out in her mind the timing for each eventuality she felt better and drove back to the house. As she pulled into the driveway David broke off from the game of football he was playing with Silas and ran up to greet her. She picked him up and gave him a good hug. When she put him down he asked her how his mum was. Mary told him that she had seen her and she had spoken to the doctor about her and he had said he would only be able to tell them about Mum in a few days' time. She also told him that she would be taking him and Daddy to see Mum as soon he came back from Salisbury. Satisfied, David ran back and told Silas the news.

Mary booked a trunk call to Paul in Pretoria. When her call came through she quickly outlined the problems she faced. He advised it would be best to use a locally based lawyer and suggested she contact an ex-classmate of his, Benjamin Kaplan, whom Paul described as a 'de-tribalised Jew', with a great sense of humour and a brilliant brain.

"He is a good friend and I can promise that he will look after you. You can bank on that."

She called Benjamin Kaplan and explained her require-ments. He immediately offered to visit her at home after work that evening. She then phoned Patrick and gave him a rapid run-down of what had happened that day. He listened carefully without comment until she finished.

"You are an incredible woman." Please be assured that I am with you one hundred per cent and of course David would be very welcome. Do whatever you feel is necessary. I will phone you back later tonight to hear what the lawyer recommends."

Mary relaxed for a while then called David in and put him in the bath to remove the dust and dirt off his sturdy young body. She explained to him that there was an important visitor coming to talk to her so he must put his pyjamas and dressing gown on after his bath and she would give him an early supper before the man arrived.

Benjamin Kaplan came much earlier than expected and Silas brought him through to the dining room where David was still eating his favourite scrambled egg supper. Mary had heard a car arrive but she was busy getting dressed so couldn't go to greet him. Shortly she heard peals of laughter coming from David and realised that Benjamin had arrived. She finished dressing and went through to the dining room.

Benjamin was a short, hyperactive man, reminding Mary of a local bird which continually hops from branch to branch, twittering rapidly every time it moved. He had told David that he had three little boys of his own and, unlike him they were all very naughty so he didn't allow them to have their supper in the dining room. They had to eat on the back veranda with the dogs. David was horrified until he saw a smile on Mr Kaplan's face and then he laughed and laughed, realising that this funny man was just joking.

"A bright lad," he commented to Mary after David had left the room. "I specially wanted to meet him as he is probably the most important person in this case and I needed to know his level of understanding and to assess his adaptability to any of the possible future changes in his life. You are obviously very fond of him, but tell me, have you children of your own, and if so how would they be affected by an addition to your family?"

"Mr Kaplan, I have twin daughters aged two and a half. They are devoted to each other and I'm certain they wouldn't be affected at all. Ours is a very stable family and David has already spent several happy holidays with us. My husband is excellent with all children. He has dealt with the schooling and training of Africans all of his life, to the extent that he now even speaks to all adults as if they were backward children. I find it most amusing sometimes. I think you would enjoy meeting him, Mr Kaplan and I hope you will do so one day."

"That is good, but before we get down to business please call me Ben or Benjamin; then I will know that you regard me as a friend."

"My brother Paul will have told you my name is Mary. I must thank you for taking on this case at such short notice. The doctor suspects that my sister-in-law Wendy has contracted poliomyelitis while nursing infected children, and, if he is correct then within a very short time she could be incapable of signing any papers or being legally able to make decisions regarding the future of her son. My brother-in-law, David's father, is presently away on business and is unaware of the latest reports on his wife's condition so there has been no discussion with him regarding David's future if his wife were to die. Please read this letter from her because it covers her concerns and wishes. As you will read, she would like to name my husband and me as David's legal guardians, and, in the event of her husband's demise, we should be his adopting parents. Could the necessary papers be prepared in advance, even though David's father, Shaun, has not yet been consulted?"

"It is a delicate question, Mary. However, technically speaking, nothing can be concluded without full consultation with him. Given the circumstances, what I can do now is to draft all of the papers but withhold them until we know Wendy's prognosis for certain. The best thing would of course be for her to tell him her wishes whilst she is still capable of doing so. From her letter it is clear that she is extremely worried over how her husband would cope with young David. Knowing both of them, what is your opinion?"

"Benjamin, I think it would be virtually impossible for Shaun to cope without a woman like Wendy. As you have read, she is seriously concerned about the effect her death would have on Shaun. He has a very demanding job and couldn't possibly look after David by himself. Wendy sees me as the only person she could entrust with that responsibility. To the outside world anything I do could easily look as if I am positioning myself to take away this child. Wendy wants me to discuss it all with Shaun. I will do whatever I can for all of them and I have my husband's full backing. I feel very concerned and anxious for Shaun. He should be back from Salisbury in two days' time."

"Mary, it is obvious to me that you are a most compassionate person and that Wendy trusts you completely. The three of you must discuss the future together. Have faith in yourself and draw on your inner strengths, as I am sure you have done throughout your life. No one could ask or expect any more of you. Don't deplete your energies by worrying about possibilities. I will have to go now but if you can come to my office tomorrow at ten, I will have all the necessary papers ready for the three of you."

Mary went through to David's bedroom and found him sitting up in bed looking through one of his favourite books. "Have you come to read me a story?" She sat down on the side of the bed, took the book and read him one of the African Aesop's fables about Kalulu a very clever and smart hare. When she had finished reading the story she kissed him 'good night', tucked in the blankets and put out the light.

Just as she was sitting down to her supper, the phone rang. Patrick was on the line from Wankie. She told him all that had happened and what Benjamin Kaplan was doing. He listened silently, as normal, only adding his suggestion that it might be wise to check to ensure that Wendy and Shaun had made their wills. Patrick assured her that the girls were thriving but as was to be expected, Lisa was 'spoiling' them in her absence. He had kept in touch with his mother, who was naturally greatly concerned that she was so far away and unable to offer help, but if needed she would come up to Bulawayo immediately. He then added, with concern in his voice, that he was missing her greatly. Reassured by his loving words, Mary had the first good night's sleep since her arrival in Bulawayo. She woke the next morning feeling refreshed and more confident to face whatever lay ahead.

Mary took David to school in her car, which he loved. It was very unusual for children to be driven to school, so his arrival always caused a stir among the young pupils. His little friends ran up to the car, standing on the running board to chat to

Mary, much of which she couldn't understand as they were all talking together.

Mary went on to the hospital and found that Wendy was off duty and wanted to talk to her. As before, they were separated by the glass doors of the isolation block. Wendy was pale but very pleased to see her and was relieved to hear that Shaun and David were coping reasonably well with the situation. Mary told her she had put the wheels in motion with Benjamin Kaplan, and that all of the necessary documents and forms had been promised for that day and she would bring them for her to read through, prior to discussions with Shaun.

"I hope that I have not over-dramatized the position Mary, but I truly sensed that I should prepare for the worst, rather than get caught not having provided properly for my little boy and Shaun. Please be totally honest and tell me if I am asking too much of you and Patrick?"

"My very dear friend, you know I would never hide anything from you. Patrick and I have discussed the possible situations at length and I solemnly promise that we would look after David and love him as much as our own. Benjamin Kaplan will ensure that Shaun retains his full parental rights, but we must wait to see what clauses he puts into the documents. All Benjamin has told me so far is that the three of us will need to talk it through as soon as Shaun gets back."

On her way out Mary met Doctor Scott and he said he would walk with her to her car. "I think it is best if I give you the full picture as I see it now. The stark facts are that the eldest child has a chance of living, but she is unlikely to regain the use of her legs. Three of our nurses are now showing early signs of paralysis. One, I am sorry to tell you, but which you will have expected is Wendy O'Connor. Only Sister Maggie continues to test negatively at present and she has no symptoms. I am aware of your situation, as Wendy has confided in me, and she asked me to keep you fully informed. I am desperately sorry that I am unable to do anything more to help her. Until a vaccine is developed, this dreadful disease will continue to wipe out hundreds, if not thousands of young children and many adults too."

Mary was shocked but understood and shared his feelings of frustration and inadequacy. She asked him if he was able to tell her any more about the way Wendy's symptoms would progressively develop. She explained that there were various papers currently being prepared by the lawyers and these needed to be discussed with Wendy's husband and then signed, while Wendy was still physically and mentally able to sign and to understand their implications.

"It is difficult to be specific but so far the paralysis appears to be progressing slowly in her legs. Later it will continue upwards through her body. My best forecast would be that her mental faculties will remain functional to the end, but paralysis will start with the legs, then the upper limbs and ultimately occur in the chest muscles. Please understand that these are the first patients I have treated for this disease, so it is difficult for me to be any more specific. I would suggest that you shouldn't delay because time is short; one to two weeks would be my guess for Wendy."

Mary thanked him very much for his kindness and candour then wept silently for her friend before driving to Benjamin Kaplan's office. True to his promise, he had a sheaf of documents ready for her. He was busy with a client so she left a 'thank you' note for him and returned to the hospital. There she read through all of the papers and noted with satisfaction that they included wills for Shaun and Wendy. She extracted a full set of copies for Shaun then sealed a large envelope and left it for Wendy at the isolation block office.

David was already waiting for her at the school gates, full of all that had happened at school that day. His energy and bright little face gave Mary a well needed boost but she couldn't prevent the dark clouds from intruding. After a light lunch of sliced ham and salads she and David rested on their beds until mid-afternoon, waiting for Shaun's return from Salisbury. Silas came back to do the ironing but she told him to leave that and asked him to play with David instead as she wanted the kitchen to herself. She prepared an Irish stew, which she knew to be a favourite dinner.

Shaun arrived home just before sundown, looking truly worn out. Immediately he asked about Wendy. "Shaun, the news is not good but you go and have a bath now. We will talk later." He returned looking anxious but a little more relaxed. He walked onto the veranda and found David waiting for him there, wanting to know where he had been, and why it had taken so long to come back.

Mary rang the dinner bell for them to come to the table. Shaun drained the last of the beer from his tankard and the two males of the family walked through to the dining room hand in hand. It was earlier than their normal dinner time but Mary wanted David to be in bed before she broke the bad news to Shaun. They thoroughly enjoyed the Irish stew and when they finished, Mary suggested that Daddy should read a bedtime story to David while she cleared the table and made coffee. She then waited patiently on the veranda for Shaun to return. Relaxed and refreshed, he thanked her for the lovely meal and for looking after David, adding that David had told him what a clever mummy she was because she had made two babies when most people only made one at a time! Mary laughed and said, "Not really so clever; and I never want to try that again."

"Shaun, I know it has been hard for you waiting for information about Wendy, but I didn't want David to overhear us. Come and sit and I will tell you everything that has happened while you were away. I have visited Wendy three times and have had two meetings with her doctor; an excellent and most helpful man. I am so sorry that there is no easy way to put this; but the doctor is certain that Wendy has contracted polio. The eventual outcome cannot be forecast but Doctor Scott has warned us to prepare for the worst." Like a wounded animal Shaun let out a heart rending cry.

"No, Oh my God not Wendy. Not my beautiful wife!" Mary put her arms around him and together they cried for Wendy.

When Shaun's sobbing finally stopped Mary said, "I'll go and make us some more coffee, then I will tell you what Wendy has asked me to discuss with you." Mary paused at the door and asked, "Would you like an Irish coffee?"

"Yes please," he answered softly as he dried the tears from his wet face.

She brought their coffee on to the veranda and gave Shaun a full account of her discussions with Doctor Scott and his prognosis for Wendy. She added that Shaun must appreciate that this information had been given to her on the understanding that it would remain strictly confidential. Mary then went on saying, "I'm sure you must have been thinking about David's future and yours. Wendy told me at some length about her concerns for both of you. If she does not survive how would you cope?"

"I honestly don't know. She has always made the major decisions for us. It's just that life seems so bloody unfair. The last six years really turned my life around; meeting and marrying Wendy, then having David. It has been absolutely wonderful and then this happens! I was very angry with her when she offered to help out at the hospital, so perhaps I am being punished for my selfishness."

"No Shaun, I'm sure it doesn't work like that. You did what you thought was best so you mustn't blame yourself or her. Wendy is expecting us to visit her tomorrow and has asked that we bring David as she wants to talk to him on his own too. She has commissioned Benjamin Kaplan, a very good lawyer, to draw up draft wills for both of you as you apparently hadn't done this yet, and there are various other papers for you both to sign, relating to David, this property, the mortgage and life insurance policies." She handed him the envelope from Benjamin Kaplan and asked him to read through the contents and sign in the appropriate places if he was in agreement with the details.

"Oh Mary, if only you and Patrick lived in Bulawayo, you would obviously be the ones to look after David, but I know that such a move wouldn't be possible. I'm positive Wendy will have given a lot of thought to our future and I trust her opinions absolutely. Please could you be there with us when we discuss it tomorrow? I will need your help and support."

"Of course I will. Now you get off to bed and try to get some rest. You look as though you need it."

First thing in the morning Shaun phoned the ESC office and told his secretary that he was back from Salisbury but would be late into the office. Mary saw to it that David was properly dressed in his best clothes and told him that his mum had asked him to come to the hospital because she wanted to talk to him. He went to the hospital in his dad's car and Mary followed at a much slower pace in hers. When they entered the hospital Wendy was already seated behind the glass door, with a two-way telephone in her hand; obviously provided by thoughtful Doctor Scott. She greeted them all with a forced but genuine smile. As previously, chairs had been placed directly opposite her and on a small table was a large legal envelope containing the documents which Wendy had already signed. Shaun's hands were shaking and there was an anxious frown on his face but this gradually eased as he read and counter-signed the papers; much to Wendy and Mary's relief. David sat quietly just gazing at his mother as she smiled at him. When Shaun finished he picked up the phone and for a long time spoke softly to Wendy. Finally he stood up, then taking Mary by the hand, he led her right up to the glass door as close to Wendy as they could get. There were tears running down his cheeks as he said, "You two are the most wonderful women in the world." Then, turning to Mary, he asked her, "Are you and Patrick really prepared to take on our son and love him as much as we do?"

Mary was totally overcome and just managed to say, "Yes we will. I promise you both." Wendy then took control and indicated that they should go now as she wanted to talk to David alone. Shaun stood silently and gazed at Wendy as if imprinting the image in his memory, then turned away hiding his tears and handed the phone to David. Shaun picked up the papers put his arm round Mary's shoulders then led her back to where their cars were parked.

It was about ten minutes later that David came running down to the car park with a secretive smile on his face. He said nothing at all about his talk with his mother, except to tell Shaun that he was to give him the framed photograph of his mum which was on the dressing table in their bedroom; because it was to belong to him now.

*

The first nurse died two weeks later, and Wendy followed a few days after that. As expected the eldest child recovered but never regained the use of her legs. Sister Maggie didn't contract the disease and continued nursing in Bulawayo for many years. The fourth nurse suffered serious paralysis of her legs, arms and some of her chest muscles but was kept alive by using a breathing tube and a portable cylinder of oxygen, until she returned to the UK for treatment.*

Shaun was devastated by Wendy's death and never really recovered from the loss of his dear wife.

---

* - See Appendix 2 for further details

CHAPTER 20

♥ 1937 ♥

Shaun and Mary were puzzled by David's lack of emotion but sensibly they chose not to ask any questions. Clearly Wendy had told him that she was leaving, and had explained that she would not be there to look after him. She had reassured him that Auntie Mary would take good care of him with some help from his daddy and Uncle Pat. When they returned to the Pauling Road house he asked Mary if she would help him to pack his clothes and toys into a box to take to Uncle Pat's house because that was going to be his new home.

"Mum told me I should ask if I could call you Mum or Mum-Mary?"

"That would be lovely," she replied, "I can then be your mum and Auntie Mary all joined up together!" He laughed and she gave him a big hug. "We will be good friends, David, and I will love you just as much as I love my two little girls."

Patrick travelled down to Bulawayo by train to collect Mary and David, bringing the little girls with him as a special adventure. He felt that they should return to Wankie as a family so that David would immediately feel part of the family; being welcomed by Lisa and Gajima, who was now at school till one o'clock every day. The school had already started giving the pupils homework, which Lisa liked to supervise, so he came back to the O'Connors' home every afternoon. This meant that he would be there to welcome David, and although there was a difference in age, the two boys were great friends and played well together.

David was given his own bedroom and straight away started unpacking his toys and putting his clothes into the chest of drawers. He put the framed photo of his mother in pride of place on the small bedside table. He sternly warned the two curious girls that they were not to touch it. Mary told him that the spare bed in his room was for his daddy to sleep on when he came to visit. David was given no instructions on how to settle in and Mary was very impressed by his initiative and self-confidence. Patrick was called in to see and praise him. This went down very well as he knew from a past visits that Uncle Pat's praise only came when it was deserved. Secretly, Patrick had always dreamed of having a son, but following Mary's problems in birthing the twins, he dreaded the possibility of her falling pregnant again. It was therefore a double blessing that David had come to them. Patrick resolved to do his utmost to be a worthy parent and to prepare the boy for any trials that life might bring.

Three weeks later Shaun came to see how David was settling in and was greatly relieved to find how seamlessly his little son had slotted into his new family environment. He was also immensely grateful and felt a nostalgic pride at his wife's wisdom and foresight, acknowledging that he couldn't possibly have arranged all of this on his own. What pleased him too was the loving reception David gave him. He ran out to the car ahead of everyone else, straight into Shaun's outstretched arms. Shaun picked him up and hugged him tightly; thankful that all thoughts he had had about David's possible resentment at being sent away were definitely unfounded. Shaun eventually put him down and said, "I've brought you your books. I think you must have forgotten to pack them. Look on the back seat of the car." Excited but cautious, he saw The Jungle Book, Aesop's Fables and many other favourites.

"But, Daddy, I thought that those were Mum's books and that she would take them with her to read to the sick children in heaven."

"No, my boy, she asked me to give them to you. You can learn a lot from them, and you can think of her when you read them."

David ran back to the house and showed everyone what his daddy had brought him, adding that although Caroline and Brigid were still quite small, he thought they would like to have the stories read to them as well.

That evening after dinner the three adults sat out on the veranda and spoke about the future. Shaun told them that he had decided to sell the property in Bulawayo and would buy a two bedroomed apartment in a new development four blocks from the city centre. It had an excellent restaurant, a lounge for residents and their guests, plus a good lock up garage for his car. All in all he felt the move would relieve him of all of the domestic chores and simplify his life.

Once the house was sold he would be looking for a position for Silas his cook and, thinking about the extra work which Mary's growing family would entail, he wondered if Mary might like to take Silas on. Mary accepted the offer gratefully. Shaun knew that they wouldn't take any payment for David's board and lodging, so he insisted on paying Silas's monthly wages and David's school fees. After vigorous protests from Mary and Patrick it was all agreed.

Next, Shaun handed them the legal papers which Benjamin Kaplan had prepared and which had been signed by him and Wendy. Mary didn't mention that she already knew the contents but asked Shaun to give Benjamin her thanks for all he had done for them. Shaun told her he had queried the small account for the legal fees and Benjamin had replied, "What do you mean my bill is too low? My fees are the highest in town. That way my clients know they are getting the best services. Ask anyone and you will find it is true. Actually, the reason is that I can then charge my friends as little as I choose. It also gives me great pleasure. Mary's brother Paul told me you were good people so let's hear no more about it."

One of Shaun's major concerns was how David would cope with the loss of his mother. Mary assured him that the boy seemed remarkably happy and until quite recently she too had been worried by his lack of reaction; it seemed a little unnatural. However, the day before Shaun's visit she had overheard, for the first time, a mention of Wendy. David had told his young cousins that his daddy was coming to visit and one of the girls asked if he was sad that he would not be bringing his mum too. "Oh no," he had replied. "My mum has gone to heaven to be an angel. She is looking after sick children there. Your mum is my mum too now." Shaun was very deeply touched and immensely grateful for the mature and farsighted way Wendy and Mary had dealt with what could have been an enormous and heart-breaking problem.

Shaun returned to Bulawayo with a feeling of relaxed contentment, knowing that his son was being very well looked after and was happily settled in a stable loving home. He promised to come again, as often as he could get away from his increasing work commitments.

CHAPTER 21

❧ 1938/43 ❧

Every night at bed time Mary or Patrick read a story to the three children. The animal stories were their favourites, especially when Patrick read them, because he could make the proper noises for all of the animals. These were very happy times, enjoyed by them then and remembered for the rest of their lives.

Gajima and David played well together. As they grew older the two-year age difference seemed to narrow and their friendship deepened. David admired Gajima's athletic strengths and his bush knowledge. They spent most of their free time exploring the wonders of the veldt together, speaking their own mixture of English and IsiNdebele. Gajima went to the mine's school, which Patrick continued expanding; adding a new class each year, until he achieved his ultimate goal of a fully equipped secondary school for the African miners' children. Gajima's natural athletic ability served him well and he captained most of the school's sports teams. With pressure from Kumbula and Lisa he also did well at his studies, generally coming in the top half dozen in the end of term exams each year.

David attended the government kindergarten school in Wankie for two and a half years and then, aged eight, went away to a very good government boarding school, known as Rhodes Estate Preparatory School. It was situated on an experimental farm which Rhodes had established at the turn of the century. It was only fifteen miles outside Bulawayo so Shaun was able to take him out on Sundays whenever possible. Together father and son explored most of the Matopos area, taking picnic lunches or, on special occasions, having lunch at the Matopos Dam Hotel. They enjoyed each other's company and it made an important break for both of them. Shaun never allowed David to visit him at his apartment in town as he didn't want him to know that from time to time he had various lady friends to stay there.

David was not a natural sportsman although he played rugby for the school's first XV team in his final year at REPS. He excelled academically with mathematics and English taking the place of field sports. Nevertheless he was a popular boy as he had a sunny nature and was always willing to help those who struggled with their homework. His excellent school reports were sent to Patrick at the end of each term, and he forwarded them on to Shaun, who treasured them greatly.

Caroline and Brigid grew into lovely, happy and mischievous young girls. They were greatly missed at home when, at the age of eight, they too made their way as boarders to Bulawayo's Dominican Convent School. They were a bright pair, causing no end of amusement to the other girls because the nuns couldn't tell them apart. Many of the pupils were not Roman Catholics and although the O'Connor girls had an Irish name, their family's religious beliefs were pondered upon but not investigated in any depth. At the end of term the pupils returning from the towns north of Bulawayo and Northern Rhodesia returned home by train, and this journey was highly looked forward to as boys from both the Salisbury schools as well as from Bulawayo and Plumtree travelled together with the girls. However, from past experience of the antics of teenagers, two nuns were posted in compartments in the middle of the train in an attempt segregate the sexes. Many stories were told of heroic attempts of boys climbing through train windows, but true or not the North Train was thought to be the most exciting part of going home at the end of term, and the never-ending envy of the convent's day scholars.

David was very protective of his sisters and, although he wouldn't admit to it, he was really very fond of both of them. However, with his logical brain he was sometimes incapable of understanding them. Mary was of little help either because when he asked her she just told him that it was a fact of life that girls were quite different from boys and there was no way of explaining how their minds worked.

Whenever possible, Shaun timed his own leave to coincide with David's school holidays. They made trips to South Africa to see David's grandmother and Uncle Des in Johannesburg and then went on to the seaside in Durban. The more time they spent together the more Shaun marvelled at his son's development. His particular interest was in how things worked. The long car journeys south passed in no time as they were spent in answering David's unending questions. Patrick told Shaun that he defined David as being a 'how, why and what' person, whereas his girls were 'who, where and what for' people.

CHAPTER 22

The Second World War had little impact on those whose who worked in reserved occupations, such as Patrick's and Shaun's. Most of the able bodied men volunteered for service. However the whole country shared in the grief of many children, wives and sweethearts who lost friends and relatives assisting in the dreadful conflicts in North Africa, Europe and the Far East. In proportion to their total populations, Rhodesian casualties exceeded those of Britain and any of the other commonwealth countries. The future prime minister of Rhodesia, Ian Douglas Smith, was one of many who were severely injured serving in the RAF.

Gajima and David discussed the wars and fighting but interestingly they differed somewhat regarding loyalties and the question of assisting remote friends if they were attacked. David said it was right to help those from whom you are descended. Gajima quoted the case of his own tribe, the Matabele, who were direct descendants of the Zulus. They had left their homeland in Natal because of disagreements over the way they were being governed. When they broke away they were pursued by the king's warriors who slaughtered many of them. As a result, the survivors felt no inclination to assist their Zulu cousins when the British soldiers fought against them in South Africa. David pointed out that the war against Germany and Japan was not quite the same, but he was unable to give Gajima any assurance that Britain would give their Rhodesian cousins any assistance if a war developed within Rhodesia, or if the country was invaded by a foreign nation. Gajima's advice was that it was best to be strong and self-reliant, then others will be very hesitant about attacking you; which is better than having to depend on possibly fickle or treacherous friends.

As adults many years later they were to reminisce over this particular conversation, especially when the British government reneged on their promises for Rhodesia's independence but readily handed independence to the lesser developed and politically unstable countries with disastrous consequences for their indigenous populations.

CHAPTER 23

∾ 1945 ∾

Life at Wankie continued normally and uneventfully until one extremely hot summer afternoon. Patrick was in his office when he received an urgent message that Kumbula had collapsed while cycling back from his sanitation and hygiene inspections. Patrick rushed down to the site, arriving just as the ambulance medics were lifting the limp body of Kumbula onto a stretcher. They shook their heads knowing the question which Patrick couldn't bring himself to ask. Patrick put his hand gently on Kumbula's chest and said the words softly in Zulu, "Go well, my dear friend. Be with your ancestors in peace, knowing that they will be proud to welcome you home."

It was a severe heart attack which had ended his life at the age of fifty-two. With dread Patrick went home to break the news to Lisa. He felt guilty for not realising that Kumbula's workload had not been reduced over the last few years to allow for his age; not that Kumbula would have accepted any help as that would have been a sign of weakness.

Lisa took the news very calmly at first but when Mary came through the two women hugged each other and wept from the depth of their hearts. Fearing his own possible loss of control Patrick left them weeping together and went out into the front garden to grieve silently for the loss of his lifelong friend and companion.

When she had calmed down, Lisa phoned the school and asked for Gajima to be sent home immediately. She met him on the road home and told him the dreadful news. He took it bravely, as she expected, but was deeply touched when he put his arm around her shoulders and said, "I'm so sorry, Mum, I know how much you loved him and you will miss him terribly. I will too. I am so sad that he will not have the satisfaction of seeing that his final work in building our school was so worthwhile."

The funeral was arranged for the coming Saturday afternoon. This happened to fall on the twenty-ninth of the month. At first sight this would have appeared insignificant, but the date didn't miss the attention of Mr Powys Davies, the mine's chief accountant.

Kumbula was universally popular so it came as no surprise that the funeral service had to be held at the sports stadium to accommodate an estimated 2000 people. They all came to pay their last respects to the man who was known and respected by every one of them. They each had, in one way or another, good reason to appreciate the assistance, advice or help he had given them over the last twenty-two years.

The mine manager, Angus Mackay, reminded the assembled mourners of the work and service Kumbula Zulu had put in for all of the mine workers and their families in Wankie, as well as for the many families in the tribal trust lands. He went on to detail the part Kumbula had played in developing the schooling and the sporting facilities plus the improvements in the township's housing health and hygiene. As each of these was mentioned the stadium resonated with the deep bass tones of approval emitted by all of the men. Angus concluded by suggesting that everyone should recognise the value of the example set by Kumbula Zulu, and to teach their children to do so as well.

After the burial, the wake was larger than any seen in the young country of Rhodesia; all races, tribes and nationalities meeting together to celebrate the life of one outstanding man.

The Wankie Colliery Company showed its appreciation by providing food and drinks for all those who attended. It was a truly wonderful send-off for a worthy man who had worked so tirelessly for the whole community.

Everyone rested on the Sunday following the funeral but on Monday, Patrick went to work with a heavy heart, knowing that his deputy's office would be vacant. He attended to a few routine tasks in his office then went next door and packed into a cardboard box Kumbula's personal possessions; a photograph of Lisa, one of Gajima as a two-year-old, a diary and some private papers. Patrick knew it would be very strange working with a new man but Patrick's policy within the department had always been that everyone was required to train an under-study to do his or her work. This obviated disruption when people went on leave and also it kept all of his staff on their toes, knowing that there was always somebody else who could potentially take over their positions. As a successor, Kumbula had been training a mature man named Elijah; a quiet and thorough person, but sadly lacking his tutor's initiative and quick sense of humour.

Patrick found he couldn't settle to work so he decided to take the cardboard box of Kumbula's personal possessions to Lisa's house. He found her holding a letter, shaking her head in disbelief and weeping quietly. Seeing him she handed him the letter and said bitterly, "The vultures have eaten the dead and are now descending on the living as well." It was a brief formal letter, dated the thirty-first of the month, giving her a month's notice to vacate the house she was occupying, as she was 'no longer the wife of a senior mine employee'. The letter was from the accounts department and had been signed by Mr Powys Davies.

Patrick was enraged by the blunt callousness of the man but was also fully aware of the company's policy on the matter. In fact on Patrick's recommendation the company had recently started providing funds for repatriating widows and their children back to their tribal homelands in circumstances such as this. The scheme also helped those women who had been abandoned by absconding husbands.

Knowing that Lisa had no tribal home nor any living relatives, and that young Gajima should be writing his Cambridge School Certificate exams in a few months' time, Patrick felt it was imperative that something be done. He handed over the box containing Kumbula's things from the office and as he did so he sensed rather than heard Kumbula's deep bass voice.

"Boss Pat, you will need a new sanitation and hygiene inspector." You cunning old devil, thought Patrick, what a brilliant idea.

He said nothing of this to Lisa but before leaving he told her not to worry about the house or to think of leaving the mine.

"Do nothing; just wait and see. I will do all I can to prevent this."

The next day he spoke to Elijah about the now vacant position of sanitation inspector. Elijah had obviously given the matter some thought already and begged not to be burdened with that work.

"Boss Pat, I am only a little younger than the one who has gone. Also, I cannot even ride a bicycle, so I would not live for long if I took on such extra work as sanitation and hygiene inspector."

"OK, Elijah, I didn't really expect you to do it but I felt I had to offer it to you. As you know I believe in fairness and trust in our office so I will tell you confidentially what I have in mind for that work; and why it is important."

Patrick then told him about the letter from Mr Powys Davies and its implications for Lisa and her son. Elijah's only comment was one of profound disgust.

"That man's mother should have drowned him in a bucket at birth."

Elijah, as a Christian you should be ashamed of yourself making such a statement. However, that might have made our lives simpler and much brighter."

"Boss Pat, I could tell Steven Jongwe and, as the leader of the African Mine Workers Union, he could ballot for strike action."

"No, no Elijah, just leave it to me. It is always better to think like clever Kalulu the hare. We will prick with a long sharp thorn. There is no need to take drastic action like you suggest."

It remained only for Patrick to convince Lisa to accept the job and then to exercise his authority by officially appointing her as the new sanitation and hygiene inspector. She readily agreed, pointing out that her work as his housekeeper was not really a full-time job any longer as Shaun's cook, Silas, had taken over much of her work, and for most of the time the twins and David were away at boarding school. She was prepared to do anything to stay on with Gajima in the home she loved and treasured.

Predictably, Mr Powys Davies objected vociferously but Patrick was able to explain to him that the new appointment had already been approved and, as no salary was attached to the position, there had been no need to advise the accountancy department.

CHAPTER 24

❧ 1946 ❧

Lisa was delighted by the news that she would be able to stay on in her home. It had been theirs for nearly eighteen years, due almost entirely to the help which she and Kumbula had received from the O'Connor family.

Now, as she sat on her veranda waiting for her sixteen-year-old son to return from his appointment with the history master, Mr Ball, she was brought back to the present day reality by the sight of Gajima, tall and slim, jogging effortlessly up the road towards her. She desperately hoped that he had heeded her advice and made his peace with Mr Ball. The broad smile on his face when he saw her waiting on the veranda told her that all was well. She hugged him and said simply, "Good. You have learnt a worthwhile lesson."

That evening after dinner, having heard all that had transpired at Gajima's meeting, Lisa said to him, "As I promised, listen and I will tell you what actually happened in the early days, long before I was born. I want you to know the truth but I don't want you repeating it to others or you might stir up a hornet's nest again. Truth is a strange thing. It is good, and yet you would be surprised at the effort some people put into hiding it.

"First let me tell you what my father told me; and I can assure you he was not a person who would exaggerate or fail to tell the truth. He was a proud man, a son of King Lobengula, by one of his many lesser wives. He became an induna at a young age, which was unusual, but his bravery, intelligence and loyalty to his father were recognised early on. In 1888 Lobengula, on the advice of a number of his chiefs, had agreed to the terms and conditions offered by Cecil Rhodes for the right to bring in white miners to dig for gold in Matabeleland. The details were written into a document which became known as the Rudd Concession†. However, within a short period Lobengula found that the gold, the rifles and ammunition which were promised in the concession, were often late or, in the case of the boat promised on the Zambezi River, they failed to materialise at all."

The duplicity of Cecil Rhodes soon became clear when wagon loads of white settlers, other than the agreed miners poured into the country. On the twentieth of September 1890 the pioneer column hoisted the British flag in what was later became the city of Salisbury. And the capital of Rhodesia.

"Lobengula was angry with his indunas for advising him badly and very disappointed in the white people such as Doctor Jameson and Cecil Rhodes, whom he had trusted when the papers were prepared. He was ashamed and angry for having been deceived by them. Arguments and bitterness set in which divided his subjects and, to put an end to it, he decided that twelve of these indunas had to be punished as an example to the others. He ordered that they be taken to a mountain a few miles out of Gu'bulawayo, the Matabele capital, and there they should be thrown over the cliff edge to their certain deaths. This mountain became known as 'Thabas Induna' (the induna's mountain).

† - See the full text in appendix i

However their executions added to the problem causing a serious split in the Matabele nation. One faction blamed the white people and wanted to take revenge on them and drive them and the miners out of the country. The other faction argued that there were benefits to be had by keeping them there because they would be stronger and better armed with white men's rifles instead of spears. There was also the prospect of becoming very rich from the gold the miners extracted from their holes they dug in the ground.

"Contrary to Lobengula's instructions, the breakaway group attacked the new European settlement of Bulawayo, slaughtering close on 200 of them. The remainder fled southwards to the safety of South Africa. Lobengula knew that troops would soon be sent to avenge the killings, and that his fighters would be no match for the Maxim machine guns the white troops would inevitably bring with them.

"It was not long before Lobengula's scouts brought news of the imminent arrival of a column of British South African troopers. They sent Lobengula a demand letter written by Dr Jameson, Cecil Rhodes' trusted friend, saying that within ten days the Matabele people must confirm their willingness to lay down their arms and to pay a certain sum in gold sovereigns to compensate the relatives of those killed in Bulawayo. If they failed to respond they would be attacked. Lobengula believed that it was a genuine offer and that he could save the unnecessary killing of large numbers of his loyal subjects if he conceded. Two of his trusted messengers were immediately dispatched with the specified number of gold coins, and were ordered to inform the BSAP commander of the king's willingness to surrender.

However, the messengers were apprehended by two BSA troopers who were scouting ahead of the column. These men killed the messengers and stole the gold. It was never recovered.

"Your grandfather told me that many years later the truth finally came out and history records that the two troopers, named Daniels and Wilson, were apprehended by the BSA police in Bulawayo. The two men were tried for the theft of the gold and for the murders of Lobengula's two messengers. The Resident Magistrate in Bulawayo, sitting with four assessors found them guilty as charged and they were each sentenced to fourteen years in prison. However, with what was to become generally known to all the blacks and the whites of the country as 'typical British government duplicity', the British High Commissioner intervened, ruling that the magistrate had 'exceeded his powers' and ordered that the prisoners be unconditionally released.

"Sadly history now ignores the fact that our King Lobengula had genuinely offered peace and the gold. Many of our own people condemned him for running away to safety instead of fighting, as was expected of a Matabele King. Not knowing at that time about the murder of his messengers, Lobengula assumed that the BSA Company had deliberately reneged on his offer of peace and he realised that he would soon be attacked, so he had no option but to trek north towards the Zambezi river in the hope of crossing to safety in Barotseland. Major Forbes sent a mounted column of one hundred men who soon caught up with him just beyond the Shangani river. Forbes then sent out a small scouting patrol under the leadership of Major Allan Wilson who found Lobengula's forces camped about twelve miles away. They numbered several thousand men plus many women and children. Their herds of cattle and goats plus numerous heavily loaded wagons had obviously slowed down Lobengula's progress. Heavy rain had been falling throughout the day and when Allan Wilson turned to go back to report Lobengula's position to Major Forbes and rejoin the main troop, he found that the Shangani river was impassibly flooded, so they were forced to spend the night in the bush, knowing full well that the Matabele had seen them and now they had the patrol effectively trapped. Three of Allan Wilson's men were sent out to try and get help but the remaining men were surrounded and killed early the next morning. It was estimated that up to 500 of our young fighters died in that brief battle. Fortunately your grandfather was not one of them.

"Taking advantage of the flooded river, Lobengula hastened on northwards and finally arrived at the Zambezi river, only to find that heavy rains had also fallen in Barotseland causing the Zambezi to flood, so he was unable to cross the river. Major Forbes had decided not to follow and thus further bloodshed was avoided. Most of the Matabele tribesmen split up and circled round, eventually returning to their former tribal areas in the south and west of Matabeleland.

"Lobengula himself fared less well and, suffering from gout and dying from malaria, he summoned all of his family members and gave them each a small leather pouch containing gold sovereigns. He forbade them from telling anyone the number of coins they each received as he wanted no dissention within the family. I never knew how many your grandfather was given but when he died there were sufficient left for my mother to pay for my schooling. Only one now remains. My mother wanted me to keep it for buying my wedding dress. However Boss Pat paid for my dress and I decided I should keep the coin for my first born child. It will be yours to keep when I go to join your father. Possess it with pride, knowing its history and let it give you confidence that you will never be poor while you have that treasure.

"I have told you all I know other than that your great-grandfather King Lobengula was a fine man, brave and noble. No one knows where he was buried as he decreed that his body should be taken by his four most trusted elderly friends to a place he had chosen, and they alone should bury him there. Many have searched that area in vain, believing that much gold was buried with him."

Gajima passed the leather pouch back to his mother, holding back the deep emotions he was feeling. Unable to speak, he put his arm around her shoulder and hugged her gently. She smiled, breaking the tension and said, "Actually, for a great-grandson of a lesser royal wife, you are not too bad a son; and I am very proud of you."

A lesson had been learnt by Gajima, and the history teacher found that the majority of his pupils were suddenly very keen to learn. He was also surprised to find that they showed him far more respect than he had been accustomed to from his former white pupils in Britain.

It was the last year at school for Gajima and he truly excelled. He captained the football team which won a cup in the inter-schools championship, set new school records for each of the athletics events involving running. He was awarded the victor ludorum; the school's highest honour for overall achievement. Lisa was bursting with pride when Mrs Jeannie Mackay presented her son with the award. The scene was actually quite comical; Gajima being over six feet tall in contrast to her diminutive height of five feet. There were smiles and light-hearted laughter from the assembled crowds when Gajima had to crouch down, nearly on his knees, for her to put the medal ribbon over his head.

Gajima then turned and acknowledged the shouts and clapping coming from his school friends, the teachers and the parents who had gathered for the end of year awards. The whole O'Connor family attended the ceremony. David was the first to run up and congratulate his long-time friend and hero. It was a great occasion and Patrick took some pride in the fact that the school which he and Kumbula had pressed so hard for had turned out some excellent scholars, sportsmen and this remarkable young man. Although the Cambridge results would not be out until January, his teachers had assured Patrick that Gajima had worked well and they were confident that he would have good results. The next hurdle would be applying for an apprenticeship, or some other training on the mine.

CHAPTER 25

❧ 1947 ❧

David and Gajima remained firm friends with shared common interests in wildlife, handcrafts and all things electrical and mechanical. Each of them secretly envied the other's special talents, Gajima's athletics prowess and David's sharp technological brain. Although David was two years younger, he would be writing his exams at the end of the following year and had set his sights on going to university in South Africa. Shaun and Patrick had discussed the future and hoped that David might win a scholarship to assist with the fees, but had agreed to share the costs if he did not. From a very early age David's dream had been to qualify as a professional electrical engineer. This and his wish to please his late mother, and his adoptive parents had driven him right from the start. He was absolutely certain that his mother was keeping an eye on him from heaven and that he would succeed in whatever he chose to do. Such positive thinking definitely paid off. He was by nature a quick learner and yet felt no need to compete with others in his class. His quiet and unassuming manner made him popular and he enjoyed helping others when they experienced any difficulties. This all made for a very happy time at school.

Gajima's exam results were good but his high hopes suffered a major setback right from the start. The personnel department rejected his apprenticeship application stating quite categorically that they would not consider him for an apprenticeship as first preference was always given to the sons of the mine's artisans. They also pointed out that he was still too young for employment as an artisan's helper; eighteen being the lowest starting age. He was extremely disappointed. Lisa suggested that he ask Boss Pat for advice.

Patrick, as always, sat quietly and listened while Gajima outlined his interests and hopes for the future. When he finished, Patrick said, "You will just have to think of something else to do for the next two years, Gajima. Tell me, how would you feel about spending a couple of years working as a game ranger/tour guide at Robins Game Farm? It has recently been declared a National Wildlife Game Reserve by the government and they have advertised for young trainees." Gajima was stunned by this idea; it was so different to what he had been planning or expecting.

Anticipating the questions, Patrick gave him the few facts he recalled from the advertisement. There were openings for two people. They would undergo instruction in tracking, identifying fauna and flora, the maintenance of pumps for water supplies, first aid, taking guests on game drives, plus anything and everything else that was necessary. A month-long probationary period without pay would apply. Thereafter a modest monthly salary would be paid until they qualified as game guides and ultimately game rangers. Full board and lodging would be provided free. Daily working hours would be determined by the clients' demands and would include weekends. There would be seven consecutive days off each month, with free transport to Wankie and back.

"Really, Boss Pat? That sounds wonderful. It would fill in the two years before I could join the mine."

"There will certainly be other applicants and you would have to go for an interview before selection. If you want, I'll phone Mr Robins and make an appointment. Perhaps we could make an outing of it; just the four of us. I will let you know what he says."

"Yes please and thank you very much, Boss Pat."

The next weekend Mary, Lisa, Gajima and Patrick set off along the dirt road for the game reserve, knowing full well that they would be covered in dust by the time they reached their destination. After their formal introductions, Mr Robins suggested that they relax with tea under the giant acacia tree in the front garden, and then, following a rest they should go for a short game drive. In the meanwhile he took Gajima off for an intensive interview. They didn't see them again until lunchtime. Mr Robins apologised for neglecting them, then spoke to Lisa.

"I think you are not going to be at all pleased with me, but I would like to take your son away from you and in the African tradition I will become his grandfather and teach him all he needs to know about wildlife and life itself. It would mean that you will only see him once a month for a seven-day break. He is a fine boy and a credit to you. I would like to offer him a two-year contract. During that time I will train him as a game guide and park ranger. He will be earning a reasonable salary with everything found."

"Thank you for your kind words, Mr Robins, and your consideration for me and my son. He is a capable boy and I am certain he would work hard, but this is a serious change in career for him and I would like to talk it over with him and Mr and Mrs O'Connor."

"Of course you should do that Lisa. Come now, everyone, and eat. I know there is something good for lunch today".

Everyone rested after the meal; a speciality of which was roast venison stuffed with bacon, plus crispy roast potatoes and fresh vegetables from his garden. Mr Robins roused them at 3.30 and loaded them all on to a pickup truck which he had adapted for game viewing. It had three rows of seating in the back, and a canvas tarpaulin secured to a timber frame to give some protection from the sun. With open sides for viewing and an opening behind the cab, guests could sit or stand and look out over the roof of the cab. It was not at all luxurious but it worked well. Mary sat in the front with Mr Robins and the rest of them piled into the back. The drive was spectacular; Patrick noted the huge increase in numbers and variety of animals since his first trip with Mary. With the official recognition of the area as a National Game Reserve, funds became available enabling new water holes to be created and, in the drier areas, for windmills to be installed to pump water into drinking troughs for the game.

For an afternoon game drive, it was unexpectedly good. They saw several herds of elephants, a huge herd of buffalos, twelve different antelope species, including a haughty sable standing close to the road showing off his magnificent curved horns. However, as a highlight to the afternoon, they saw a pride of four lions with three cubs. The lions paid no attention to them and they were able to spend twenty minutes just watching the cubs play-fighting while the parents completely ignored them and the spectators. Shortly before sunset Mr Robins pulled in at one of the small dams and brought out sun downers for everyone while they watched the last of the animals coming down to drink. Lisa noted with pride that, without being asked, Gajima immediately stepped forward and helped Mr Robins pour the drinks and hand out plates of snacks. Mary leaned over and quietly spoke to Lisa.

"You have taught your son well."

"Yes, I hope so. I wonder what he will decide to do? We are going to discuss it tonight and, if you can spare us the time, we would like to talk it through with you and Boss Pat. It is a big decision and we value your thoughts."

After dinner, Mr Robins excused himself, leaving the four of them in the lounge to discuss the pros and cons of the game guide proposition. The two males were in favour whereas Mary and Lisa expressed their reservations. All agreed that the offer and the conditions were very good. Patrick's opinion was that Gajima would gain valuable experience in dealing with people and that learning how animals think and behave would teach him more valuable lessons than he would get from temporary work in Wankie. Gajima had not had the benefit of going to boarding school but here he would learn self-reliance, initiative and discipline under Mr Robins' watchful eyes. The women folk expressed their concerns that Gajima was too young to take on the responsibilities for the lives and safety of the paying tourists. There was also the issue of his youth and inexperience in handling the advances of predatory foreign female visitors. They had heard various disturbing stories about such things.

Patrick then invited Gajima to tell them what he thought. Gajima was a little embarrassed to be speaking about himself but after thanking them all for being so concerned about his future he was able to express his thoughts.

"As you know, I have always enjoyed the bush and wildlife but truly my first love is engineering. I would have liked to go with David to university but of course that was not possible. I now hope that I will be able to follow the same path as Boss Shaun and become an apprentice electrician when I turn eighteen. So, to me, this chance to become a game guide is a good opportunity to learn something new and interesting. However, I don't see it as a long-term career. I like Mr Robins and I know I can learn a lot from him. I would like to accept the job if he will take me on, knowing my long-term plans."

Everyone agreed that Gajima should explain to Mr Robins exactly what his final ambitions were. He then went through to Mr Robins who listened carefully and said, "It is not often that I come across a young person like you and I would be very happy if you will come and work with me; even if it is only for a couple of years. Who knows, I might even persuade you to make a career of being a game ranger one day." Together they went back to the lounge to tell the others the good news.

*

When they arrived back at the mine Patrick gave Gajima two large duplicate books and suggested that he use the one to record the facts of what he did, learned, or saw each day. "This will help you with your weekly reports for Mr Robins, and the other one you can use for your personal letters. You will find that as you grow older your memory can become too selective, one way or another. These details could be of help if one day you decide to write about your adventures in the bush."

CHAPTER 26

ℰ❍ 1945/49 ℰ❍

Shaun O'Connor's lack of a conventional home in Bulawayo meant that he saw very little of David for most of the year. However, he generally took his annual leave to coincide with David's school holidays over the Christmas period. Occasionally he made the journey up to Wankie, but he became aware that they were slowly drifting apart and it was at these times that Shaun missed Wendy more than ever and he was acutely aware that his son was a different boy with his brother's family in Wankie. Although Shaun was careful to keep his affairs with various women from David, he sensed that David was not ignorant of them and this didn't help matters.

When visiting Mary and Patrick, Shaun envied their relationship. He was very proud of David's maturity and progress at school and yet he knew that all credit had to go to Mary and Pat for that. Alcohol, parties and Shaun's women friends had done little to alleviate his loneliness and the dreadful feeling of futility in his life. Mary and Patrick did their best to help him but they could see no solution to the problem.

When David was ready for senior school, Patrick, as his guardian, was able to apply for his admission to Plumtree School, whereas Shaun, living in Bulawayo would have had to comply with school zoning rules and send his son to a local day school. The family were delighted but not surprised when

David was accepted and immensely proud of how handsome he looked in his new school uniform and green blazer. Theo and Joanna Odendaal had unfortunately left Plumtree when their first son was born and were now teaching in Bulawayo, so they were unable to welcome him to his new life. However, David knew several Wankie boys who went to his new school, and from them he learnt the initial tricks of arriving at Plumtree on the train. "Never worry about your tin trunk or bike in the guards van. As soon as the train stops, run up to the house that you had been allocated to and secure the bed in the dormitory as far away as possible from the prefect who is in charge of the juniors' dorm. This will ensure that you would not have to get up early to bring the prefect his hot coco drink every morning"

Similar to REPS school, Plumtree operated with few set rules, relying on every boy using basic common sense. The school grounds were virtually unlimited and the dining hall would provide a picnic lunch for the groups who wanted to spend the whole of Sunday in the veldt. Swimming in the dams was discouraged because of the risk of bilharzia but if a home-made canoe capsized, it was not a punishable offence. The only requirements were that the groups should stay together and be back at school in time for supper at 6pm. Failure to do so could result in punishment.

David thoroughly enjoyed his four years at Plumtree. With only a few exceptions, the teachers were superb. He was put into the 'A stream' at the end of the first term which meant that he would be able to write his Cambridge exams at the end of four years instead of five. He worked hard and steadily. The exam results were published in the Bulawayo Chronicle and

The Herald in Salisbury. David and a boy from Prince Edward School tied for top marks in the country. The O'Connor family members were delighted with his achievement. Brigid and Caroline bragged about their brother, but secretly knew that they would be hard pressed to match his achievements when their time came. An interesting highlight during the year was the Royal Visit to Rhodesia when the Royal Train stopped at Plumtree and the two young princesses walked with their parents along the platform then went on to officially open the school chapel. Princess Margaret, being younger, was a great favourite and commented that she had never been photographed by so many cameras in her life. Nobody had told the boys that 'close up' photography was not permitted.

Following the good news about the exam results, David was extremely disappointed when Shaun, Patrick and Mary decided that, aged sixteen and a half, he was too young to go to university, even though his exam marks qualified him for immediate admission. He was very keen to get started but the family insisted that he should stay on at school for a further year and write the bursary exams. For the first time in his life he felt that he had been unfairly overruled and that, had his mother been there, she would have been on his side.

With hindsight it was a wise decision as the engineering faculty was still overloaded with fairly wild ex-servicemen from the 1939–1945 war. The South African government had very generously awarded free places to any ex-serviceman with the required entry qualifications. These 'older men' could have a bad influence on the young students.

One night at home for the Christmas holidays, David went to bed quite early and just before dozing off to sleep he became acutely aware of a woman's perfume in the room. Then a short while later he had a weird feeling that his body was shrinking and shrinking until it was the size of a small boy's. Next he felt himself being lifted up into a woman's arms and he recognised it was his mother. She hugged him and he distinctly heard her gentle voice saying, "You have been such a good boy, David, and I am very happy for you. Don't worry, the delay is all for the best; you will see this later." He tried to speak to her but found he couldn't make a sound. Tears of sheer joy filled his eyes as he remembered his mother's voice and her perfume. Slowly his body returned to its normal size and his mother had gone. He wakened fully, sobbing and crying deeply for her. It was the first time he had done so since she had died, all those years ago. Exhausted, he finally went into a deep sleep.

When he wakened the next morning, he was filled with a wonderful feeling of freedom, happiness and love for everything and everybody. David tried hard to hide his high spirits but one by one each member of the family noticed and commented on his obvious happiness. Determined not to speak of the previous night's happenings, he made various excuses. Mary, however, with her keenly developed senses, realised it was something much deeper. She waited, knowing that he would share it with her when the time was right. Her intuition was correct and that afternoon, after Patrick was back at work, Lisa was off duty, and the girls had gone to see a film at the local bioscope, David joined Mary for afternoon tea under the trees in the garden.

Hesitantly at first, David told her all that had happened the previous night. She listened to every word without comment and when he was finished she surprised him by saying, "Oh

David. This is absolutely wonderful. I've waited for years hoping to hear that you have finally been able to acknowledge your sadness and allow yourself to grieve for your mother. For all of this time I have had to hold back my own feelings of loss, for fear of upsetting you. Now we can share the loss together and I will be able to tell you all about her and you will get to know what a lovely person she was."

Seeing the tears in her eyes, David put his arms around her and said, "Thank you for looking after me. You will always be so very special, and I will always love you. Nothing will ever change that."

Back at Plumtree for a further year, David had little to look forward to other than the bursary exams at the end of the year and the weeks seemed to drag by. Girls became an interesting diversion and in spite of his natural shyness, David started corresponding with girls he knew; at one stage writing to three of them. These letters helped him to understand a little of the female mind in the years ahead. He found that he had a lot of time to study and by the end of the year he was well prepared for the bursary exams. The results came out just before Christmas and with them came notification from the Alfred Beit Trust that he and one of the girls he had been writing to had been awarded top bursaries for Rhodesian boys and girls. This meant that not only would a major part of the university fees be met by the Trust but also that he would now be certain of admission to Witwatersrand University. There was great celebration in the O'Connor household with Shaun joining them in the family party. The girls teased David unmercifully, calling him 'brains bum' but, enviously they acknowledged that their brother was not as dumb as they made him out to be.

*

David decided to go for an early morning run, as he had often done with Gajima when they were younger. When he reached the footpath on the outskirts of town, he saw the tall slim form of his friend gliding effortlessly towards him. As the gap closed Gajima shouted to him.

"What are you doing up so early, little boy? Did you wet your bed?"

David laughed and answered, "I came to see if an old man like you can run any faster than Kamba, the lazy tortoise in the book of African Aesop's fables. I hear that you don't walk or run any more because you spend all your time driving beautiful foreign girls round the game park in Mr Robins' pickup."

"David, you should know better than to listen to idle gossip, and maybe you are very envious." They laughed together then Gajima became serious saying, "Congratulations, Mother told me last night about your bursary. I am really happy for you. It is great news. Now you will find out that you will need to do proper work; not just gentle school lessons."

Gajima then told David that he had completed his two year contract and had left the safari job and was hoping to start as an apprentice electrician. The two agreed to meet up later. David went home for breakfast with the family, inwardly very pleased to know that his friend was about to enter his chosen career.

CHAPTER 27

☙ 1950 ☙

The university's date for registration and enrolment was only in mid-March so Shaun asked David if he would like to come down to Bulawayo for January and February to do a spot of 'real work' for the Electricity Supply Commission. The ESC had introduced a scheme whereby students could benefit from practical experience during their long Christmas vacations. The young men were each allocated an electrician who taught them how to use tools, learn good safety practices and to develop confidence in directing the semiskilled workers and unskilled labourers. They all worked a normal 7am to 5pm shift and were paid two pounds two shillings per week. David accepted the offer instantly, saying that he would love to do it. However, Shaun warned him that it was real work and would be out of town, but that he might possibly come back to Bulawayo for weekends, if the workload permitted. He should travel to Bulawayo on the overnight train on New Year's Day and be ready to start work on 2nd January. Shaun immediately started making arrangements for David's visit. He phoned Bill Anderson, one of his electrical foremen who was in charge of a project near Gwelo and asked him if he would be prepared to take on his son for the two months. Bill, a long-time associate and friend readily agreed.

On arrival at Bulawayo station, a tall and upright Mr Anderson, with a well suntanned face and a ready smile was waiting for him. David introduced himself, aware of the powerful grip as they shook hands. After putting his suitcase into the back of the ESC's pickup truck they set off along the main road towards Gwelo. Mr Anderson asked him many questions about his aims and ambitions and listened with interest to his replies. Shortly after passing through the small village of Lalapanzi (which means a place to lie down), they turned off onto a very rough dirt road and twenty miles later arrived at their destination; the Good Hope Gold Mine.

Mr Anderson had told David that their job was to complete the erection of a transmission line and step-down transformer substation to provide power for the mine. Most of the overhead line work was nearing completion and their target was to be ready to switch on by the end of February. A temporary wire mesh enclosure had been erected for housing all the equipment awaiting installation. Also included in the fenced area was a wooden hut/office, three canvas tents, a five-ton lorry and last but not least a wooden long drop out-door toilet. It all looked very primitive to David but wisely he made no comment.

Some distance away the steel framework of the mine's shaft sinking headgear could be seen, with a scattering of pipes, rails, coco pans and the paraphernalia common to most small gold mining operations. David was intrigued.

"The accommodation is not the height of luxury," Mr Anderson commented, "but you will find we live quite well out here. I have one linesman, installing the overhead copper conductors and I will give you a spell with him but I want you to work with me for most of the time. Don't hesitate to ask any questions. It is better to ask and be thought to be an idiot, rather than not asking and remaining ignorant." David realised that this was a man from whom he could learn a great deal. Overalls were found for David and suitably attired he started work.

Mr Anderson turned out to be a patient and thorough teacher; highly skilled and totally confident in his own ability. He taught what he knew to be the best techniques, or as he put it, the only way to do things. They worked long hours and though often dog-tired, David really enjoyed the tasks he was given. In the evenings they sat round an open fire, cooked their supper on the coals, and discussed a wide range of subjects from trade unions and apprenticeships to people, politics and pensions. They slept in the tents and were awakened at 5.30am by the 'cook' bringing tin mugs of steaming hot coffee. David thoroughly enjoyed the whole experience, especially the adult male company.

Normally they worked through the weekends, but at the end of the month Mr Anderson invited David to spend a weekend in Bulawayo with his family.

"It will give us a chance to have proper baths, and for you to meet my two teenage delinquents."

Leaving the Good Hope early on Friday afternoon they drove to the Anderson's homestead in Bulawayo's Hillside suburb; a few miles west of the city's centre. It was located near the top of a kopje overlooking the Hillside Dam; a favourite picnic spot for the city people. Mrs Anderson, a well-built jovial South African lady, overflowing with hospitality, welcomed them in and after looking them up and down and laughed heartily.

"What you two need are good hot baths! Don't touch anything on your way through. David, I have put fresh towels in the children's bathroom. Bill will show you where it is. The kids are out just now, making plans for tomorrow, but they should be back soon.'

Feeling greatly refreshed after his badly needed bath, David joined Mrs Anderson for tea on the front veranda.

"Our two children, Rosemary and Peter, are not really as bad as Bill makes out. They are a bit of a handful but they are young yet. Rose is sixteen and Pete will be eighteen in a few months' time, so there is still time for improvement. Bill tells me you are going down to my home town Johannesburg to study at Wits?"

"Yes, Mrs Anderson, I leave at the end of February and I'm beginning to feel a little nervous as the date approaches."

"There is no need for that. I took my teaching degree there and although Wits is huge, the professors and tutors are excellent and you will soon make friends there. My advice to you is to steer clear of politics, avoid booze and don't skip any lectures, because it takes simply ages to catch up."

Rosemary and Peter arrived and were introduced to David. Rosemary lost no time in telling him that they were going to see a film at the newly built 20th Century cinema on Saturday afternoon, and then would be going on to a friend's party that evening.

"Please come with us. Pete is bringing his current girlfriend and I don't want to look like his chaperone."

"Sure, I would love to, as long as it is not a 'dress-up' affair, because I didn't bring any smart clothes."

"No, it's very casual and should be good fun."

It was indeed so. Rose was a lovely bright outgoing girl and good fun to be with. Pete's current girlfriend, Helen, was a quieter but very attractive looking girl. David enjoyed their company and the party that evening was great.

Breakfast on Sunday morning was, by long-standing tradition, Mr Anderson's responsibility and, in deference to their children's Saturday night outings, they ate at nine o'clock. David and Peter wakened quite early and went for a swim in Hillside Dam. It gave them a chance to talk without Rose being present. Peter confided to David that he was keen on Helen but felt there was little future in it for him because she was going to Cape Town University to take a BA in fine arts.

"You know what that means? She's bound to be snapped up by some long haired arty guy down there and I'll never see her again. It really hurts just thinking about it."

"You're probably right, Pete. She's bound to meet many interesting guys but don't give up. She will be coming home for her vacs and you can make up for lost time then. You never know how things will turn out. I reckon girls choose who they want, and we actually have little say in the matter. I would advise you to keep in touch by writing to her often and just see what happens. It must be hard for you but it's no good making plans so far into the distant future."

"I suppose you are right. We had better get on home now, or we will miss Dad's elaborate Sunday breakfast. Thanks for the chat; I'll take your advice on-board."

*

In the remaining weeks the electrical installation at the Hope Gold Mine was completed, tested and finally commissioned. Satisfied with the work David had done Mr Anderson gave David some good practical advice while driving back to Bulawayo.

"Your safety and the safety of those working with you, or for you, are of paramount importance. So, don't allow anyone to deflect you from carrying out all the tests and precautions which are necessary. Treat all electrical equipment as being 'live' unless you personally have isolated and locked off or earthed it. Don't accept anyone else's word for it. Also, when in the proximity of open 'live equipment' keep your hands in your pockets. This will stop you touching things in order to check if they are live. Believe me, although it sounds silly, the temptation to do so is very strong. It looks so innocent and passive. I saw the remains of one of our engineers after he touched a live 33000 volt terminal. It is a sight I will never forget. His footprints were burnt into the concrete flooring and all that was left was a small pile of ashes. Finally, when operating any electrical circuit breaker, regardless of whether you are switching it on or off, assume it might explode. Stand back as far as possible, after the first check to make sure it is the correct one, and then look away from it while switching. Fire from an electrical short circuit is a dreadful thing; temperatures of 1000 degrees centigrade or more are normal and you can be roasted in a fraction of a second."

David told Mr Anderson about the conditions at Wankie, mentioning that fire prevention measures were not considered essential underground at Number One Colliery. Electric arc welding was even permitted. The mine was classified as non-fiery because their coal was top grade anthracite and the mine was methane free. Mr Anderson was shocked to hear this.

"Believe me, David, fine dust of virtually any hydro-carbon compound when mixed with the right volume of air is definitely explosive. Just last year the Gloria Flour Mills, here in Bulawayo, had a massive explosion in one of their wheat silos. The dust was ignited by a small spark of static electricity. If I were you I wouldn't go down that coal mine or any other mine for that matter. There is an old saying 'Only ants, rats and bloody fools go down holes in the ground' and I believe it, so I refuse to work underground. My life is worth more to me and my family than all the gold, coal and other minerals in this rich country of ours"

David made a mental note to pass on this advice to Gajima when he next wrote to him.

David thanked Mr Anderson for his patience, advice, hospitality and kindness then made his way to the ESC office in Selborne Avenue. It was midday and Shaun was in his office waiting to take him out to lunch before he boarded the train to Johannesburg for the start of four years of intensive study at Witwatersrand University.

CHAPTER 28

✄ 1950/54 ✄

David found the university and the city bursting with energy and vitality. Compared with sparsely populated Rhodesia, to his mind it resembled a disturbed ants' nest. People seemed to be rushing everywhere to catch trains, trams and trolley buses. The roads were filled with non-stop streams of cars, all travelling at high speed, seemingly regardless of the danger to pedestrians and themselves.

The university was widely spread over an area known as Milner Park; formerly an estate belonging to Lord Milner. Each faculty was housed in its own building but due to the large number of ex-servicemen who had enrolled under the South African government's scheme, it had been necessary to erect large so-called Nissen huts for many of the lectures. As lecture theatres these wooden buildings were not very successful; the lighting was poor and the acoustics dreadful. Added to this there was a total absence of any heating and the Johannesburg winter could be bitterly cold. Once into their third year the students were well catered for. The laboratories and lecture halls in the main buildings were excellent. The various gold, diamond and coal mining companies generously donated all kinds of laboratory equipment and, in addition, sponsored the electrical, mining, mechanical and civil engineering faculties. For engineering degrees Wits University was regarded as the best in the whole of South Africa.

The largest building of all was in the centre of Milner Park and it contained numerous lecture theatres for mathematics, philosophy, languages, the arts and classics. It also housed the huge examinations hall and the Great Hall which seated up to 1000 people. Students streamed in and out of these building from morning to evening. David found it stimulating and at times exhausting but he soon joined the crazy rush and enjoyed it greatly.

The South African people have a reputation for their generous hospitality and David soon made a number of good friends and was frequently invited to visit them at their parents' homes in and around Johannesburg. The workload was unbelievably heavy and to keep up David found he had to put in three to four hours every night for writing up the day's lecture notes and the various lab reports. It was difficult at first but he soon adjusted to having only six or seven hours sleep a night. He made a strict rule of taking the whole of Saturdays off for leisure and entertainment but Sundays were generally spent preparing for Monday's classes.

CHAPTER 29

∾ 1949/51 ∾

Although Gajima had enjoyed his time in the game reserve with Mr Robins, and had been treated very well, he was ready to return to the colliery. On Patrick's advice, he reapplied for an apprenticeship. His application was submitted on the basis that although he was not the son of an artisan, his father had given twenty-one years of outstanding service to the mine and his mother continued to do so. The application was rejected without comment or explanation so Patrick asked Steven Jongwe to covertly find out precisely how many of the sons of mine electricians had applied for apprenticeships. The answer was not a single one. The four current vacancies for electrical apprentices remained unfilled.

At the next heads of department meeting Patrick 'innocently' enquired if there had been a good response to their general advertisement for the new intake of electrical apprentices. The European personnel manager said it had been disappointing, adding the observation that the majority of artisans seemed to actively discourage their sons from following into their fathers' trades. "As I see it," Patrick commented, "in the near future we will have no artisans left and will have to tap into the African labour force. Some of the youngsters in our school are very bright and would jump at the chance to train. They could become good tradesmen in time."

"Patrick, we know you are very proud of your black school-boys but it will take years before any of them will be able to grasp the fundamentals of the trades," said the chief buyer.

"I have only one further query then, unless we take on additional electricians, who are going to fill the gap and do the work which the apprentices formerly did; namely the fetching, carrying and helping of the electricians?"

At this point Mr Mackay intervened and told the meeting that he would take the matter up at his next meeting with the mine's foremen and the trade union representatives.

It was not the result Patrick had hoped for but at least the seed had been sown to create a new category of employment for people like Gajima. The unions and the foremen flatly rejected full apprenticeships for black applicants, but a new grade of artisan's helpers was proposed and accepted. The rates of pay for this grade were increased quite substantially, and although the rejection was disappointing for Patrick, it was at least a step in the right direction.

Telling Gajima the outcome was not easy. Patrick knew exactly how the young men would feel and only hoped they would not become embittered by the rejection; which Patrick knew was based entirely on the false premise of their inferior abilities and their unreliability. All Patrick could do was to explain to the disappointed Gajima and the others how and why these prejudices had arisen. They stemmed from the time when the black and the white races had first started working together as employer and employee. The main problem had actually been due to poor language skills of the white people, coupled with the black people's inborn dislike for working for anyone other than themselves. Patrick assured Gajima that things would inevitably change; but this would only happen when the whites began to appreciate the real value of their workers and when the blacks demonstrated their own skills and reliability. He estimated that it would possibly happen within the next two or three generations.

"Go and think about things, Gajima. Try to put aside your anger and resentment. It will do you no good. You have always wanted to work with machinery and electrical equipment. If you take the job as an artisan's helper you will actually be doing the job you want and will only be missing the dubious title of 'apprentice' and their slightly higher pay. From what I have seen, some of the electricians are lazy blighters and will be only too pleased to have you do more than they would have previously allowed for apprentices. You can still learn a great deal by observing and thinking for yourself. Ask David to pass on some of his technical books to you and study them well. I know he would be only too pleased to help you."

Gajima thanked Patrick and talked the matter over with his mother. The following day he put in his application and two weeks later was offered a position as an 'Artisan's Helper', at a salary well above his expectations, thanks largely to the unofficial advice Patrick had been given by Steven Jongwe.

During talks with Steven, Patrick also heard more about the ordering of sub-standard switchgear and other electrical equipment by the buying office. This equipment was being bought cheaply through unknown Eastern European manufacturers. Steven told him that two good electricians had resigned following arguments with the buyers over these issues and yet no positive action had been taken.

Gajima had spoken to several of the other electricians' helpers before his first day at work. They warned him that some of the electricians were OK but others were, as they put it, 'professional bastards', and it was just the luck of the draw as to whom you were allocated. If you were unlucky you got a South African. Gajima was paired up with Hendrik Joubert; an Afrikaner from the Transvaal, who frequently asked for the 'replacement' of helpers because, in his words, "They were lazy, stupid or just no bloody good for anything."

Before he went to work that day Lisa had given him some sound advice. "Treat your boss with respect and he will respect you. Do as you are told and speak only when you are spoken to. Don't ask too many questions or he may think you want to take over his job. Finally, be careful and don't argue, even if you know you are right."

Dressed in his new mine issue boots, overalls and hard hat he collected his cap lamp and handed in his mine number token, which the cap lamp attendant hung on the board. This acted as a check on precisely who was underground at any time of day or night. The token was returned to him when he returned his cap lamp for recharging at the end of each shift.

The underground foreman introduced him to Hendrik Joubert, a six foot tall ex-provincial rugby player from the Transvaal. Hendrik looked him up and down with a critical eye.

"I will call you Jim and you should address me as Maneer Hendrick or Baas Hendrik. You understand?" Gajima politely lowered his eyes and answered smartly.

"Ja, Baas Hendrik, I understand."

"Good, Kom nou, we've got work to do and mustn't stand talking."

As they walked down the haulage Gajima was told what they were going to do that day. It involved a relatively simple job of running the cables from a distribution board to supply permanent lighting in a new section of the haulage-way. At every stage Hendrik explained exactly what they were doing, and how it needed to be done. Although it was quite straight forward work, Gajima found it satisfying and at the end of the shift he looked back with a feeling of pride at the work they had done. Hendrik noticed him doing so.

"You did OK, Jim. I will try you out for a week then we will decide."

"Thank you, Baas Hendrik, I would like that."

After handing in his cap lamp, Gajima went into the changing rooms and showered, washing off all of the black smears of fine coal dust. There he met a couple of the other 'artisan's helpers' who were keen to know how his first day with Hendrik Joubert had been. Knowing their opinion of his new boss, Gajima was careful and casually answered that it wasn't too bad and that he only shouted at him once.

That evening Gajima started on his own programme of learning, using the first of the elementary books David had sent up to him from Johannesburg. It was not possible for him to attend the mine's night school as that was only open to apprentices, but he was determined to keep pace with the best of them.

Lisa was very pleased and reported back to Mary and Patrick accordingly. Hendrik Joubert was already known to Patrick as there had been several complaints made in the past about his abrupt manner and intolerance of what he saw as laziness. Patrick was pleased that Gajima was working with Joubert as he personally found him to be a stern but fair man. If they got on well together then Gajima could learn a lot, provided he was careful and worked hard.

The development of Number Two Colliery entailed the installation of electrical supplies on a grand scale so Gajima was kept extremely busy and the years passed by very rapidly. He had been upgraded several times so his pay was at the top rate. Even after contributing towards housekeeping costs he was still able to save a fair amount each month.

CHAPTER 30

☙ 1952/54 ☙

Mary and Patrick's twin girls finished school at the end of the year and achieved good results; Caroline excelling in the science subjects and Brigid, by contrast, did well in languages and the arts. They both qualified for Matric Exemption and hence would be eligible for entry into any of the South African universities. Mary and Patrick were delighted by their achievements, but quite honestly they had not given any serious thought to the possibility that they might want to follow in David's footsteps and go to university. Although Mary and Patrick were reasonably careful people and had built up their savings, it came as a shock to them that nearly all of this would be swallowed up by the fees, travelling expenses and boarding costs for their daughters if they went to university.

The girls took after their mother in colouring and were attractive, tall and slim, with tanned complexions and long dark hair. They got on surprisingly well together, not because they were compatible, but rather because they were complementary. Caroline was by nature a little shy and quiet, but self-reliant, and very efficient. By contrast Brigid was boisterous, very sociable, a born mimic, a quick thinker and non-stop talker. Patrick claimed that she hadn't just 'kissed the blarney stone', she must have created it.

Caroline was interested in medical research and the sciences, whereas Brigid's interests fluttered like a butterfly's over far wider fields; people, languages, travel, photography and journalism, to name but a few. From babies Patrick had insisted that Lisa spoke to them only in Zulu. As a result they both found it easy to pick up other languages. At school they learnt Afrikaans and French and later in South Africa they gained a useful smattering of 'Xhosa'.

After long discussions and careful analysis of the family finances, Patrick and Mary eventually decided to offer the two girls the opportunity of going to Rhodes University in South Africa. The decision was not based on sound financial grounds. They couldn't really afford it but were prepared to gamble on two things: Caroline applying for, and being successful in getting a bursary or a scholarship, and, although they didn't tell her, on Brigid deciding to quit before completing her degree course. Mary and Patrick were prepared to take this risk on the basis of knowing and understanding their children. Mary was also keen to avoid any possible future criticism for favouring David over her girls, although they knew that his fees were covered by his bursary and also by a substantial monthly cheque from Shaun. Patrick believed very strongly in the importance of higher education for both, boys and girls. His daughters were told that finances were very tight and that they would have to manage on few luxuries and would have to get paying jobs during their vacations. They were overjoyed by the prospect. Admission applications were sent off immediately to Rhodes University and full acceptances were received for them both a month later.

One of the disadvantages of working in a mine was that accommodation was fully provided by the company, and this gave the employees the impression that their earnings were well above average; but in actual fact they were faced with a serious financial problem when they retired and had to purchase their own houses elsewhere. Their mine pensions and their savings did not take into account inflation, particularly the inflation of property prices. Unlike some countries, Rhodesia did not have any social security system so employees were expected to plan for their own retirement and old age. Most of them did so; the alternative being the embarrassment of having to rely on their families for support.

From David's fortnightly letters home the family learnt that he had met the 'love of his life' in Johannesburg. Her name was Helen MacDonald and she was a Rhodesian from Bulawayo. He had written the following:

It is indeed a very small world. I met her briefly at the Anderson's two years ago, just before I came down to varsity but at that time she had intended going to Cape Town University to study fine arts. So I never gave her another thought. Luckily for me there had been a change in plan because the family wanted her to be closer to home, so she had come to Wits instead. I find it amazing that although we have about 16,500 students here, I never bumped into her until a month ago. Just by chance I happened to meet her when she came to our annual Engineers Ball. Like me, she is half-way through her degree course. I'm sure you will love her; she is a gorgeous blonde and looks quite a lot like my mum! With luck we will both graduate at the same time, and then who knows?

"This sounds serious," said Mary as she handed David's letter over to Patrick.

He read it and agreed with her saying, "He's a sensible young-ster and we must trust his judgement. We will only know in two years' time, after they both graduate."

*

Those years passed quickly. On completion of the exams and his thesis, David felt reasonably confident of qualifying for his Electrical Engineering degree and was finally able to propose to Helen, his long-term girlfriend. She had supported and helped him through some hard times and a deep loving relationship had developed.

Both families were very pleased with the news of their engage-ment and looked forward to a wedding in Bulawayo early in the new year, subject of course to their final exam results.

CHAPTER 31

Helen and David both passed their final exams and their wedding date was set for early February. Ignoring the advice Mr Anderson had previously given him about working underground, David had secured a position on the Antelope Mine in Northern Rhodesia, and was due to start work there on 1st March.

Helen was the MacDonald's only daughter and her father wanted the very best for her. Over the years his industrial building construction company had expanded and prospered, so no expense was spared for the wedding. Several of the O'Connors' close friends from Wankie were invited as were Shaun's workmates. Although Shaun's invitation included a partner, he came alone to the celebration. Mr MacDonald generously booked the entire O'Connor family into rooms at the Palace Hotel, Brigid and Caroline basking in the unexpected luxury. David and Helen had invited Lisa and Gajima but they had politely begged to be excused. David was disappointed and phoned to try and persuade them. However, Lisa was adamant saying that they would feel uncomfortable being the only Matabeles there, but asked instead if David and Helen would call in to see them after the wedding, on their way through to Northern Rhodesia.

Mary kept her eighteen-year-old promise by giving David his mother's wedding ring for Helen. She also gave him the oval stone which the old woman at the Rhodes Hotel had given to Mary for the protection of her third child. Mary had already given Caroline and Brigid the small round stones for protecting them when they went off to university. These stones meant a lot to Mary, who believed implicitly in their protection, so she was relieved when they were accepted without undue comment.

The wedding ceremony took place at the Bulawayo cathedral. Helen was attended by her best friend Rosemary Anderson and two flower girls. With the benefit of her artistic training, Helen had designed and made her own wedding dress plus the dresses for Rosemary and the flower girls. The styling and colours were absolutely stunning. Helen's own dress was in white French lace and she looked divine. David couldn't believe his eyes when he saw her coming up the cathedral's long aisle with her father. He felt very emotional and had difficulty holding back the urge to throw his arms around her and hug her when she rather shyly stood beside him at the altar.

The wedding reception was a very lavish function which was held in the MacDonalds' large and immaculately kept garden, in the fashionable suburb of Khumalo. With their families and the MacDonalds' numerous friends, they catered for nearly two hundred guests, seated in an enormous marquee which had been erected on the front lawn. Mary and Patrick were very proud of their son and took to Helen immediately. They did their best to help Shaun, who looked rather lost and was obviously desperately missing Wendy at this important time. Sensitive to his feelings, Helen spent a long time talking to him after all the speeches and toasts had finished. She made a friend for life and succeeded in lifting his spirits dramatically by asking him if he would dance with her after the first waltz with her new husband. Shaun was deeply touched and waited impatiently to get onto the dance floor with his beautiful daughter-in-law. Mary, Patrick and David looked on with pride as Shaun elegantly demonstrated his remarkable dancing talents.

David enjoyed talking to Mr and Mrs Anderson whom he had not seen since his start at university. They congratulated him on his beautiful bride, as well as for getting his electrical engineering degree.

"I hear you are going up north to the copper mines," commented Mr Anderson. "This is a much better plan than the coal mines, but don't forget the advice I gave you about ants and rats going down holes in the ground."

"No, Mr Anderson, I haven't forgotten and indeed I have passed it on to many fellow students as well as a boyhood friend of mine who works underground at Wankie Colliery. I will be working mainly on the surface and will be involved in the installation of the electrical equipment for their new copper refinery. It feels strange to think that I will be working for the same company as my father did when I was a baby."

The wedding celebrations went on well into the night. The people of Bulawayo truly know how to party. Bulawayo was a town which grew slowly and naturally. It was the industrial centre of the country and it was said that everyone knew everyone else; unlike the capital, Salisbury, which was regarded as being rather 'snooty and superior', populated by civil servants, politicians and lawyers.

Helen and David had a short honeymoon at Troutbeck, in the Eastern Highlands, before the long journey back to Wankie to see Gajima and Lisa. Helen gave her a few pretty boxes of wedding cake plus several photographs taken at the wedding. She was thrilled and promised that she would keep them forever. Gajima's congratulations were very touching. He told David in all sincerity that Helen was the most beautiful white girl he had ever seen. David's heart swelled with pride and happiness.

CHAPTER 32

❧ 1955 ❧

Angus Mackay, now sixty-seven and well past the normal retirement age, decided that it was time to return to his beloved Scotland. Jeannie was delighted by this move as life on the mine was not as friendly as in the old days when she knew most of the employees and took an interest in their lives.

Patrick was deeply concerned over Angus's decision and although he still had eight years to complete until his own retirement, he felt that it would be extremely difficult working under someone else, so he also handed in his notice. Four other senior members plus twenty-eight of the mining and engineering staff submitted their resignations, taking with them the knowledge and expertise of many years of working on a coal mine in Africa.

The farewell parties were sad affairs, attended by several directors and long term friends. Generous cheques were presented to Angus, Patrick and to the others for their loyalty and long service.

Patrick and Mary bought a fifteen acre smallholding on the outskirts of Nyamandhlovo and as it was only twelve miles from Bulawayo they planned on raising chickens and pigs for the butchers in the city. The Umguza river flowed through the lower section of the property where the soil was good for growing vegetables and tropical fruit. Their close neighbours were Joanne and Theo Odendaal who were now running the farm belonging to their late parents. It was through them that Patrick heard of their own property.

Lisa and Gajima stayed on at Wankie in spite of the departure of Hendrick Joubert who had proved to be an excellent teacher to Gajima, and whose thoroughness and dedication would be an example to the young man for the rest of his life.

CHAPTER 33

Gajima had fallen madly in love with a very pretty young girl named Naomi and had nearly saved enough to pay her parents a deposit for the girl's lobola (the bride price, charged by parents for the hand of their daughter). The couple had been going out together for nearly a year already and were both very keen to marry. Lisa was pleased he was happy but gave only her reluctant approval of her future daughter-in-law. She made allowances because she desperately wanted grandchildren of her own, while she was still young enough to appreciate them. She was also rather envious of Patrick and Mary 'going farming' as she called it.

After the departure of Angus Mackay, Mr Powys Davies was in his element, because the new managers wanted to know precisely where every penny was spent, and he was the one who could provide that information. "Knowledge is power," he boasted to the hard pressed workers in his department. "Every requisition and order must bear my counter signature, no matter how small or large the value is." The wry joke on the mine was that every sheet of toilet paper had to be signed by Mr Powys Davies himself. Some humourists offered to return the used ones to him just to prove that they hadn't been wasted.

Up until the closure of Number One Colliery the mine was virtually free of methane gas and it had been classed as non-hazardous by the mining inspectors. This meant that smoking was permitted, equipment did not have to be to flame-proof standards and open arc welding had even been allowed underground. However, the new Number Two Colliery was different in several important respects. The coal was fractured and pockets of methane gas were present and yet the mine had not been reclassified by the inspectors. It should have been regraded from 'non-fiery' to 'fiery'. Head Office must have known, or at least should have known and paid attention to these facts.

Adding to the potential dangers, was the mine's policy of buying electrical equipment marketed in Rhodesia by new importers who employed sales reps with very limited technical knowledge. Most of the older more experienced electrical fore-men had left the mine and no attention was paid to complaints from the electricians. The switchgear was made from flimsy light gauge sheet steel and although it could carry the normal daily load currents, it was not rated to interrupt the maximum currents which would flow under short circuit conditions. It was neither flameproof nor explosion proof; as was required for most coal mines worldwide.

There had already been one circuit breaker failure and fortunately it had not injured anybody nor did it start a fire. Gajima worked on the installation of the replacement switch-board but it had not been his responsibility to file a formal report. The electrician logged the details but didn't bother to write an official fault record as he knew nothing would be done about it. However, Gajima did mention the incident in a letter to David. In reply, David used some very uncomplimentary language about cost cutting, and sent Gajima useful details of how to calculate the magnitudes of the currents which would flow under those particular conditions. Providentially, he also reminded Gajima again to always stand well back and off to one side when operating any of 'those rubbishy foreign circuit breakers'.

Helen and David spent three years in Northern Rhodesia and after completing the copper refinery project, David had worked his way up to Section Engineer (Surface). He was enjoying the work and the challenges it entailed but he was unhappy about the rapidly worsening political developments in Northern Rhodesia. Totally unexpectedly he was approached by a visitor from AMI's consulting office who asked if he would be interested in a consulting engineering position in their Salisbury office.

Ever since qualifying, David's ultimate goal had been to work in a consulting capacity. In his opinion it was the pinnacle of the profession. This seemed like a golden opportunity.

Without mentioning it to anyone other than Helen, David quietly researched the background of AMI and found that it was indeed a highly respected heavy industrial consulting practice. They had a reputation for demanding the best and they only employed top quality engineering staff. The company had started from humble beginnings in Australia. Over the years it had developed into a major player in the industrial world. David and Helen decided it was at the very least, worthwhile applying for a position with them. He felt ready for wider experiences and he knew that Helen would welcome a change. She was becoming tired of the limitations of life on the mines, both socially and culturally.

David relished the challenge and at the first opportunity discussed it on the phone with his father. Shaun's feeling was definitely to go for it.

David was overdue for long leave and had been thinking about a seaside holiday in South Africa. He talked over possible plans with Helen and after careful thought they finally decided to submit an application for the AMI position and, if called for interview, they could then travel via Salisbury rather than Bulawayo on their way south. Three weeks went by with no response from AMI, and then David received a phone call from the personnel department inviting him for a preliminary interview the following week. David explained that he couldn't possibly make that date as he had to hand over his projects to his deputy who would become acting section engineer. This would take a minimum of ten days. The AMI personnel officer seemed rather put out by this but agreed to make it a week later. This suited Helen and David much better as it gave them time to organise their holiday plans, arrange kennelling for their dogs and find house-sitters for their mine house.

Unexpectedly, in the mail the next day was a wedding invitation from Caroline. She was getting married in four weeks' time to Doctor Gary Pienaar, a surgeon who worked with her at Groote Schuur hospital in Cape Town. In a brief covering letter she wrote:

"I know it is a hell of a long way to come but we sincerely hope you two will be able to make it. Brigid will be home after her photo assignment in Israel so will be back in time to be my bridesmaid and I would love Helen to be my matron of honour. Mum and Dad are definitely coming down. You

will love Gary, he is our kind of person. His ancestors were Huguenots who arrived here from Holland a hundred years before ours did in 1820, and he has the cheek to call us 'new South Africans'. We will arrange accommodation and everything else for you here. You must come.

Love C.

PS I will phone Helen one evening soon to talk about dresses, colour schemes, etc.

The dates allowed sufficient time to attend the AMI interview in Salisbury and still have a fairly leisurely journey down to the Cape. It had been their intention to travel through the Transvaal to Durban and around the coast to Port Elizabeth and possibly on to Cape Town, but now they would go the other way round instead, travelling via Johannesburg and the Orange Free State and on through the Karoo to Cape Town. Helen was delighted at the prospect of the holiday and the wedding.

David phoned Patrick and established that they would be arriving in Cape Town at about the same date but that they would be spending a couple of days with friends in Beaufort West, on the way down. Lisa had agreed to travel down from Wankie to Nyamandhlovo to take care of their smallholding while they were away. She had assured them that Gajima was quite alright, but added, "That Naomi girl will no doubt be moving in with him the moment my back is turned." Lisa looked forward to the month away from the heat of Wankie and the chance to talk to 'normal' non-mining people again.

*

At the AMI offices in Salisbury David's first impression was very favourable. He was conducted up to the third floor and handed over to a very smartly dressed, good looking girl with a lovely smile.

"I am the personnel manager's secretary and I will be filling in endless forms with your details. Don't worry about all the interviews; they are quite painless, just relax and know that it is the same for all of you. This is an efficient but happy place and I'm sure you will like it. You are the fourth of sixteen electrical engineers being interviewed so let's get started." She took a folder from her desk and put his name on the front cover then ran through the completion of endless forms and a detailed questionnaire, noting all of his answers. At the end of it she said, "That is all done, next you will be interviewed by the personnel manager, the consulting mechanical engineer, the consulting mining engineer and finally the consulting electrical engineer."

It was an unexpectedly harrowing business. It took the best part of three hours. By the end of it he felt quite certain that he would be rejected. When he was ushered back with the personnel manager he asked when it was likely that a decision would be made, as he was going to be away in Cape Town for the next four weeks.

"Not for quite a while," was the reply. "We will let you know if you are on the shortlist and then there will be full technical interviews of those applicants."

David left, impressed with their thoroughness, but disappointed that he would have this issue hanging over him during the wedding and their holiday. Helen was anxiously waiting for him in the lounge at Meikles Hotel and between thirsty sips of a cold Castle lager, he told her all that had happened. She was sure that he would be selected, in spite of his cautious pessimism.

Early the next morning they set off southwards, aiming to cross the Limpopo river at Beit Bridge and staying overnight at the Mountain Inn, a beautiful little country hotel high up in the Soutpansberg mountains. It overlooked the northern Transvaal town of Louis Trichardt. They had travelled about 600 kilometres, approximately half the way to Johannesburg, which would be their next stop. It was a crisp cool evening and a blessed relief after the heat of the Rhodesian low veldt. After dinner Helen and David went out into the gardens to see the twinkling lights of Louis Trichardt a thousand feet below them. The journey for the next day would be through the farming areas of the Transvaal high veldt, pleasant but less interesting and not as spectacular.

They again made an early start the following day; having ordered a picnic lunch from the hotel. The twin lane, dual carriageway South African roads were a pleasure to drive on after the narrower, but now fully tarmac Rhodesian roads. They made good time and, being familiar with Joburg they easily found the home of their varsity friends with whom they would be spending a few days. They had passed the midway point of their journey and had only another 800 kilometres to reach Cape Town. It was a long and uninteresting route through the Platerlande which translates as the 'flat lands' and it was precisely that. However, the approach to Cape Town made up for it. They travelled through the Hex River Mountains with its beautiful yellow, red and purple wild flowers now covering the mountain sides and the valleys below. From there the road snaked its way down through the Hex River Pass and into the famous and vast Cape vineyards. Each of them had retained their traditional Cape Dutch homesteads, built three hundred years earlier. From there on it was an easy run down to the magnificent city of Cape Town.

The accommodation arrangements were truly luxurious. As promised, Caroline had rented two of the vacant flats in her apartment block, one for Helen and David and another for Mary and Patrick. Brigid had moved in with Caroline. Right from the start it was very happy and light hearted affair. There was the usual rehearsal at the church the day before the wedding. Brigid, always up to a prank, put on one of Caroline's dresses and met Gary at the church. They rehearsed the various wedding procedures and when the parson said, "Now at this point I will say to you, 'you may kiss the bride'," Brigid shrieked with delight threw her arms round Gary's neck and gave him a long loving kiss. Gary was completely taken aback, and of course had no idea that he was being kissed by his future sister-in-law.

An instant bond formed between the Pienaar and O'Connor families; Gary and David had much in common, especially their love for Caroline. Mary and Gary's mothers found that they shared several distant Eastern Cape relatives plus a wide knowledge and love of gardening. Patrick told the young couple that they were very fortunate in both having the perfect mothers-in-law as well as fathers-in-law.

The wedding was a splendid affair. Caroline looked absolutely stunning in a classical wedding gown. Patrick proudly led his daughter up the aisle followed by the four flower girls with Brigid and Helen shepherding them along. The reception was held at the prestigious Mount Nelson Hotel and was attended by many members of Gary's extended family; the couple's numerous friends from Grahamstown, as well as several of the medical staff from Groote Schuur hospital.

It was only during the speeches at the reception that Gary found out the truth about the deception at the wedding rehearsal. He was teased unmercifully about not even knowing which twin he had just married.

Mary and Patrick were very proud of the way the girls had matured and progressed. Their university careers were precisely as they had forecast; Caroline had won a scholarship which had helped with her university fees, and Brigid had left university at the end of her first year and had already become a successful photo journalist. It had been a very worthwhile gamble that Patrick and Mary had taken.

CHAPTER 34

ᘒ 1959 ᘒ

Gajima's day started like any other, except that pretty little Naomi made his breakfast for him. He was feeling a little guilty that she had insisted that they slept in his mother's double bed the night before. It was a week since Lisa had left for Nyamandhlovu to take care of Boss Pat's property. He thought of her affectionately as he walked along the underground haulage way to the job they had worked on the previous day. It was nearly complete, with the new switchgear installed and the cabling connected up and energised. All that remained that morning was for Gajima to lift the cable from the floor and secure it to the cable racks which ran along the haulage side walls. He had just opened his tool box when there was a loud crashing noise and he saw a derailed coal truck veering off the rails towards the side of the haulage way. Fortunately there was nobody in its path. Next the steel wheels of the truck ran over the new cable he was working on. Gajima watched in horror as smoke started coming out of the squashed cable. Seconds later there was a stream of sparks and the cable caught fire. One of the white miners nearby shouted to him, "Wena, vala getzi, tshetsha." (Hurry and turn off the electricity, quickly.)

Gajima ran back to the newly installed switchboard and, standing slightly to one side he reached for the operating handle of the main circuit breaker. As he did so, there was an almighty explosion in the switchboard. The flash would have been in excess of 1000 degrees centigrade. The flimsy front panel blew off and a white hot flame of electric arc followed, straight onto the left side of his face and body. He staggered backwards, and blinded by the flash he then fell onto the rail tracks. He felt no pain at that time but realised that the front of his overalls was on fire. With the loss of the power supply, all of the lighting had gone out. The only illumination came from his burning over-alls. The next thing he felt was a blast of cold water as a quick thinking worker turned his high pressure water hose onto him, extinguishing the flaming overalls. The smell of roasting meat and burnt clothing choked him. Excruciating pain followed and mercifully he then lost consciousness.

An hour later he woke up in hospital. He tried to speak but couldn't move his lips. In dreadful pain and desperation he let out a wailing sound and a nurse came running up to his bedside.

"Don't move! I'll bring you water." A short while later she returned with a small bowl of water and a wad of cotton wool. She dipped it into the bowl and gently dabbed it onto his lips. He tried to lick his lips but couldn't open his mouth. The nurse continued dripping the water and it eventually softened the charred skin sufficiently for a trickle of water to run unto Gajima's mouth. He swallowed gratefully. The pain was almost unbearable.

"There's been a bad accident and you have some serious burns. The doctor will be here soon to examine you. I must tell you, it is going to be very painful. We have put temporary dressings on your burns but we will have to take them off for Doctor to see what needs to be done. I am Nurse Dube and I will be looking after you. I'll be back soon to give you an injection to relieve the pain."

When she returned she gently lifted the sheets and Gajima saw a blurred image of his left arm and leg covered by bandages. After the injection he pointed to his mouth and the nurse fetched more water. With deep concern in her eyes she explained that the left side of his face and his left arm were burnt but luckily his left eye appeared to be OK. The left arm was seriously burnt exposing the bone. She assured him that the doctor would be able to repair his lips. Tenderly she held his right hand and promised she would do everything possible to help him. She told him that she had nursed many African children who had fallen into their open cooking fires and some of their burns were horrific.

He began to feel drowsy from the injection and his thoughts turned to his mother, to Patrick, David and Mary, all of whom were away and un-contactable. It was dreadful to be so alone. Somehow he knew that pretty Naomi probably wouldn't be able to give him much support.

The doctor arrived and, assisted by two nurses, slowly removed each of the dressings from Gajima's charred body. They found that the burns from his overalls were relatively minor but his left arm was badly burnt. Fortunately he had instinctively acted on David's advice about switching and had turned his head away to the right, otherwise he would certainly have lost his sight.

The doctor concluded his examination and decided that the injuries were much too serious for them to treat at the mine hospital. Major plastic surgery would certainly be needed and this could only be done at the burns unit of the Memorial Hospital in Bulawayo. The doctor gave instructions for Gajima to be sent down there by ambulance the following day. Nurse Dube readily volunteered to travel with him and see him settled in the hospital. Finally, the doctor gave him an anaesthetic to relieve his pain.

When the doctor left, Gajima indicated to Nurse Dube that he wanted to write. She brought a pencil and held a note pad for him. With a very shaky right hand he wrote, 'Stop at O'Connor's house'. Nurse Dube read it and asked, "Your mother?" He nodded slightly and she continued, "I will find out the address from the office and arrange for the ambulance to call in on our way to Bulawayo tomorrow morning."

Exhausted, Gajima was just getting back to sleep when he heard raised voices and, on opening his right eye, saw four men arguing with the very irate Hospital Matron.

"I've told you already, he is seriously injured and he's in no condition for you to question him. Your accident report will just have to wait. If you don't believe me, take a look for yourselves." She lifted the sheet.

"Now do you believe me? He cannot talk or answer any of your damn fool questions. He is lucky to still be alive and yet you want him to tell you what happened. You had better get out of my hospital now, before I get really angry." They hurriedly left.

Naomi was very concerned when Gajima didn't return from work that afternoon. Then, when she heard there had been an accident, she decided to go to the hospital in time for the evening visiting hours. She dressed in one of her prettiest dresses and with some trepidation made her way to the mine hospital. A nurse warned her that Gajima's accident was serious and said she should be prepared for it. She showed her to the men's surgical ward and then directed her to Gajima's bed. All she could see was a figure covered in bandages. She had an absolute horror of illness and couldn't bear the sight of blood but summoning her courage she walked up to the bed and softly called his name. On hearing her voice Gajima turned his head towards her. All she saw was his charred mouth, half open, where the doctor had separated his lips. She let out a hysterical scream and dashed to the sluice room where she vomited violently; then ran from the hospital sobbing uncontrollably.

She made her way back to the house, slowly packed up her things and walked to her parents' home. She felt ashamed but knew that it would be impossible for her to ever live with Gajima, no matter how much they had meant to each other in the past.

Heavily sedated, Gajima had a relatively restful night, except for a dreadful nightmare of being naked out in the desert with no water and the midday sun scorching his bare body. The next morning Nurse Dube fed him porridge thinned with milk and sweetened with a little sugar. Then she replaced the dressings on his suppurating burns. It was a slow and very painful business but one which she managed as gently as she could. At eight o'clock the mine's ambulance men wheeled him off to the waiting vehicle for the 200 mile journey to Bulawayo. Nurse Dube brought a case containing the medical supplies she might need for her patient, a small overnight bag and lunch for the driver and herself. She had also prepared a nutritious beef broth and cold drink for Gajima.

On arriving at the small village of Nyamandhlovu, they asked a local man for directions and easily located the O'Connor smallholding on the banks of the Umgusa river. The driver parked the ambulance in the shade of a large tree in the front garden while Nurse Dube went and knocked at the front door of the cottage. Lisa opened the door, greeted her and invited her inside, anxiously noting the ambulance and Nurse Dube's uniform. As gently as she could Nurse Dube explained what had happened and why they were there. Lisa listened without comment until Dube was finished.

"Oh my God. This is a dreadful thing to happen to anyone, but for my only child… It is absolutely heart-breaking. Thank you for what you are doing for him. I can tell he is in good hands and I am very grateful to you. I would like to speak to him, if that would be possible, but first let me get you and your driver some refreshments. That will give me a little time to compose myself."

"Yes, of course. I will go and tell him you are coming but I must warn you his condition is serious. You will have to be very brave. He is young and I can assure you that he will survive this ordeal."

Lisa brought them large glasses of cold homemade lemon syrup to drink then went into the back of the ambulance. She crouched down next to her son and placed her hand in his. He opened his right eye and slowly drifted back into full consciousness.

"Ah, Mame," he whispered in Zulu, wincing with pain as his lips moved.

"Don't speak, my son, just listen. Remember how I told you when you were small that with determination you can do anything? This is one of those times." Gajima nodded his head. "Nurse Dube says you will be in hospital for a long time but I will try to come to Bulawayo every four days, until Boss Pat and Miss Mary come back. You must go now but remember what I have told you." He nodded again, squeezing her hand. He closed his eye to hide his tears as she clambered out of the ambulance.

On their way back to the cottage Nurse Dube hugged Lisa and this small act of compassion released their restrained emotions and they cried uncontrollably together.

Back in the house, Lisa counted the money she had in her purse. She calculated that she had sufficient to travel to the hospital every two days, if she took the bus into town but walked back; it was twelve miles.

Nurse Dube handed her patient over to the hospital staff and saw to his formal admission then waited for the doctor to arrive. The elderly sister in charge of the burns unit listened carefully to the details of Gajima's accident and made a number of notes on his record sheets. Then in answer to Nurse Dube's queries about the doctor she told her that he was an excellent man and had worked in a burns unit in Britain during the Second World War. He had also developed new techniques for skin grafting, mainly for air force personnel who had received burns when their planes crashed and caught fire. He had come back home to Rhodesia at the end of the war.

The doctor was delayed in the operating theatre so, after saying a brief farewell to Gajima, Nurse Dube and the ambulance driver left for the return journey. It would be four long months before she would see him again.

*

On their return from the wedding in Cape Town, the O'Connor family were devastated when Lisa told them of Gajima's accident. After visiting him at the hospital, Patrick arranged to obtain a copy of the official accident report, using the services of the ever devious but useful and resourceful Steven Jongwe. Accompanying the report was a recommendation from the Accounts Office that the mine should pay Gajima his normal salary for the period he was in hospital, but thereafter his services would no longer be required 'in view of his illegal actions which had endangered the safety of the mine'. Patrick was absolutely astounded by what he read. However, he felt that Gajima should not be told about this until he was very much stronger mentally and physically. Lisa stayed on at Nyamandhlovu and, with Mary and Patrick, visited Gajima frequently.

The accident report itself was very brief saying that the derailing of the coal truck was caused by a heavy steel crowbar which had been accidently left on the rail track by persons unknown and it was just unfortunate that the coal truck had run over the power cable. The conclusion was drawn that the injury to Gajima Khumalo Zulu was due to him performing an illegal act, namely operating a circuit breaker; work for which he was neither authorised nor qualified.

The report praised the man who had been washing down coal dust from the haulage. It stated that his prompt action not only saved the life of the electrician's helper but, significantly, it also mentioned that his washing down activities had prevented the ignition of the coal dust, which could otherwise have resulted in a major underground explosion. This was a very strange statement in view of the fact that the mine was still classified as 'non-firery'. There followed a short technical statement by the underground electrical foreman confirming that the circuit breaker was of the correct rating for the proposed load but that the fault current which flowed into the damaged cable was many times greater than that. He quoted the manufacturer's name and gave technical details of the circuit breaker. Patrick was determined to get to the bottom of the accident and to see that Gajima was cleared of blame and was adequately compensated. He started building up a dossier of all the data he could find in relation to the accident.

Anticipating their future needs, Patrick immediately engaged a local contractor to build a couple of rondavels (thatched huts) on his smallholding in readiness for Lisa and Gajima, when he was discharged from hospital. With his knowledge and experience Patrick was certain that there would no longer be any prospect of Gajima being able to hold down a regular job, even in the unlikely event of an offer from the colliery. Patrick felt that the only realistic prospect was to employ Lisa to help in the house and Gajima to work in the garden and orchards. It was certainly the end of a promising career for young Gajima. What really troubled Patrick was the long term future as their smallholding was barely bringing in sufficient to cover their own living costs, without paying additional wages.

CHAPTER 35

∽ 1959 ∽

After Caroline and Gary's wedding Helen and David spent a few days sightseeing and shopping in Cape Town before the long but leisurely return journey back to Salisbury for the next interview by AMI. They decided to follow the beautiful 'garden route' through the Eastern Cape Province, with a week's break in Durban, before motoring via the Kruger National Park to Rhodesia. They felt the holiday was quite an extravagance, but as David pointed out, if he was selected by AMI, it would be at least a year before they would be entitled to any leave.

The holiday had been simply magical and they arrived in Salisbury a day before the interview. David was rather dreading it as he had not really looked at any of his technical books since leaving university and felt a little rusty on theory. However, he need not have worried as most of the interview focussed on good practical engineering matters. He found out later that a number of the other short-listed applicants, who were possibly superior to him in their own highly specialised fields, lacked his all-round engineering knowledge.

At the end of the second day of questioning he was called into a meeting with the personnel manager and invited to join the company. He was told that they would be offering him a certain salary and it was up to him to accept or reject it.

There were strict conditions of service which meant that he must never disclose his salary nor must he ever indicate to any other employee whether or not it had been increased. Failure to comply with these company rules would result in instant dismissal. He handed David a sealed envelope and offered him his congratulations saying he hoped that David would accept their offer. A confirming phone call was all that was required.

David put the envelope in his pocket without opening it and drove back to the hotel where Helen was anxiously waiting. Together they opened it, not knowing what to expect. It was a very pleasant surprise; thirty-five per cent more than his current salary, with unbelievably good leave conditions, free medical and dental treatment and a very good pension at age sixty.

"Oh my love, I'm so thrilled. I just knew you would get it. I can hardly wait to be back into civilisation again." David was very pleased by her response and hugged her fondly.

"I know how bored you've felt living in a mining town."

He phoned the personnel manager and confirmed his acceptance of AMI's offer. "By the way," the personnel manager said, "you should keep all of the receipts for your relocation and removal costs; we meet all of those. I'm sorry I had forgotten to mention it to you."

*

They heard the horrific news of Gajima's accident when they called in to see Mary and Patrick. Lisa and Patrick had just left for the hospital so Mary gave them the details of what actually happened, as well as Gajima's present condition. They were completely devastated by the news but decided it was too late to visit him as they needed to get home before dark.

David gave in his notice to the mine and following the usual farewell parties, and the packing up, they set off back to Salisbury to a very different life. On arrival they booked into a residential hotel and put the dogs into kennels while Helen set about finding a house to rent. Although Salisbury had many lovely suburbs, finding suitable accommodation was not a simple matter as her specifications demanded a fenced one acre garden in a good area of town, a minimum of three bedrooms, zoning for a good primary school, ease of access to David's office and a modern house. She travelled miles and was becoming quite desperate after four days of searching. Eventually, on the day before their furniture was due to arrive, she found what she wanted in the suburb of Borrowdale, about five miles from the centre of the city. With great relief she signed up a year's lease agreement.

David settled in easily at AMI. He found three Wits graduates already there; one electrical engineer two years his senior, one metallurgist and a chemical engineer. He was handed a major project on his first day. This settled the pattern which certainly was challenging but very interesting. He loved it and looked forward to going to work each day. It gave him excellent experience and prepared him for reaching his ultimate goal of having his own private consulting practice.

CHAPTER 36

It was two months before Gajima was considered by the Memorial Hospital doctors to be well enough to give his evidence to the accident enquiry team. As agreed earlier, the doctor notified Wankie personnel department and a week later, the Mine replied saying that his evidence was no longer required as they had already reached their conclusions and the matter was now closed.

The plastic surgeon had performed minor miracles of skin grafting, resulting in much of the side of Gajima's face being basically healed but was now a patchwork of black and pink, the colours which characterise burns on African peoples' black skins. Gajima never spoke of it, but it must have been traumatic for him to see his own face in the mirror for the first time after the accident. He was ashamed of his disfigurement and avoided people as much as possible. He could only imagine how others felt when they saw his face now. He was less concerned at the loss of his lower left arm, feeling that it was not a disfigurement but only a handicap to be overcome.

Gajima was eventually discharged from the hospital after four months of plastic surgery, which involved the removal of skin from other parts of his body and grafting small sections of it onto the burnt areas. Sometimes these grew success-fully but many did not and so the whole process had to be repeated. Gajima's staying power was tested to the limit. The loyal support and encouragement he received from Lisa and the O'Connors, plus regular letters from Nurse Dube, helped him greatly. For the whole of that time Nurse Dube had seen to the maintenance of their mine house but she wrote and told Lisa that the housing authorities were pressing for their possessions to be cleared out as soon as possible. Plans were made for removing their household goods and personal effects, as well as for collecting Gajima's sick-leave pay from the mine.

Before putting Lisa and Gajima onto the train for Wankie, Patrick advised them to both go in person to the pay office, to collect the money due to Gajima. Further, he told them they must not discuss the accident with anyone, nor should they speak of compensation claims. Finally, and most importantly, they must not sign any papers, especially those relating to settlement of claims. If pressed they were to say that the lawyers were looking into the matter.

"Don't hide your face, Gajima. Allow them to see the damage you have suffered. I still don't believe that you were responsible for this accident, nor do I think you acted illegally. I only wish that we could prove it to them. I think you have been treated unjustly. I want to take this matter further."

*

Going back to their former house was not easy for Lisa or Gajima, but they enlisted the help of friends, sorted out what they knew would fit into their new home and packed everything into wooden crates for railing down to Nyamandhlovu. The remaining items they gave to their friends and neighbours. After thoroughly cleaning the house they arranged to spend the night with close friends. That evening Gajima took the opportunity of visiting Nurse Dube to thank her for her letters and to show her the good work the doctor had done on his face and the remainder of his left arm. She was most impressed; praising him and the plastic surgeon for their perseverance. She told him that she was thinking of leaving the mine and applying for a position in the Bulawayo hospital; hoping to work with the surgeon in the burns unit. Gajima was very pleased to hear this as it might mean that he could see her occasionally. She was the only person in whose company he felt truly at ease, as she apparently did not find his appearance repulsive. When he told her this she laughed and said, "Gajima, if you had seen the burns I've seen you would think yourself 'slightly over cooked', but actually quite good looking." Smiling she added, "I hope you will come and visit me if I get work in Bulawayo."

The next morning Lisa and Gajima went to the pay office. Several of the workers there put hands to their mouths to stifle their gasps when they saw Gajima's face. Ignoring them he gave in his mine number and asked the clerk for the pay which was due to him. The clerk looked up the records then returned saying that there was a note on the file saying that Mr Powys Davies was to authorise the payment of his wages but that they needed his date of discharge from the hospital. He gave the date and was asked to wait. Fifteen minutes later Mr Davies appeared from his office with two papers in his hand. Gajima walked back up to the counter to meet him. When Mr Davies looked up and saw Gajima's face, he scurried back into his office like a frightened rabbit, shouting for a clerk to come to his office. Gajima overheard him telling the clerk, "I can't face this. Give him his money and these papers and be sure to get him to sign the second one." The obedient clerk did exactly that. He gave Gajima the money and the papers and asked him to sign the second page. Gajima carefully counted the money then borrowed the clerk's pen and signed the papers. He thanked the clerk, put the money and the papers into his pocket, and walked out with Lisa.

In an anxious hushed voice she said, "Gajima, Boss Pat told you not to sign or admit anything!"

"Yes I know, Mother, but don't worry." He patted the pocket of his jacket. "I just feel sorry for that poor clerk when Mr Davies finds out what he has done."

It was later that Mr Davies realised that the clerk hadn't brought back the mine's disclaimer. He called the clerk in and asked him for the signed paper.

"Well?" said Mr Davies impatiently. "You did get him to sign the paper, didn't you?"

"Yes Mr Davies I did exactly what you said. I gave him the paper and I made him sign it, just as you told me to." Mr Davies' blood pressure rose and he flushed with anger.

"You bloody idiot. You shouldn't have given that paper for him to keep. It was a very important paper and I must have it back."

"But Mr Davies, you told me to give him the money and the paper to sign. You said nothing about bringing the paper back to you."

With their crates of possessions delivered to the station, Lisa and Gajima said goodbye to their numerous friends and took the night train down to their new home in Nyamandhlovu;

taking with them all their treasured happy memories, leaving behind the sad ones and Kumbula's grave.

When they arrived at their new home Gajima read the paper and found that it was an undertaking that, having been fully compensated, he would make no claims nor take any action against the company for his injuries. He gave the document to Patrick for filing in the future claims dossier.

CHAPTER 37

∽ 1960 ∽

AMI was a major shareholder in one of the local building societies and after completing two years with the company, David qualified for a mortgage from them at a special low interest rate. So at last they would have the opportunity of owning their own home. The search started for a suitable house in the right area. Prompted perhaps by the 'nesting instinct' and much to David's surprise Helen fell in love with a very large house on nearly two acres of ground. David questioned her choice but she pointed out that it would comfortably accommodate them, their future children, plus Mary and Pat. In addition there was a separate cottage in the back garden for Lisa, so although it would need modernising David readily agreed on the purchase. A month later Helen fell pregnant, and in due course produced their first child; a beautiful daughter. Fifteen months later, for an encore, their son arrived. They named them Dawn Mary and Peter Shaun.

CHAPTER 38

✌ 1969/70 ✌

Shortly after setting up his own consulting practice David was called in to advise a client at Victoria Falls on problems they were having with their electric motors. He easily located and rectified the cause. Having some time to spare he called in to see Leslie, an old friend who was now the electrical foreman at the Wankie Colliery. When walking past the old scrapyard David saw the remains of Gajima's infamous switchboard. To his trained eye it was immediately apparent that the operating handle of the main switch was still in the closed position. This meant that in fact the switchboard must have exploded before Gajima's hand had even touched the operating handle. The switch contacts had obviously welded together by the fault current. Gajima's actions could certainly not have contributed to the accident, nor in fact had he performed any illegal act.

"Leslie, I have a favour to ask. Please would you ensure that that old switchboard is not moved from the scrapyard? It could be needed for evidence in a court case."

*

As soon as David arrived back in Salisbury he contacted Patrick and gave him the full details of what he had found.

"David, can we be absolutely certain that this would stand up in a law court?"

"Without any doubt," David replied.

"Alright then, I will get the lawyers onto it immediately."

Within a week the general manager at Wankie summoned one of their senior electrical engineers from their Johannesburg office and he wrote a full report confirming David's findings. A letter followed apologising and offering full compensation to Mr Gajima Khumalo. He would receive a substantial lump sum for his injuries plus monthly payments of his former salary for the rest of his life. Gajima readily accepted the generous offer and immediately proposed to Dube knowing that he was now in a position to support her as well as his mother. Their marriage was a simple affair with only family and close friends in attendance.

CHAPTER 39

❧ 1972 ❧

To the nation's horror on Tuesday, 6th June 1972 the local radio and TV announced the news of a major mining disaster at the Wankie Colliery.

"At 10.30 this morning a massive underground explosion occurred at the Wankie Colliery and it is feared that over 400 mineworkers may have been killed, or are still missing."

CHAPTER 40

ᐃ 1972 ᐁ

At David's request Patrick sent details of the mine disaster, collected from various newspaper reports and comments made by some eye witnesses. They made grim reading but gave some indication of the magnitude of the devastation which had occurred underground. Patrick selected some of them for David's records and information as follows:

The Cap Lamp Superintendent who was stationed near the entrance to the shaft at Number Two Colliery, heard the rumble of a far off explosion followed by two very loud ones nearby. The whole building shook so he went quickly outside and saw some smoke coming out of the shaft entrance. Suddenly there was a roar and dust rushed out of the shaft at high speed. He saw people lying in the dust; some were blinded and were trying to crawl away. He assisted one African who was covered in blood and dust but he died soon afterwards. Three others he successfully pulled away.

The policeman who was in a brick-built hut near the pit head was blown away fifty yards and died instantly. The hut was totally demolished.

The underground explosion had collapsed the supporting pillars of the old workings and hundreds of tons of overburden crashed down, releasing methane gas and blocking the haulage ways.

Tremendous columns of smoke and gases poured out of all the shafts, rising hundreds of feet into the atmosphere. The Kamandama incline shaft was completely blocked by falls of roof and twisted steel girders.

For nearly four days rescue teams made determined efforts to reach possible trapped survivors. They cleared an incline shaft sufficiently to permit the entry of proto teams and their equipment. Forty-one hours after the explosion a fan was brought back into operation and a sluggish ventilation current was established in the hope that it might possibly help the trapped workers.

The proto teams, working in relays, penetrated 2000 metres into the mine among scenes of the most appalling devastation. Explosions were heard at frequent intervals and freely burning fires were encountered.

In the end the rescue attempt was abandoned and the teams were withdrawn. It had become obvious that nobody could have survived the holocaust underground where 427 persons had died.

The entrance to the mine was sealed by building a concrete and stone wall. It was declared a burial ground and plaques bearing the names of all the men who had died were set into the wall.

Very generous payments were made to the wives and families of all of the workers who lost their lives in the disaster.

CHAPTER 41

✌ 1972 ✌

D.expectations that David and Helen had envisaged.

The owner of this piece of land was an 'Old Rhodesian' generally known as Mr T, but Patrick was told that his name was Bill, and within the first day these two men, much the same age, found that they had a lifetime of memories to share and discuss. Mr T had been a cattle and dairy inspector until his retirement from the Public Health Department fifteen years earlier. He proudly took Patrick and Mary over the twelve acre site that he was offering for sale, pointing out several important aspects of the property, including the jewel of a sparkling mountain stream that ran through the property. Patrick was astounded by lushness of the vegetation and assumed that this was because it was the middle of the rainy season, but Mr T assured him that the river never dried up. Once Mr T realised that he was talking to a really interested buyer, he opened up to additional aspects of the property, including a 'water furrow' built by 'the ancients' which never silted up. But the more interesting bonus was a so called 'slave pit' at the entrance to the property, overlooking the valley below. The slave pit intrigued Patrick and he felt sure that David would be greatly interested too, but as it was to turn out it was Gijima who immediately picked up on its existence and simply could not hear enough about it.

Mr T and his wife ran their home as a small guest house, which delighted the senior O'Connors as this meant that they could drive up to stay with them for a few days at a time, on each occasion learning more about that part of the world – so unlike the west of the country which had been their home for most of their married life.

Agreements of sale were signed, and plans for two houses were submitted to the Council for approval. Dube had set her heart on a modest house with an attached granny flat for Lisa. This was to be set in an existing orchard of apple, pear and plum trees, fruit that simply could not be grown in other parts of Rhodesia, but which thrived at this altitude of over 6000 feet. With Lisa's love of gardening, they knew how their mother would enjoy her remaining years in what she would think of as a piece of heaven.

The O'Connor house was to be built overlooking the river, with little outlook but with the sound of constant running water. It was a spacious dwelling, allowing accommodation for guests and family at the same time. A large workshop had been included, which was to be David's pride and joy as he planned on making wooden toys, furniture and kitchen gadgets to be marketed in the area. The building contractor was very quick and within seven months the two houses had been completed, but of course David and Helen would not move permanently until such time as he was ready to retire.

Dube, Gajima and Lisa settled into their home before the final painting was complete, putting up with the inconvenience just to be in their own home. Shortly after their move, Lisa's lifetime dream of becoming a grandmother was fulfilled; Dube producing a fine son and heir which after interminable discussion was named Mililo David Khumalo.

Gajima's deep interest in the slave pit increased, and he pestered Mr T for more information, which was freely given. However, Mr T had to point out that most of the literature he had read concerned Great Zimbabwe – the famous ruins near Fort Victoria and to the best of his knowledge little had been written about the actual slave pits of Inyanga. He said that there were five 'pits' in the immediate area, and all these looked out onto the valley, but of course there were many others suitably placed to enable the occupants to pass signals over vast areas of the land. The basic structure was expertly constructed of stone and they were all roughly the same size of about sixteen feet across. Each had a tiny stone entrance only wide enough for the occupants to crawl through. Mr T added that even with the heavy rainfall in Inyanga, the pits never became waterlogged, in fact the drainage was amazingly efficient. As an afterthought he said that many years ago he had read a book written by a Bulawayo businessman, interested in the paranormal, conducting a séance at Zimbabwe Ruins, and suggested to Gajima that he get a copy from the library in Inyanga village.

Very interesting information came through at this séance session, especially as to where the people originated before landing at Sofala on the east coast of Africa. At this stage Gajima was fired with enthusiasm, feeling at last he had found something worthwhile to study and write about.

Gajima lost no time in following Mr T's advice as to the possibility of there being informative literature at the local library, and the following week he made the journey by bus to Inyanga village where he was directed to a small but well stocked library.

While he was filling in his membership forms, a middle aged man entered the building, and the librarian immediately introduced him as Mr John Munasa, the headmaster of the local school. When Mr Munasa heard that Gajima had come from Wankie, he immediately wanted to know what the situation was like there, after the horrific disaster, and whether Gajima had personally been involved. The two men sat down in the 'reading' section of the library, and Gajima told Mr Munasa exactly what had happened, and because of the headmaster's obvious interest, he found himself relating most of his own life, including his time with the animals at Robins Camp, now renamed Wankie Game Reserve. They sat talking for over two hours after which Mr Munasa asked if he would visit him at the school as he felt that he could offer him a position on his staff. "I desperately need someone to teach the children about the animals in our country, for as you are aware there is little wildlife in the mountains, apart from baboons and the odd leopard. I am also looking for a retired artisan to interest and guide the older boys into an electrical career."

By the beginning of the new term, Gajima had secured a very worthwhile job. He was well respected by the pupils and being a natural athlete was admired for his running speed. It never ceased to amaze him how a chance meeting at the library had changed his life.

His mother and Dube were naturally delighted that Gajima had so unexpectedly found an interesting position at the school. Dube offered her services to the local hospital in Nyanga village where she was immediately welcomed. Lisa thoroughly enjoyed the rearing of her grandson, and it went without saying that she had found her bit of heaven. She took enormous pride in her vegetable garden but the thieving baboons in the mountains continued to anger her. This amused the locals greatly, and it is said that the baboons blushed with shame when they heard her foul language.

CHAPTER 42

ᕫᕫ 1975 ᕫᕫ

One day, while David and Helen were about to leave for Salisbury, one of the gardeners told him that there was an important man wanting to speak to him. This person would be waiting at the Tsanga River Bridge. When asked who he was, the builder said he didn't know but that it was very important.

When David went down to the bridge a young man approached him asking if he was the son of Mr Patrick O'Connor. On receiving confirmation, the man led him into a small pine plantation. Waiting there was a middle-aged man who introduced himself as Steven Jongwe. He told David that he had worked for Mr O'Connor in Wankie and had now risen to the rank of lieutenant colonel in Robert Mugabe's 'liberation army'.

"I made a promise to Patrick O'Connor that I would repay my debt to him one day. That opportunity has now presented itself. I have given orders that all members of the O'Connor and Kumbula Zulu families must not be molested in any way nor should their properties be damaged. Please convey my best wishes to your father, and assure him that now you can all live safely in this beautiful part of our country." Having said this he turned and retreated into the pine forest behind him.

David had absolutely no idea why this promise had been made to Patrick, but accepted it with enormous relief as there had been several terrorist attacks on farms in the area. Being on the Mozambique border the area had become the best route for infiltration of Robert Mugabe's political terrorists. David had not relished the idea of living behind a high security fence and having metal screens fitted on all the windows for protection against hand grenades. On returning to Salisbury, David asked Patrick if this man could be trusted to keep his word, and the reply was, "I cannot make any promises but I think he is proud enough to keep his word."

David's father Shaun only visited the Nyanga property once before suddenly dying of a heart attack. It was a happy release from his loneliness, having never fully recovered from the death of his beloved wife. His last will and testament specified that Patrick and Mary should inherit his estate, except for his wedding band which should go to David.

Steven Jongwe kept his promise and ensured that the families were not molested in any way.

✌ EPILOGUE ✌

On 18th April 1980, the Rhodesian flag was lowered to be replaced by that of the new Zimbabwe. Robert Mugabe was elected as the new prime minister but sadly the lack of basic knowledge coupled with greed and cronyism resulted in the rapid decline from being one of the wealthiest countries in the world to one of the poorest, exactly as the last Rhodesian prime minister and all of the tribal chiefs had forecast.

APPENDIX 1

THE RUDD CONCESSION

Know all men by these presents, that whereas Charles Dunell Rudd, of Kimberley; Rochford Maguire of London; and Francis Robert Thompson, of Kimberley, hereinafter called the grantees, have covenanted and agreed, and do hereby covenant and agree to pay me, my heirs and successors, the sum of one hundred pounds sterling, British currency, on the first day of every lunar month; and, further, to deliver at my royal kraal one thousand Martini-Henry breech-loading rifles, together with one hundred thousand rounds of suitable ball cartridge, five hundred of the said rifles and fifty thousand of the said cartridges, five hundred of the said rifles and fifty thousand of the said cartridges to be ordered from England forthwith and delivered with reasonable despatch, and the remainder of the said rifles and cartridges to be delivered as soon as the said grantees shall have commenced to work mining machinery within my territory; and further, to deliver on the Zambesi river a steamboat with guns suitable for defensive purposes upon the said river, or in lieu of the said steamboat, should I so elect to pay to me the sum of five hundred pounds sterling, British currency. On the execution of these presents, I Lo Bengula, King of Matabeleland, Mashonaland and other adjoining territories, in exercise of my council of indunas, do hereby grant and assign, jointly and severally, the complete and exclusive charge over all metals and minerals situated and contained in my kingdoms principalities, and dominions, together with full power to do all things that they may deem necessary to win and procure the same, and to hold, collect, and enjoy the profits and revenues, if any, derivable from the said metals and minerals, subject to the aforesaid payment; and whereas I have been much molested too late by diverse person seeking and desiring to obtain grants and concessions of land and mining rights in my territories, I do hereby authorise the said grantees, their heirs, representatives and assigns, to take all necessary and lawful steps to exclude from my kingdom, principalities, and dominions all persons seeking land, metals, minerals or mining rights therein, and I do hereby undertake to render them all such assistance as they may from time to time require for the exclusion of such persons, and to grant no concessions of land or mining rights from and after this date without their consent and concurrence; provided that, if at any time the said monthly payment of one hundred pounds shall cease and determine from the date of the last payment; and further, provided, that nothing contained in these presents shall extend to or affect a grant made by me of certain mining rights in a portion of my territory south of the Ramaquaban River, which grant is common known as the Tati Concession.

This, given under my hand this thirtieth day of October, in the year of our Lord 1888, at my royal kraal.

Witnesses:

    CHAS. D. HELM

    LOBENGULA X his mark

    C. D. RUDD

    ROCHFORTMAGUIRE

    F. R. THOMPSON

APPENDIX 2

In actual fact one of the nurses who contracted polio was sent back to England for treatment and many years later she became known to the author. On arrival she was placed in a newly developed apparatus known as the 'iron lung'. This device enabled her to breathe. After four months she was able to reduce the time spent in the iron lung and ultimately her muscles strengthened and she was able to breathe naturally again. Eight years later she returned to Rhodesia to live with her sister. With leg irons fitted she was able to walk if someone held her arm to assist her balance. She could feed herself using one arm to lift the other hand. She was one of the brightest and most cheerful ladies that I have known; a great listener and advisor for people who had problems. She died very peacefully, aged eighty-one, about fifty-five years after contracting polio in Bulawayo.

ABOUT THE AUTHOR

Robert Kidd grew up in Rhodesia, attending Plumtree Senior School from where he qualified to study heavy current electrical engineering at the Witwatersrand University in Johannesburg, South Africa. After graduating he married his Rhodesian girlfriend, and they moved to England for two years of valuable practical training in electrical and mechanical engineering.

On his return to Rhodesia he joined a large international firm of consultants, which paved the way for reaching his ultimate goal of setting up his own consulting practice.

Rhodesia being rich in minerals, much of his work centered on the mining industry.

On retirement he built his dream house amidst the beautiful mountains of Inyanga, but after fifteen years he and his wife felt that the time was right to join their grandchildren in Scotland, where they now live.

Lightning Source UK Ltd.
Milton Keynes UK
UKOW05f1014240617

303985UK00003B/48/P